STOCKINGS REQUIRED

TALES OF A CIGARETTE & CANDY GIRL

KARRYN NAGEL

To Cake,
Every once in a while,
I miss that galactic kiss
with a vengeance.

Cover Art Director – Amelia Hogan
Illustration by Leo Zandro Leonardo
Editing by Mali Apple and Rebecca McLeod

☙Dedication❧

This book is for the men and women who work the night shift in San Francisco.

Thank you for your patience, humor, and most of all, your tough love.

☛Acknowledgements

I had no idea writing a book would hurt so much.
And feel so good.

Or, maybe I knew, and thought I could get away with not doing it. No such luck.

For help in getting down the bones (in no particular order),

Dee, Brenda, Chris, Scott, Niki, Amy, Michelle, Tara, Sierra, Hunny, Wendy and so many more friends and family.

For editing brilliance-Niki, Victoria, Wendy, and Mali.

For the dream come true, Sean and Tamera.

On the home front, the inimitable Brown Bear and Pandora, specifically The Stroll station.

And for the creative spark, the Muse herself.

Chapter 1

The building in front of me was unremarkable. If you could say anything at all about this particular building, it was simply that it blended perfectly with the other buildings near it, especially in the grey light of a late San Francisco winter. But that's SoMa for you. You can walk down the street playing duck-duck-goose – only here, it would be called boring-boring-sketchy. Or perhaps more accurately, office-office-office-Bed, Bath & Beyond.

I was standing in front of the third out of five "borings" on this block, wondering what the hell I was doing here. My life had taken on the usefulness of a stalled car on the freeway, and in an effort to jolt myself out of this rut I'd decided to do something incredibly brave or astoundingly stupid, depending on how you see that sort of thing. I might end up falling spectacularly on my face. Or, it might just make my life soar.

The first 26 years of my life hadn't exactly been worthy of a billion dollar Hollywood screenplay: I was just a girl trying to get by in San Francisco after moving here from the tragically ordinary Modesto. I did the obligatory college undergrad work. I bounced around a little bit with some odd jobs, trying to pay down my student loans. I moved here two years ago looking for something special, something that made me feel free, something I was passionate about. The thought of taking a normal job again made me squirm, which was what I told my best friend Jana every week when she called to check on me.

The last time she rang, I'd had news.

"I found something on Craigslist, something really interesting. I think this is It," I said as an opener. When you are best friends, sometimes it's nice to ignore the long distance by acting as if you see each other every day. We didn't bother with Hello, How are you, I'm fine, I need to talk to you, Do you have a minute. We saved those pleasantries for when there was something serious on our minds.

"Ok, hold on, let me cancel my conference call, I'll be right back."

I waited on hold, listening to bad remakes of good songs from the 70's while she got rid of responsibility, in order to live vicariously through my "carefree" (read: desperate) existence.

"Hey, sorry about that. Okay, Pale, what have you got?"

"I sent you the link, check your Yahoo."

Silence on the other end as she clicked into her email account to look over the link I'd sent her. The next few minutes passed in silence as she read and I chewed on my lip and nails.

"I don't know, girl, really? It doesn't seem like you. If you do it, though, I think that's great! Be careful, though. When I bartended, I saw some crazy shit out there. Did I ever tell you about the guy who ... "

I tuned her out as she launched into story after story about her bartending days. She hadn't come right out and said that she thought I couldn't do it, but she didn't say I could, either. A familiar voice inside of me suggested that she was right; I would never, ever, ever in a million years do something like this.

But then a second voice fought back. “Not like me? Why, that was practically a dare! She's dared me to try this job; I can't back out now!"

And that’s how I had come to be standing here in front of a nondescript building South of Market on a cold February night. Taking a deep breath, I plugged in the 4-digit code I'd been provided over the phone by a sensual-sounding French woman.

I stepped through the door, ready to start my new job as part of the nightlife of San Francisco.

Chapter 2

The office was humming with murmurs, costume rustling and zippers. Young women jostled each other in front of a mirror, surrounded by haphazard stacks of makeup bags, hair products and shoes. A few dusty bulletin boards were crowded with photos taken at least a decade ago, judging from the hairstyles, and some more-recent additions were tacked casually in the upper corners. A few girls looked up at me or scoped me out in the mirror when I came in, but no one said anything.

I stood around for a minute, wondering what I should do next, when a tall, beautiful woman came over to greet me.

"*Bonjour*, and welcome, Pale!" she said in a teasing manner. When she had called me about my application earlier that day, I had jokingly answered the phone in French. Mistakenly thinking I was native to her country, she'd started chatting rapidly, leaving my high school freshman language skills far behind. I felt myself blush at her reminder.

Selene must have been at least 6 feet tall, and she had platinum blonde hair and warm, chocolaty brown eyes — eyes that were right now smiling at me in a friendly way. I didn't stand a chance; my girl crush was instant.

"Let me get you started with a quick video about what we do, then we'll get you into make-up and costume, and count out your inventory," she said briskly, leading me to a small sitting room in back, where an older TV/VCR combo was set up. No one else joined us.

While she got the old technology up and running, I thought back to last week when I found the ad for this gig. I nervously pulled my printout of the Craigslist ad from my pocket for a quick refresher.

EXCELLENT SECONDARY SOURCE
OF INCOME

Are you an entertainer, or just like to ham it up? Do you want to have fun while making money? Do you want to experience the nightlife of the City? Then you should come to work for us as a Candy Girl!

Tawny's Tarts has been in business for over 15 years and have steady accounts (60 gigs per week on avg.) We provide everything you need: the gigs, merchandise, transportation, costumes, etc. It costs you nothing to start! Make an average of $10 - $30, cash, per hour. As a general guideline, expect to make $50 to $150 for a five-hour gig. You take the money home, in your pocket, at the end of every night.

This position requires skill in sales (you will be hawking name brand items, treats, novelties, etc.) and acting (as you play the part of an authentic cigarette/candy girl of yore).

By donning the alter ego of a candy girl, you automatically inherit the right to be outrageous, courageous, witty, spontaneous, flirtatious, fun, charming! Give it a try — call today!

I had been intrigued. Scared, and intrigued. Put myself out there? Talk to strangers? Going to bars, cold selling, relentlessly pursuing cash, stories, and a flashy present tense I could finally count as a meaningful life – this was exactly the kind of thing I would never do. This was, I guessed, why I was sitting here.

The video was dated and crudely edited, blending images and video from the 80's and 90's, as well as some current footage from a few years ago. I saw Selene posing with a tray, her enigmatic Mona Lisa smile reminding me that confidence was not always feigned.

While some of the training video was laughable, there were definite elements of classic sales incorporated in their technique. I started to get nervous again, to see the legacy stretching back all these years, which also reminded me that I was about to don this same iconic image. All these girls, chasing notoriety and adventure, using nothing but their street smarts and sex appeal to carve out their own piece of the pie...I said one more internal prayer, praying that I didn't embarrass myself.

When the video ended, I headed out of the training room and into the main lobby, which was filled with girls in various states of readiness. Some had just come in and were storing their things in the closet, others were counting merchandise they'd spread over the tables they'd commandeered, and still others were crowded at the mirror, primping and perfecting their look. Some were quietly focused on their tasks, but others were chatting with each other or talking loudly on their cell phones.

Selene pulled me behind the front desk and directed me to a small side room.

"Pick out a color that you like, and we'll get you changed."

I was standing in what looked like a very colorful coat-check room. In front of me were two long clothing racks filled with uniforms in every color: baby blue, turquoise, red, pink, yellow, and purple. The long-sleeved tops were draped with braided rope, and the short satin A-line skirts had black satin trim down each side – very burlesque meets band camp. Selene explained that they were modeled on the bellhop persona.

A small scrap of matching fabric was pinned to each costume, too big to be a wristlet, and too small to be a belt.

"What is this for?" I asked.

"That's for your hair, instead of the pill box hat. We switched those out just a few years ago. It's more modern, yes?"

Selene explained that the costumes were provided by the company for free and were laundered regularly. We were allowed to put together our own outfit, but it had to have a consistent theme and had to meet with Selene's approval.

"Your costume is everything we can see on you, so wear a complete costume from head to toe! The overall look that we are going for is classy, sexy and professional.

"You should always wear a comfortable but dressy pair of black shoes or boots. No pirate boots; they should be urban. Shoes need to have elevated heels, be clean and in good condition. Stockings are required with every costume; nude, black or fishnet pantyhose are acceptable. No holes or runs. I would definitely bring a second pair with you." She rattled all this off quickly, straightening costumes, adjusting accessories, and kicking stuff on the floor to the corners.

I was feeling overwhelmed, but Selene wasn't finished with me yet.

"Your makeup must include foundation, eye shadow, lipstick and mascara, yes? Glitters and fake eyelashes are allowed, if you wish to use them. Your hair should be brushed and styled — bobby pins, hair ties, styling products, that sort of thing. We have feather clips if you don't want to wear the matching hairpiece."

I was distracted slightly by how much information was being thrown at me, and I interrupted Selene to ask her if she expected me to remember all of this. She laughed musically.

"Of course not, though you are absorbing more than you realize! Besides, that fresh meat aspect is one of the things that will help you sell tonight. Now, back to your look.

"The goal is to look authentic. You picked that up from the video, yes? Since this is your main tool when you are out, the costume is one of the two most important things you possess. Of course, the other is your attitude."

At the moment, my attitude was cowering under the clothing racks, but I did my best to appear enthusiastic and competent.

"Basically, always arrive on time for work, with a professional appearance. Treat this like you would any other legitimate job. The management reserves the right to veto any part of your look if it's inappropriate. Any questions?"

Though I did have questions, I shook my head no. Selene was still slightly intimidating.

"You are running a little behind since we still need to get your merchandise counted. Go ahead and get changed as quick as you can, and I'll get your inventory started."

I thought for a moment what my dad would say if he knew I was doing this tonight. I gave Selene a big grin, and chose a pink bellhop uniform.

I headed back through the crowd of girls in the main lobby and into the training room. I closed the door, but there was no lock, making me nervous. About halfway through getting my top on, I discovered to my dismay that it zipped all the way up the back, which was a torture device in women's fashion invented for the double-jointed. On my most bendy days, which were generally limited to days that I helped someone move or when I'd managed to get a little booty the night before, I could've still only gotten the zipper a little over halfway. Of course, the door opened just as I'd gotten the zipper midway up my back, with my chest hanging out. Of course.

I heard a stifled laugh as I turned to check who was coming in. A very short, dark-haired girl shut the door quickly as she slipped into the room and turned to look me over. She had dark curly hair that was big and thick, equal parts curly and fuzzy. Her eyes were also dark, but as she looked me over she was smiling at me like we'd just gotten away with deep-frying Twinkies. She was really short – she couldn't have been more than 4'10 – busty, and young. Despite that youth, her eyes were intelligent, and amused.

"My name's Meredith. Do you want some help with that?" she asked good-naturedly."

"I don't know. Aren't we going to dinner first?" I shot back with a sly grin and raised eyebrows. She laughed, and gestured for me to turn my back to her.

"My name is Pale. Thanks for the help. It's my first night, and I'm crazy nervous."

"No kidding? Pale's an interesting name. That's not a stage name, is it?" she asked, tugging at the zipper on the back.

"Nope. Just parents who had a strange moment. I guess Blake was considered, but they decided Pale was more feminine." I adjusted my outfit in the mirror as Meredith struggled with the back.

"Why did you ask if it was my stage name?" I asked over my shoulder.

"Oh, I guess I gave myself away! I'm a singer."

"I love singing! I was just crazy for it when I was little. So, are you performing right now?" I asked.

Meredith laughed and closed my top.

"Not really, unless you count the coffee shop I'm working in part time." She turned to stash her bag under some props and tables. "They have an open-mic night, but I'm trying to get more evening gigs. You have to know the right people, yadda yadda. It's taking more time than I anticipated, so I thought this job would be fun, and might help the singing career a bit." I turned back to the mirror and slipped on my skirt and shoes.

"So, it's your first night, huh?" she asked.

I nodded yes to her reflection, as she had moved back to the door and was headed back out to the main area.

"Don't worry, you will do great. Most girls are nervous at first, but it wears off quickly. You ought to do fine, as long as you don't get falling-down drunk, lose your money, or wreck the costume!" She flashed me a smile and stepped out to the lobby.

I followed her out and took an empty spot at the large table in the center of the room. It was hard not to check out the other girls: they were obviously in pre-show time excitement and dressed so beautifully, they were magnetic. They were all wearing the iconic uniform, but each girl had added some aspect of herself that showed me more about her than she realized. There was another tall blonde in the corner, with long, reedy legs. I could tell she'd seen her share of tough times by how casually she used her makeup, like she'd done this hundreds of times before. Her makeup was a bit cheap and heavy, even for nightlife.

The short-tempered rockabilly girl with the tattoos was carefully going over heavy black eyeliner just above her pupils, adding a long slash at the end. She'd already snapped twice at a girl who'd bumped her at the mirror. Over and over she ran the brush across her eyelid, unsmiling, focused, and serious. I could tell she had other things on her mind.

There was a short, jumpy Indian girl complaining about her inventory, requesting replacements for item after item, all the while on the phone. She was carrying on what appeared to be a totally one-sided conversation to her boyfriend.

Selene brought over a large tray and plunked it down on the table. She pulled out an inventory list and started teaching me the ropes of counting each item. We checked batteries for the light up rings and toys and divided the items by category. The sheer number of items we carried was dizzying, but I managed to take in most of what she was saying.

"Now that you have the gist, get all this counted, yes? Go see the drivers if you need to change anything out. The boys can help you with questions, too, as I need to get back to the desk." Selene gave me another confident smile and patted me on the shoulder. Her hand seemed to linger for a moment, but I might have been imagining that.

I counted the items and logged them on my inventory, trying to move briskly but not to make any mistakes either. Girls all around me were tucking their belongings into the training room, their trays counted and set aside, ready to be picked up on the way out the door. They stopped at the mirror to put the final touches on their hair or adjust their hems.

I found two items with dead batteries, plus a candy bar broken in half. A few Tarts were standing near the main desk, at what looked like an inventory closet, so I headed over there with my defective product.

"What do you need?" asked a lanky, tired-looking guy with white dust in his sandy brown hair. He was about 6'1, and hunched over to look at me through the pass-through. His eyes were dull from exhaustion. He had the look of someone who was used to being asked for too much.

I hesitantly stepped closer to the large cutout where a window used to be, to look at the boxes behind him. The shelves were filled with cases of cigarettes, cigars, gum, mints and candy, as well as large bags of rings, necklaces, spinning light rave toys, and all manner of other items. On the floor, buckets of water held roses.

"Hi. Sorry. It's my first night, so I'm still getting in the swing of things. My name is Pale. I have two rings that have dead batteries and a broken wrapper on this Snickers."

He was very cute, and while he did give me a small encouraging smile, he ignored my introduction and turned to get me what I requested.

"These should work for you," he said as he handed me the replacement items. "Good luck." He looked away, done with the conversation.

Obviously I made a huge impression.

Though I was dressed up as much as the other girls, I suddenly felt insecure, and went to check my reflection before I headed out the door into the night with these strangers. Other than Meredith and Selene, I was not exactly feeling the camaraderie I had hoped for. I had envisioned a team of glittery, enthused girls going out to take on the adventure and nightlife of San Francisco. It turned out this gig was about *me*, taking on the crowds.

I was not exactly a bombshell like Ms. Rockabilly Eyeliner, and I didn't have Meredith's spunky good nature, I thought to myself as I stared into the mirror. But I had a certain presence of my own. I'd just have to show them what I was made of.

Shine on, you crazy diamond, I whispered to myself.

Chapter 3

I stepped onto the sidewalk and turned to see a mid-90s commuter car that looked like it had just finished doubling in the "Bring Your Own Big Wheels" race down Potrero Hill. It was covered in a film of pollen, awkwardly dented, and painted bright yellow. Well, it had been bright yellow; now it would be poetic to call it mustard. The door fought me as I tried to open it. It couldn't look less like something a sexy woman in fishnets would step out of. I briefly daydreamed how much better I would look stepping out of a golf cart than this car.

The jumpy Indian girl and Meredith got in the backseat. Looking impatient, the driver gestured for me to get in the front seat, which was the last place I wanted to be. I slid in, and realized that the entire car smelled deliciously like a bakery.

Our driver was the same man from the inventory counter, the one with specks of powder in his hair. Mr. Congeniality. He waited wordlessly until we settled our trays in our laps and got buckled up.

"Listen up. My name is Thom. I am your driver. I know there's only one new girl here, but you others need to hear this too. You will follow every instruction I give you to the letter."

"If you intentionally ignore my instructions or piss me off, this job will end immediately. Yes, Selene knows I talk to you this way, and she agrees with me. I don't take any shit from anyone. This is my car. Here are the rules." He ticked them off his fingers, one by one.

"One: You can eat cold food or wrapped food, but no wrappers on the floor. Two: Don't spill any fluids, for ANY reason. This means puking too. Three: Don't be late, ever. Four: Check you have all your shit. I will not bring it back to you once I drop you off. Five: Respect me, and we'll get along just fine."

"Any questions?" he asked rhetorically.

"Where exactly are we going, and how do I know when to meet you?" I asked, ignoring the rhetoric.

Pulling a scrap of paper from his pocket, he handed me a list of what looked like band names.

"When I dump you at your drop point, I will hand you a list of bars for that neighborhood. You do as many of those as you can, ideally all of them, in the time I give you. Sometimes that's 35 minutes; sometimes it's 60 minutes. At the end of one run, I pick you up and take you to the next one. You manage your own time; don't call me unless you get lost or something happens. I will call you if I'm going to be late. I'm sometimes late getting back to you from getting the other girls, but you should always *be on time*."

He glared at me, but I could see he was mostly just tired. The smell of Thom's car had my mouth watering for a raspberry danish pretty much the instant his speech started, and I realized that the white dust in his hair must be flour.

The other girls in the backseat rolled their eyes at Thom when I turned to check in with them.

"Hi, my name is Pale. I'm the fresh blood," I said to the Indian girl.

"Hi, I'm Rehka. Don't worry about Thom. He's always trying to scare the new little lambs," she laughed. "It's the hours. They kill him over at his second job, since he works so early in the morning making pizza dough." She gave Thom a sly look.

"I'm not a dough rat, Rehka," he snapped. "I work in a bakery, and make things you wouldn't believe existed, they are so heavenly," he said firmly, and started to join traffic.

The girls in the back started clamoring, begging and pleading for pastries from heaven and the joys and wonders contained in them. Thom silently maneuvered through traffic, ignoring them. This was clearly a regular request, consistently denied. After several long and loud moments, the girls giggled and sighed, giving up the chase of Thom's goods. I could hardly blame them in either regard; he was very cute. I snuck a glance out of the corner of my eye, taking in his soft blue eyes, long hands, and sunken posture. I turned to the girls in the backseat and they both winked at me, letting me know they approved of me scoping him out.

"So! Let's make sure you know all the prices, and I'll give you some tips on what to say tonight that will help," Meredith chimed in, leaning forward and smiling, her dark eyes on me.

The rest of the ride was a chatter of selling techniques, costume tips, and pointers on exploiting sex appeal to my advantage. I also learned some of the back-story on my fellow passengers. Meredith had been at the job for about three months, but already acted like a pro. This was likely because she's one of those people that everyone loves. She grew up on the East Coast with several brothers, but after starting college, she realized her passion was singing, so she dropped out, packed her things and came out West. Rehka was a college student who just started a few weeks ago, and was nearly kicked out in her first week due to her constant calls to her boyfriend.

"He needs me! I have to talk to him several times a day or he gets fragile!"

Meredith and Thom both rolled their eyes at the same time. I noticed that Rehka was very jumpy about any little noise she heard.

We bumped and soared through the streets of San Francisco, Thom maneuvering like a New York taxi driver. At least he was taking his wrath out on the road instead of me, I noted gratefully. The streets were flashing different flavors of the city. The edgy, hip leather and whip of South of Market faded as we passed the austerity and tension of FiDi to take Rehka over to Pier 23. I was curious how she was supposed to spend a full hour working a single bar, but didn't press the point with Thom.

Our next stop was for Meredith, who would be working bars in the flamboyant, sex-steam-rising Castro District. Although it was not obvious she was a singer, she was obviously talented. The boys of Castro Street worship at the altar of talent, happy for any chance to brush knuckles with I Knew Her Then, so I figured this was a good run for her.

Meredith had one last thing to say to me.

"It's your first night, Pale, and you want to share that with everyone you meet. Don't discount the pity sales! You will make a lot of tips that way. As a matter of fact, it will likely be your 'first night' for several months." She winked at me and sauntered away.

Thom drove on, finally pulling up in front of an Irish bar just outside an entrance to Golden Gate Park. Thankfully, the Little Shamrock looked fairly unintimidating. He pulled into a yellow loading zone, and put the car in park.

"This is the first stop on the West run. You've got 20 minutes, then I'll meet you right back here to take you to the rest of the run." He stared forward, not meeting my eyes.

I sat there for a minute. When I realized he was not going to give me a much needed you-can-do-this, I opened the car door and stepped out into the night as if I'd done this before, posing like a cherry on top for the passers-by on the street.

I stepped up to the bar and sidled in. I stood there in the entrance, taking a moment to get my bearings. To my left was a small, intimate, warm-wooded bar, and to my right there was a smattering of round tables squeezed up close to a fireplace. I made eye contact with the first several groups who caught my eye, then decided to move in on the men parked at the bar, as they looked like they must be regulars.

Though their backs were turned to me, to a man they all rotated slightly so they could hear over their shoulder what I was about to say.

"Good evening! How are you tonight?" I began a bit too brightly, looking down.

"I'm still here, lass, and that's saying something."

The middle-aged man was grey in his face, hair, and clothing; he appeared to blend into the environment without effort. But when he glanced up from his tumbler, his eyes were a shockingly bright blue. Despite the drink in his hand, he was obviously sober.

I was distracted with wanting to talk to him, to find out his story and what brought him here, but I realized with a flash that I looked like an exotic flower who wandered into barren grassland.

A little more gently, I said, "It's my first night, and you are my first customer. I'm not sure how to talk to people I don't know. Do you mind if I just chat with you for a moment?"

He gave me a long slow look, never moving from my eyes, though I could tell he was taking in the rest of me. I looked away at first during his assessment, then realized that if I couldn't make this sale, then there was no point in being out here for the next 6 hours. The moment grew longer and at long last he broke into a grin that was both new and mischievous, like a joke's punch line delivered for the first time.

"A fresh mermaid, is it? And me, yer sailor helplessly wooed by the sound o' your sultry song!" he laughed, booming it out for the whole bar.

A quiet breath that the room was holding was released, and I heard sounds brighten before me, clinking glasses, moderately loud music, and doors and chairs, scraping their pub-time melody once again. He was the King, and they were the court. I was amazed; I hadn't realized that one regular in a bar could determine the way the rest of the room would react, but there it was, a golden path laid out before me. My Sailor King had made it clear: I could be trusted, I could work the room.

I spent some time bantering with my champion, and we warmed to each other. He laid it on thick with compliments and propositions, while I volleyed back sassy refusals. He bought me a shot, and even though I knew I should stay sharp, I couldn't help myself – I tossed it down with sexy flair. He laughed throughout the whole exchange, as if laughing, slurring, and flirting all at once was the easiest thing in the world. I've been around enough Irishmen to know that, for them, it is.

He leaned in and handed me a $5 tip after buying some smokes, and said, "I wish you the luck of the Irish tonight, lassie. I'm happy to help a Tart like you, especially with your blushing cheeks. Keep a hand on your drawers, if you know what I mean." He winked and turned sideways into the room, passing me the money as if everyone couldn't see, though of course they were enjoying every move.

I moved on to my right, closer to the fireplace, to a large table of college-aged kids unwinding for the weekend. Starting conversation with them was easy, and soon we were all laughing. I took a few orders from them, then worked a circuit around the bar, leaving the rest of the regulars at the bar for last. I knew I was taking too long, but I couldn't help it; my anxiety had vanished. I was euphoric that I'd conquered the invisible shield that divided my audience from me. What I first thought of as the societal equivalent of a ravenous wolf pack had been revealed as a bunch of frisky, nervous puppies out for a frolic in the concrete jungle.

Though the requests for product were fairly solid from the tables, the guys closest to the booze were content to just tip me and not take anything. This was solid gold for me, pure profit. Even better, my grey gentleman winked at me again on my way out. Every once in a great while I fantasize about taking an older lover. I think it's Jean-Luc Picard's fault. Perhaps that old rogue at the bar was picking up on those dormant thoughts.

I shook my head and hurried out to the yellow abomination, where Thom was waiting behind the wheel.

"Did you get it out of your system? Being late?" Thom asked.

When I looked up from jostling my way into the car, I could see he was actually giving me a smile. He was even looking me in the eye. I smiled back, to soften my retort.

"I'm two minutes late; throw me in candy jail."

"Good, now we can continue on your run. I assume you aren't pissing drunk? Didn't lose anything? Broke down and cried, did you?" He was back to business mode, grilling me to make sure I'd make it through the next few hours.

I regaled Thom with the delicious moments of my first time out, despite his disinterest, and soaked in my happy confidence as a bolster for wherever we were going next. Though my anxiety had retreated, it was waiting to come out if there was a new opportunity. Anxiety was like that, always willing to give you a shove from the top stair if you slipped on ice and grabbed for the rail.

Thom pulled up in the air/water section of a gas station, across from a corner bar with a bright green sign over the door that read "Sam's." He pulled out a package of Post-Its and quickly jotted down the names of eight places, all bars. I started to feel panicky at getting them all done, but took a breath and reminded myself that Thom barely knew me; he wouldn't sabotage me this early in the game-I couldn't possibly have annoyed him so much so soon. He ripped off the Post-It and ran through the bars on the list.

"You need to work through all of these in the next 40 minutes. I'll meet you a couple of blocks down the street, outside of Evergreen." He pointed vaguely to the right outside the car.

"All of these? Are you serious?"

"You manage your own time. I don't care if you spend all your time in one bar; just be outside Evergreen in exactly 40 minutes."

Did he realize he'd just given me a clue on how to do this? I wondered as I slipped out of the car. I didn't think so. I smiled at Thom's slip-up; I thought I was required to go into every bar he gave me, but as it turned out, I could go into one, two, none of them, or all of them. Whatever was the best sale for me! Of course, I had no idea which bar would be the best sales, but knowing that I got to make that decision gave me some control, which was comforting at the moment.

I felt weirdly exposed, standing in a gas station lot. I glanced at the list and tried to memorize the names, so that I didn't have to constantly refer to it while I was out working the run. The atmosphere out there wasn't the safest, and I didn't want to make it look like I didn't know where I was going. I felt like a bright pink button with "PUSH ME" written on my chest in shiny white letters.

I sized up the first bar on the list as I headed across the lot to the corner. Even though I was under the washed-out gas station and streetlight glare, I took my time crossing the street, putting a little saunter into it. I was rewarded with several honks and catcalls, which drew the attention of the packed bar-goers pressed up to the windows.

Though I did it to bolster my flagging confidence, my performance alerted the bar that I was coming. It turned out that this was a good thing, because inside it was absolutely packed, hot, and deafeningly loud. I had to throw my voice about three times louder than usual.

I started working through the bar, which stretched out like a galley kitchen to my left. People made room for me the best they could, but the room was as full as a Japanese subway at rush hour.

The patrons weren't as encouraging as those at the Little Shamrock. Once I got to the back, however, I was rewarded by a large group of clean-cut guys who scooped up several packs of cigarettes, gum, and candy, and tipped me well on top of that. They were very nice but all business, no flirting. It felt strange that they didn't want much of the candy-girl personality, but I took the hint and plunged back into the human sardine can.

I decided there was no way to do better than I just did in the back, so I weaved my way back through the crowd toward the front door. On my way out a guy stopped me to purchase some smokes. I reached the door at last, and saw that the whole trip had taken me ten minutes. I headed for the next bar on my list, happy to be back out in the cool night air.

I made it through four bars in the next 20 minutes. At each stop the bouncers were polite and attentive, opening doors, winking, holding back thick curtains, and pushing extra-drunk people out of my way. My experience with customers turned out to be a strange blending of the first two stops, along with some boredom, rudeness, and compliments thrown in.

I quickly learned that the same technique didn't apply to every bar. Some customers liked sarcasm, while some liked to be flattered. Some wanted you to sit down and join them, share stories — basically, be their personal entertainment. Some really just wanted to buy you a drink. Recalling Selene's warning not to drink too much, I refused every one.

When I realized that I had ten minutes to visit the final three bars, I rushed through the next two so that I would have some extra time at the last place, Evergreen.

I realized my mistake as soon as I entered Evergreen. While the last bar — which I made a single, quick lap through — had been huge, Evergreen was tiny and didn't look promising.

The walls were matte black, and there were a few weakly lit candelabras along the wall. Instead of creating a romantic atmosphere, it felt more like those lights should be put out of their misery. The bar, tables, and stools were all chosen so carefully as to not offend anyone, that they had no personality, making them unbearably boring. I could tell that they were trying for understated elegance, but it just felt empty. With my pink satin costume and the blinky lights on my tray, I looked like a walking Christmas tree in this setting. I'd be finished with this place in mere minutes.

Sure enough, the girls in this bar all looked down their noses at me. I shrugged it off; I guess I must have seemed like trashy competition compared to their pressed linen pants, designer shoes, and cackling hyena-pack laugh. I decided to head to the bathroom to check my makeup and take a break from having the tray around my neck.

The bathroom had a large mirrored wall, and a table for me to set the tray on. I adjusted my makeup, and washed my hands, which had gotten strangely dirty. I assumed it was the money, but maybe it was the environments I'd been working in.

I glanced down at my watch again, pulled myself together, and headed out to find Thom.

"Not bad so far. Don't let those trophy wife bitches get you down," I chuckled to myself as I stepped back into the currents of the night.

Chapter 4

Thom was waiting for me at the curb. He had Rehka in tow, camped out in the front seat. She was swaying in her seat and reminded me of a wind-blown poppy, especially since she chose a red outfit tonight. Apparently Rehka wasn't concerned about losing sales by drinking heavily.

Thom seemed strangely satisfied, even though she was making it impossible for him to drive: punching buttons, opening and closing doors, and talking loudly to him, me, and — I presume — the ever-present boyfriend on the phone that was also being waved around. I captured Thom's glance in the rearview mirror, and he was barely containing his laughter.

"I'm taking you to the Haight run, and Rehka is headed over to SoMa. If, of course, she makes it that far. I might have to come back and get you to take over her shift if she can't finish it." His grin expanded and turned wicked. Rehka was getting into a lover's quarrel on the phone, and wasn't paying the slightest attention to the implication.

"What's so funny?" I asked.

"Well, besides this totally shameless display, I just made $50 bucks." Thom glanced over at Rehka, who was now hanging out the window and trying to yell incomprehensible insults at passing pedestrians.

"What do you mean?"

"We have a bet going in the office on how long it takes certain girls to get three sheets to the wind, and it looks like I won for tonight." Thom pulled out his cell and took a ten-second video of Rehka, who was still oblivious to the luck she'd just rained on Thom.

His insurance complete, he snapped his phone closed.

"That's so...callous. And awesome," I grinned at him, happy we'd found some common ground. "So, you guys bet on the girls often?"

"Sometimes."

"Well, I'll do my best to earn you some spare cash."

"Thanks." Thom put on extra speed around a corner so he could hear Rehka squeal and laugh.

We pulled up in front of Hole in the Wall Saloon, and Rehka teetered dangerously out of the car, swinging around to lean in the driver's door.

"Thooooommm! You are soooo-OOOO cuuu-UTE!" she wailed, an ice cream truck song, echoing down the street.

"See you in 45, Rehka. Keep your phone close," he called out.

We jetted back over to the Haight/Ashbury district, rich with the history of consciousness-altering dating back 40 years. The lines those hippies crossed, the ideas they fought for, the discomfort and changes they made to themselves and the world around them, live on in the brick and concrete of the area, both symbolically and literally in the colorful stains of the sidewalks. I could see the tradition of littering the area with broken boundaries had sadly carried on by the children and grandchildren of those radical fighters.

Being in the Haight was like the one-trick pony at the circus: it was old, and you pitied the creature, but you didn't expect it to be anything other than an old, tired pony that smelled like old hash/donkey sex, with a saggy knit hat and a dirty blanket thrown over its back. Maybe a tie-dyed blanket; it depended on whether you were in the Upper or Lower Haight. Despite these feelings, or maybe in an effort to recapture the purity of the time before, the moth-drawing, magnetic quality of this famous place brought people here.

Thom slowed down as we the reached the top of Haight Street, just outside the entrance to Golden Gate Park. He eased into a parking space in front of a bar with double doors and an orange neon sign. I glanced back behind us at one of my favorite touristy attractions in the Haight: Kan Zaman Café. They had belly dancers, hookahs and wonderful food there. It had been one of my first and happiest experiences moving to San Francisco; it had seemed so exotic and lively to me. I felt a little happier knowing I might get to go in there on this run.

Thom went through the same steps that we did before with the Post-It, and gestured to the double doors. "You'll start here at Milk Bar, then move on to the rest on the list. This is a shorter run; you'll only have 20 minutes. I'll be back to take you to the rest."

Standing outside Milk Bar, something about the name made me hate it already. I wasn't as nervous as I had been when I started, but I also didn't feel like I was going to do very well with the clientele. Just a hunch.

I opened the door and took in the white tables, white walls and pastel lighting along the skinny bar.

Even though it was a Friday night, there were only eight people in the whole place, though they were well into party mode. My first instinct was correct: the vibe was awful. I made a cursory pass to the customers, but their noses were already turned up by the time I got to them. No sales; time to hit the next one.

My next location, Alembic, felt more like something I could work with. It was wedged between the Red Vic movie theater and the beginning of the mixed-bag businesses that pepper the lower Haight. These start with a generic Tibetan import store named Land of the Sun, followed by a whole lineup of stores that cater to a schizophrenic taste in clothes and accessories: rockabilly/West Coast Swing gives way to Classic/Purist Hippie, followed by cutting-edge Suburban College Uniform, which only sells one white and two plain cream t-shirts (with a waiting list for those three shirts). The white one had a penguin on it.

I stepped into Alembic and broke into a big smile. They were playing a great song on the loudspeakers, and I paused a moment to enjoy the music. As I began to scope the room, a guy immediately jumped up to come over to me. He was so grateful to find some minty gum because he was feeling lucky with his second date; he tipped me well and bought her some chocolate. After that, working the room was pretty easy. Even when people didn't buy, they were still incredibly friendly. I left the bar feeling really good.

I headed down the street, carefully not making eye contact with the various transients and homeless, as there were some dangerous addicts in the Haight. Now that I was carrying some cash, it made me feel exposed. Having a 25-pound, awkward load balanced on my hips and hanging around my neck, along with the bulk of the neck pillow, made it hard for me to keep my eye on all corners.

I continued my sales in Zam Zam but passed by Hobson's Choice, since it was not listed on my Post-It note. As I headed on to the Gold Cane, I pondered why some bars didn't have a deal with the company, and whether I should stop in and give it a try anyway.

My sales after Alembic weren't exactly amazing, but I had some great interactions and received some nice compliments. The bars were mostly filled with regulars, rather than tourists or shoppers, which seemed to make for a laid-back feel that was very easy to blend into. One older lady was very excited by my Superman pez dispenser, and showed her appreciation with a tip and a spontaneous hug.

Finishing my run, I doubled back to the spot where Thom said he would meet me, and I made it on time. He rewarded me with a begrudging smile, and we took off down Haight Street towards downtown.

"SoMa?" I asked simply.

"Yep, Rehka's too drunk."

"Ah."

Thom was quiet on the drive, but seemed more comfortable, less tense. I decided to attempt some conversation.

"So, why exactly do you smell even better than my dad's cinnamon rolls on Saturday morning?" I started gently, giving him an encouraging smile.

Thom laughed, and relaxed slightly.

"I work at a bakery when I'm not here. It's what I really love to do. But the hours between both jobs make for a damn long day, so I often run out of patience by the time I get here," he admitted.

"I take it the bakery doesn't pay you enough to live on?"

"The money's okay, but I've had some big expenses in the last year, so I'm driving you girls around to make ends meet."

"Wow, that's intense. Doesn't leave you much time for sex and rock-n-roll," I joked.

Thom was silent for a long while, so long that I thought I might have overstepped my bounds.

"Yeah. But I have to do it," he mumbled. It seemed like he was shutting down, so I backed off and changed the subject.

We talked about other parts of the job: the company history, the owner, the routes and the general take on holidays. Thom was actually quite pleasant when he wasn't being prickly. He jabbed playfully now that we weren't talking about him, and I was glad I backed off of whatever was making him uncomfortable.

We moved quickly across the city, and soon we were South of Market. Thom dropped me off with another list of bars, and said he'd be back in an hour. He gave me a smile as I smoothly exited his hellish yellow turd of a car. I was getting the hang of it, and it seemed I'd passed some sort of test in his eyes. I think that Thom just wanted some respect. That's not hard from where I sit, but it made me sad that he hadn't been getting much of it before now.

As I moved toward my first stop, Icon Lounge, I reflected that this should be the more profitable part of the night. It was getting close to rowdy o'clock — that time around midnight when many people get their second wind, stepping up their games to get lucky. The first sheen of makeup and cologne has worn off, the first layer stripped away. The dance was what mattered.

And now that I knew the basic steps, no one was keeping me off the dance floor.

As I finished up at Acme, I reflected on the whirlwind that had been the past hour. At Icon Lounge the patrons had all been really brassy, and practiced a contrary, friendly-yet-insulting nature. I didn't get very far showing respect; in fact, I found that the more I tried to push people's buttons, the better my sales had been. I was learning that it was a game to them, the one-upmanship: how intelligent was the cute girl who's peddling her wares? I'd seen the dumb girls at the bar getting crushed to a pulp socially, ignored and jeered at for being exactly what they appeared to be: arm candy.

I'd been keeping up my 'It's my first night' line, which sounded cheesy, but it was earning me more tips. A number of people asked me what happened to Rehka; she was apparently a regular on this run. Her customers all laughed knowingly when I told them that she was "indisposed." In the short time since she'd started, she'd already left a strong impression.

I was yanked back to the present as a guy grabbed my arm and leaned in to whisper to me. His breath was so pungent, I nearly gagged. He was dressed sharp, but his eyes were hostile. "All you girls are the same...seducing us, tricking us, manip-...." He lost track of what he's saying; he was so busy trying to hold himself upright by leaning on my arm, tightening his grip painfully.

"Manipulating?" I said sarcastically. I figured he wouldn't hear the tone, but he was starting to piss me off.

"Yeah, exactly! ManIPulating us into believing that you care, when yuuurr just waiting to RIP our heaaarts right out..." he trailed off, looking in the direction of the street where the main door was.

"Miss, is this man bothering you?"

I heard a deep rumbling thunder, and looked toward the door for what I assumed would be a thunderstorm outside. Bizarre, the weatherman had predicted a mild evening.

The voice cut across the hall as a figure strode toward me, almost casually. It was one of those moments where everything appeared to be easy-going, but in actuality, a fight was about to break out.

I was looking at one of the biggest men I'd ever seen: a bouncer built like a two-story brick doghouse, all muscle and the towering certainty that goes with it. He was wearing a perfectly cut black blazer over a bright blue shirt stretched taut over his chest, complete with tailored black pants and big black shoes. I mean, a girl has to catch her breath for a moment, because lordie, those are some big black shoes.

"Miss, is this man disturbing you?" he repeated, leaning down toward me, with concern and menace. I hoped the menace wasn't meant for me.

"He really is," I said, in what I hoped was an I could-take-care-of-this-myself, but-wouldn't-it-be-so-much-cooler-if-you-did-it tone of voice. A tone of voice that conveyed confidence, intelligence, female fragility, and the guarantee that my panties just dropped.

I thought I was starting to get the hang of how this worked.

Before I could even draw my next breath, Big Black Shoes had grabbed Slurred Speech and thrown him bodily down the hall. Though the movement was impressive, what was even more so was that he didn't even look, he just bowled him down the hall, and we both watched him skid to the door with a small fwoomp as his head lightly concussed the doorframe.

Big Black Shoes turned back to me and gave me a wide grin. "I'm really glad he was. I needed that excuse. And he needed to meet the floor, not you. You? You are meant for me."

This entire speech was delivered with such density and rumbling, I thought I was caught in some sort of audio avalanche. I guess if we were to tumble into bed, he would likely shatter my eardrums. I took a second look down, and considered it worth my life.

"My name is Vincent. And you should know, since I've never seen you before, that while you are in this place, I'm looking after you. Always." He gave me a wink and walked away, headed back to the front door, looking every bit the protective sphinx.

"I'm Pale!" I called after him. My own voice sounded ludicrous in the aftermath of those rolling syllables.

"Yes, you really are. I'll see you next time, sugar." He chuckled to himself, giving a small wave of his hand over his departing shoulder.

He doesn't know I've heard that a thousand times. But in his case, he can say it. All. Night. Long.

Chapter 5

Thom was waiting for me at our pickup spot. I was beaming, despite how tired I was. He told me we were headed to my last run of the night. We drove west up Mission Street, the desperately colored tacos looming into view, flavored with street scams and the invincible young.

The feel of the city had shifted again. I sensed the pressure of people trying to impress, swindle or protect each other. The dance was so furious and intricate, my mind flashed through images of martial arts fights from the movies. The high from my last run seeped from my bones, draining my mood from happy-but-tired to simply tired.

I saw the telltale rainbow flags as we approached the Castro, the hub of free expression for the entire United States. People from all over the country came here; and not just gay men and lesbians either. Trans-gender, trans-sexual, non-affiliated, those Identifying As. The family members, friends and lovers who show their support. The streets were lined with hybrid boutique shops selling boy shorts and oven-fresh cookies. Here the clubs, the stores, and even the bumper stickers cater to the niche market of Tourist Gays.

I was nervous again; after all, the men weren't interested in me, right? I fretted aloud to Thom, who gave me a pitying smile.

"Trust me; you'll enjoy yourself more than you think." Another list appeared from his pocket, and we reviewed it briefly together.

I found myself reluctant to move. It was way past my usual bedtime, and I couldn't find a comfortable spot for the tray to sit on my shoulders, no matter how much I shifted about. My feet hurt, my legs were cold, and the longer I wore the costume the more binding it was, with its high collar and long sleeves. Even if I could've ripped it off right then, I still would've needed some help getting out of the zipper. It was like a sexy straightjacket.

I found myself wondering silently if this was the right job for me. Sure, I'd done well in sales, at least I thought so, and it'd been a bit adventurous, but now it was a real effort to keep my energy up. I wondered if it was often like this, getting cranky and tired and short-tempered as the night stretched on.

I took a few deep breaths, and exited the hideous parody of a motor vehicle.

My first stop, Rød, had a cozy exterior. The window sign was fire-engine-red neon, and it looked like a wine bar.

I stepped through the door and was immediately confronted by a sea of red velvet; it even covered the ceiling and walls. Black-light paintings decorated the walls, while dainty blood-colored crystal chandeliers hung from above and miniature fabric lamps threw their red-gold light on the tables closest to the walls. I was mesmerized by how audacious, classy, and masculine the whole thing felt.

I heard a pounding steady beat towards the back, and was drawn past the bar to a dance area. The darkened doorway created the illusion of a large space, but when I stepped into the room I discovered it was a small, pulsing dance floor. A raised platform was wedged tightly into a corner, and the DJ stared intently down at his work while bouncing to a silent rhythm in his headphones. He was shirtless, though that was hardly remarkable.

The dance floor was filled with half-naked men undulating together, a hypnotic movement of grace and power, swirling and crashing like waves on a stormy beach. Some of them, many of them, were in tune with each other. A few had fallen off-beat, and struggled to find the break in the flow, so they could fit themselves back into the group's intense energy.

I scanned the room, trying to figure out how to navigate the crowd when it was this cramped. I considered heading back to the front; it didn't seem like there was any use in trying to talk when the music was this loud, and when everyone's focus was on the music. I heard a shout, and all of them turned to look at me, their attention like a floodlight. They broke into huge grins, jumping up and down excitedly. They beckoned me toward the dance floor like a puppy they were trying to entice to their side. I shook my head No, but kept smiling, hoping one of them would want something if I stayed toward the edge of the room. Four of them leapt toward me, pulling me into their cacophony of lust, laughter, joy and chaos.

They spun me around, playing with my hair, and caressing my face. I was jumping, giggling, clutching my cash box and the corner of the cigarettes, all while I tried to find a current of fresh air among the hardened, sweaty chests curving around me. It was so magnificent; they practically lifted me in the air with their enthusiasm. I lost track of time and purpose, torn between my job and the total surrender a crowd in a good mood can inspire.

Though it only lasted a few minutes, it felt longer. I gestured to my five-minute best friends that I was headed into the other room, and their shallow dismay that I was leaving lasted only a moment. As I turned back to the main bar, one of the dancers gently tugged at my sleeve.

"You are so beautiful, darling. Thanks for coming into the deep end with us. Most of you girls won't even get back this far," he shouted in my ear, over the music. The DJ really pulled out all of the stops, quickening the beat.

I must have showed surprise, as he started laughing. He handed me a $20, pulled out some gum and a candy bar, and said, "Come back and see us sometime." He winked, and then plunged back in.

I made my way slowly back into the red room, trying to straighten my disheveled look and checked my cash box, just in case. The saucy boudoir feel of the main bar was a relief after the intensity of the dance floor; it invited you to just sit down and have a brandy. The front was peppered with couples, mostly older men with other older men, but a few with younger companions.

Two older gentlemen were drinking from snifters, and looked at me in a bemused manner. The couple gestured to me like you would for peanuts at a ball game, though they both had elaborate hand waves, their fingers drifting through the air like they were brushing against a soft kitten.

"So, she survived the pit, eh?" one said out of the side of his mouth to the other.

"Yes, though it looks like she barely made it out," replied his partner.

"They must have pulled her in quite deep; she's practically panting."

"Who can blame her darling? Their chests are built like the David."

I found it hilarious they were talking about me like I wasn't standing in front of them. It would've been easy to think they were trying to make me look like a fool, but I could tell from the way they started the conversation that what they really wanted was an audience. I was to watch, not perform. They bantered back and forth for a while, and I gave my best enigmatic smile, feigning a mystery I didn't think I actually possessed.

Finally, the first gentleman leaned closer and said, "Thank you for not being rude. We do enjoy fresh meat like you when going out on nights like these, which are so rare, my plum. My partner is quite sick, you know, and just the sight of you brings such joy and happy memories to the surface. We started talking about you the moment you came in. There was a time when we were quite the riot about town, and you girls were one of the highlights of our nights."

"I'm sorry about your partner," I said, knowing that it was inadequate.

"Aren't you a dear?" he replied, his eyes sliding sideways to his boyfriend.

"I have all kinds of..." I started to say, but his eyes snapped back to me, and he waved his hand in the air again to interrupt.

"Is there a juicy memory from your childhood you could share with us, strumpet?" he inquired, giving me a smile of encouragement. The boyfriend's eyes sharpened as he turned to me, leaned forward and gave me an interested look.

"I think I know what you would like," I answered, pulling a thought from the past, one of the sweeter moments with my dad from long ago. It felt like the wrong time and place to share such a memory, but I figured why the hell not.

"I'll share a story my father likes to tell. When I was little, maybe four or five years old, my dad would take me to the park. It was just the two of us; my mom left us when I was a baby. He's a quiet man, but he was a good father, and he often took me outside to play.

"One windy day, I had tired of the playground and digging in the dirt, so I took shelter under a nearby willow tree. When my dad came to find me, I was gently holding the branches of the willow tree; as they swayed in the wind, I swayed along with them. My dad says he asked me what I was doing, and I told him I was dancing with the trees."

I could see the gentlemen were moved by my story, as they were holding hands very tightly. The first one pulled a ten out of his wallet and reached for a small pack of gum.

"Thank you for that lovely piece of you, dear. Good luck out there, and be safe," he waved me away this time, again with an airy flourish.

As I left the bar, my mind turned over something the gentleman said, about giving him a piece of me. It was an interesting turn of phrase. I started to wonder if that was the real trick of this job, giving away pieces of me for the sake of entertainment. I'd have to consider this further if I decided to come back out another night.

¤ ¤ ¤

Thom met me at quarter to two at our designated spot, and I was a bit frazzled by the time he pulled up. The rest of my run — Blush Wine Bar, Q, and Badlands — went relatively smoothly. Everyone I met was polite and sweet, even though they declined to buy anything nearly every time. Each bar was different in its own way, but I found myself too tired and confused about how to work these crowds to notice much detail. I got a bit lazy and cut myself some slack for surviving my first night. I had no idea how well I did, but it could hardly make a difference now.

For the first time, I realized begrudgingly, I was happy to see the yellow road stain of his car, if only to get away from the pounding music. It was very quiet in the car. Loud quiet. I waited for my ears to adjust.

Thom glanced at me, and then took off without a word.

"What?" I demanded.

"Nothing. Just seeing if you are cut out for this. Not many people can do this, you know. If you don't enjoy it, cut your losses."

I was irritated that Thom was back to his Eeyore impression. "I'm just tired. I had fun. It was kind of hectic tonight though, right?"

"Suuu-ure, but it's often like this. Hey, I'm not trying to say you can't. Just that maybe you want to find something better, you know?" he finished. I could tell he was mostly talking to himself, but I was too thin on sympathy after walking around all night to comfort him about his future. I said nothing.

We drove back to South of Market through streets that were now empty, aside from the occasional taxicab.

Thom dropped me off in front of the office. I punched in the code, and headed inside. The place was once again bustling, as girls shimmied out of outfits, counted out their merchandise, and packed their bags. In one corner a few girls who were loud and a bit drunk were comparing notes from the night. The rest of the girls were quiet, and several seemed to have had a bad night; they looked like they were nursing minor heartbreaks.

I wondered what I should be feeling. I couldn't even tell. Did I do well? Did I tank? I sat at an empty table in the middle, and the chair tipped me partially forward, which was why it was vacant in the first place. I decided to get it over with quickly.

Selene was nowhere to be found, so I went up to the dark-haired man who sat behind the managers' desk, punching the keys of a computer. His clothes, eyes and hair were all black, completely black. He wore silver jewelry of skulls, turquoise beads, and various animals, but there seemed to be a theme of horses. He turned to me, and just stared. It was not a reassuring feeling.

"Hi, I guess I need to count my tray, and am not sure where..." I started to say.

Suddenly he came out of his reverie, and turned to the desk.

"What's your name?" he asked briskly.

"Pale."

He handed me the original inventory sheet I had filled out earlier. "Have one of the girls show you what to do," he said, turning back to the computer. He was already lost in thought again.

I just stood there, but he didn't spare me another glance.

I walked away, feeling brushed off. I was at a loss, but went back to my reality-tilting chair. One of the quiet girls came over and walked me through my checkout process: how to note the amount left over of each item, what to write if I'd sold out of something. It wasn't rocket science, and soon I had an accounting that matched what was left in my tray. I looked around and noticed a bunch of other girls counting and sorting their cash, so I did the same.

I joined the queue of girls at the front desk, where the black clad manager was calculating and checking girls out. The other girls chatted to each other, comparing stories of success or failure. I ended up standing behind Meredith.

"Hey there!" she said, still friendly but more subdued than earlier. I was definitely feeling the same, so I gave her a tired smile.

"How did you do tonight?" I asked her.

"I think I did pretty well, but it dragged tonight. My rhythm felt off..." she trailed off as she stepped up to the desk. I listened closely as she and the night manager joked back and forth a bit. I heard her say his name, and wondered if I heard it right; it sounded weird.

When she was done, Meredith was smiling, and she had a wad of cash. It turned out she had a talent for plucking greenbacks from those slippery pockets.

Happy for her, I stepped up, grinning.

"So, your name is...Ransom?" I asked.

"What?" He stared at me.

"Your name. Is it really Ransom?" I repeated, not sure if I should even be asking.

"Yeah. What's your name?" he asked me, looking down and taking the sheet from my hand.

I passed the tray over the counter. "I'm Pale, we just met a second ago? It's my first night."

"Yeah, I can tell," he said absent-mindedly. He was busy punching in my numbers from my inventory.

I waited quietly, letting him concentrate. And truthfully, I was too tired for chitchat.

"You did pretty well, actually." He handed me about $80 in cash. "We deduct the cost of the items, take the company cut, plus a rental equipment fee, and anything left over is yours, so you always leave here with cash in hand. Assuming you made a profit. You want to be careful out there, it's late and it's dangerous. I shouldn't have to tell you that, but sometimes girls get robbed, so don't be one of them," he said in a flat tone. I got the impression he wouldn't bother telling me this if I had done poorly in my sales.

A bit overwhelmed, I just stood there. "Is there anything else I need to do?" I asked.

"Your costume." He looked me over.

"What about it?" I said, stupidly.

"Turn it in to me, at the window to my left, once you've changed," he said, staring at me again, like I was an idiot.

"Right! Right. Sorry. Just...tired."

He smiled in a sarcastic and indulgent way, and took the paperwork from the next girl. I used the training room to change into my street clothes, and then passed my costume to Mr. Black-and-Moody.

All my tasks completed, I was ready to leave. There didn't seem to be anything to say, or anyone to say it to. It was rather anti-climactic: we came together as a team so early in the night, but we left as strangers. I walked outside, acutely aware that I was on my own, with all this cash.

I hailed a cab, and the driver tried to strike up a conversation, but I was not having it. I gave him my address, and we bumped along the streets like abandoned trash carried along by a cold breeze, the remnants of the night stories we didn't tell each other.

Chapter 6

I woke up very late the next morning, foggy-headed. The phone had rudely turned its volume up to 10 — or so it seemed — as it shrieked at me from the kitchen. I staggered out of bed and shuffled to the phone, wondering what on earth could be so important.

"WHAT," I growled.

"My goodness! Big night, Duchess?" said my best friend, sounding pleased with herself for waking me up.

"Jana, seriously, what are you doing calling me so earl-" I barely got the words out before she started laughing.

"Early, sweetie? Is that what you call 11am? I waited as long as I could to hear all about the big First Night, but some of us have been up since five, so SPILL," she commanded.

No rest for the wicked, I thought wearily.

"Fine, but can you give me five minutes? I just got out of bed. I need to put some clothes on." I wandered back to my bedroom-living room-dining room area — it's a pretty small studio apartment.

"Ok, but I want to hear everything! Spare no details." She hung up.

Had I known she was going to be so demanding, I would've held out and bargained for the afternoon. But once that girl sets her mind, you can forget about not giving her what she wants. She was a brat, but she was my brat, and it was one of the things I loved about her. She somehow managed to always get what she wanted. I wish I were more like that.

Twenty-five minutes later, I was happily showered, eating a late breakfast of cold pizza, and describing my night to my best friend. I embellished a little, and felt triumphant that I made it through such a strange experience, and managed to make money on top of it all. When I went to bed last night, I wasn't sure if it was something I wanted to continue, but now I was convinced I could do this. It was not exactly easy, nor was it the best income in the world, but at least I could use my sex appeal, and end up with some fun stories to share.

Jana seemed impressed with my ability to navigate the Castro, though she played it cool.

"Honey, you've never been around gay people in your life, living out in the middle of Nowhere, USA! Did you embarrass yourself asking questions? Did you do that thing you do when you get nervous? You know, that thing with your feet?" she poked at me lovingly.

"Shut up! I don't do that anymore. I was totally cool. I acted like I'd been to the Castro every day. It really was great, Jana. I met the most wonderful older couple…." I launched into the next details of my night. Jana loved this kind of stuff. I was delighted she was so supportive.

After another 20 minutes of this, she finally asked "So, are you going to work tonight?"

"I don't know, I guess so. The night manager didn't say anything about it, and I was pretty out of it by the time I left. I assume I should talk to Selene."

"Yeah, you might want to call first, check and make sure what the next step is. Though, it sounds like you did well enough, financially.

"Pale, listen: I know you've been restless lately because of ... you know, this last birthday of yours was sort of important, with your birth mom and everything..." she said gently. "I get it, you are trying something new. It's fine if you don't want to talk about that. Just be careful, and have fun."

I ignored her comment about my birth mother. After all, what was there to be said? Jana was right, I'd just turned twenty-six, which was the same age my birth mom was when she...found me a new home. Except for my first year before my adopted mom ran out on us, it'd been just my adopted dad and me since I was a baby. It was just weird and painful to think that I was the same age she was when it all happened.

I snapped out of my thoughts when Jana said, "I have get back to work, but I also want to talk with you about boyfriend stuff. Can you free up some time soon?" I could hear her roll her eyes at the term "boyfriend." It sounded like she needed to vent. Jana and Alex were in love, but they had recently moved in together, so they were still "magnetizing," as she put it, and this process had caused some friction.

"What are best friends for?" I said, and agreed to a day later in the week.

Selene answered when I called the office. We chatted for about 10 minutes about inconsequential things, and then she asked how my night went. I gave her a truncated version of what I told Jana. When I got to the part about whether or not I should come back, I suddenly got nervous.

There was a pause on the phone, then Selene said, "Well, I was looking at your numbers from last night, and they look fine, especially for a Thursday. I'd say you did average for a girl on her first time out. I want to bring you back in tonight, and for the rest of this weekend also. We will see you tonight at 6:30 p.m.?" she asked confidently.

"Sure!" I said, relieved.

"Great. Bonsoir!" she said and hung up.

So, that's it? I thought. I was employed. Just like that. I was pretty certain that "real" jobs required harder work: snazzy resumes, sweat-inducing interviews, agonizing waits by the phone, all that awful stuff that went with finding the right company to work with. But just like that, based on sex appeal and some sales? This'll be like taking candy from a baby.

Next I called my dad, relieved that I finally had some good news to share. He'd been down on me for several months over my directionless life, and I wanted him to back off about the job, especially. He wanted me to go back to school and finish my degree and had been nagging me about it — a lot — but the prospect of school just seemed unrewarding, at best. I think he was just lonely, because ever since I moved to San Francisco, he'd been calling more and more, and even threatening to come and stay to, as he put it, "get me back on track."

The phone rang over and over, and on the 12th ring he picked up.

"Hello?"

"Hi Dad, it's me."

"Oh. Hello honey," he said after a pause. I sighed. He was not exactly sharp today.

"Dad, I've got some great news. I started a new job last night, and it went really well. I am going back again tonight, and am working all weekend!"

"What kind of job are you working at night? Is it security? Or a call center, like here in Modesto?" my dad asked. His family came here from Germany when he was a boy, so his questions were very direct, and came out sounding a little abrupt. The accent didn't help either. He didn't mean to be intimidating, and would often soften his tone for me.

I also knew he didn't mean to ask me if I took the most Boring Job Ever, but I couldn't help it, I lashed out.

"Dad! That's why I left Modesto, so I wouldn't have to take crappy jobs like that! No, it's more exciting and interesting than all that! God, sometimes I think you want to freeze me in carbonite, like Han Solo," I said, exasperated.

There was a pause as Dad shuffled around the kitchen. I heard the clanking of jars on the counter and dishes in the sink. I could practically see the dirty yellow countertops, coupled with the dark brown 70's wallpaper. I sighed again.

"I'm sorry. I just don't want the same things that you want. Can't you be happy for me? It took me a long time to find work, and I am going to try really hard to make money."

There was another long pause on the phone, more clattering. I knew he was trying to think of the right thing to say.

"I don't want to carbonite you, Pale. But I don't want you to get into danger and jail and such either. I am your father, it's my job to tell you these things, okay, Chewbacca?" I could hear his smile at the end. *Star Wars* was our favorite movie to watch together, and Chewbacca talk at the dinner table was one of the ways we would deal with our loneliness, together.

I smiled, and laughed softly. "RAWWWWRRRR!" I said back, doing Chewy's roar.

We both laughed.

"Okay, you be careful out there, and tell me all about it in a few days, ja? Don't make me use The Force!" My dad the comedian, ladies and gentleman, I thought silently.

"Okay, Dad, sure thing." I hung up, and didn't give it a second thought. After all, danger was exactly why I took this job.

I packed a bag full of makeup and hair-styling supplies while humming that old song, "I Want Candy." I walked out the door, excited for tonight's adventures.

Chapter 7

Meredith gave me a smile as I came in, and concentrated on her eye shadow application in the mirror. The tall reedy-legged blond woman I saw yesterday was in the corner coaching a timid, average-looking girl on hair techniques. The blond was teasing up the hair of the mousy girl who looked like she wasn't used to the attention.

I pulled out a seat and dumped my bags, then camped out at a spot at the mirror on the wall. Before I knew it, the blond had come over to me, and was staring at me in the glass.

"I can see how those eyes are going to work for you," she said playfully, with a raspy voice.

I looked more closely at her. She looked like she was in her mid-30's, or probably older. She was close to 5'10, spindly, and had the look of an older hippie kid in her tie-dyed dress and bright turquoise and pink eye shadow. There was fringe on her leather purse, and woven peace bracelets on her wrists. A Buddha necklace hung limply on her bony collar.

"What's your name?" she asked with authority. "I'm Susannah. I've been here the longest."

"Thanks. I'm Pale. I just started last night."

"Back for more, hmm? Well, I've been at this a long time, honey, and I know ALL the tricks of hard selling. You've got questions or get stomped on, talk to me. I take care of the girls who can stick it out.

Consider me the assistant manager to Ransom. *Toujours gai*, you know?" She turned to go back to her own makeup station.

"Ok, thanks," I called out. "What was that last thing you said?"

"Always joyful!" she cackled, and did a little dance.

Susannah went back to the mousy girl, who was bent over her tray, concentrating on counting inventory. She was looking a bit more the part in her costume and makeup.

I turned back and got to work on my look.

I looked in the mirror, and tried to gauge the appeal I could play up the most. My hair was a wavy dark brown, nearly black in this light. It was thick, and fell to my shoulders. My skin was pale, a creamy white with no freckles — well, except for the one that's almost never seen, because it's inside my left elbow. My eyes were a medium light gray. They tended to intrigue or alienate people, I'd learned the hard way, and were one of the first features that people noticed about me.

I was not as petite as Meredith, but I didn't tower as tall as Susannah, either. I had really tiny feet. Most people didn't notice that. I was not strong, but I was flexible. I had the kind of body that's good for acrobatics. I was using the company's uniform tonight, so I couldn't do much to change the way my body came across. I would need to rely on hair and makeup to develop my allure.

I decided that I would play up my eyes with heavy charcoal eyeliner and a turquoise uniform. Last night the customers were mostly intrigued, and no matter what, those colors would help make my persona stand out. Jana said that I looked amazing in turquoise and I agreed.

Susannah came over to talk to me. She'd changed into a different kind of uniform than the bell hop style, a tie-dyed outfit that was slightly too big for her — it was cute, but I was a bit surprised Selene had approved it — and she had a giant feather in her hair. The lights she was selling were all on, rings and necklaces all blinking a slow, hypnotic rhythm.

"Do you have a tip jar?" she asked.

"What? No. Do I need one?" I replied, jolted out of my stare.

"Of course! It's how we make half our profit! You need to play up the pity, definitely. If you don't, you won't make it, sugar." She walked over to the vending machine, and bought a bottle of water. She opened the water, poured it into a canteen she had, and handed it to me.

"Here you go." I looked at her blankly.

"It's perfect!" she said, explaining patiently. "You just cut off the top portion, add a tip sign, and stick it in the front corner, where everyone goes to look at the cigs. You've got a flashlight, right?"

"Not yet. Apparently I need one?" I asked, hesitating. I wondered how many other accessories I was going to need. It wasn't like I had planned to sink a bunch of money into the outfit.

Susannah saw my dismay. "Don't worry, pumpkin. It's just a few small things to make the sales come in guaranteed. Use the flashlight to highlight the product, right? Like in the training video!

"Definitely you need to make yourself a tip sign; there are pens and supplies on that desk over there. Keep it simple. A really popular one is 'Tipping is Sexy.' EVERYONE likes being sexy!" She waved me across the room, and went back to her routine.

I looked around and saw that the regular girls all had tip signs attached to battered water bottles. I grabbed a pair of scissors and started to cut mine in half.

As I cursed under my breath and tried to get the right angle, I heard a drawling, amused voice just in front of me.

"You look like you are enjoying yourself while destroying that, but do you want some help?"

I looked up and saw the most beautiful face grinning down at me.

He had hazel eyes, dark brown hair with red highlights, and a tall, solid body. His leg was bumping my leg gently, punctuating his teasing and breaking me out of my stunned state. His face was a bit fierce, and I struggled to answer. I couldn't believe no one told me such a complete hottie was working here. I deserved a memo, at the very least.

"Yes, help would be great. I need to cut this in half," I managed, proud of myself for keeping my cool.

He shot me a glance, seeing through me. He laughed and took the tools from my hands.

"So, you're the new girl. I saw a new name on the dry erase board." He gestured to a white board on the wall I hadn't noticed before. I saw the names of all the neighborhoods across the top laid out in a grid, with columns underneath to insert the names of each girl going out that evening. My name was listed under "SoMa."

"Fresh meat! I love it. First night or second?" he said rapidly. He was looking down, concentrating on cutting through the plastic easily and in a straight line. He finished the cut, and then scraped the edge of the scissors along the top so the edge was dull.

"Second night," I said, looking him over closely.

He beamed another huge, disarming grin, handing me everything back.

"Well, I'll be driving you tonight, Miss Daisy. Try and keep to the schedule; we leave here in 20 minutes." He sauntered back to the counter where the supplies were kept. I felt an absence as he walked away, like a cold spot of air in a warm hallway. I turned around and caught Susannah staring at me. She turned away abruptly, so I ignored her.

I dressed more quickly than last night, and got my tray with my inventory sheet. It went faster than I expected. It must've been nerves that clouded me yesterday. I knew the night would be long, but I was more excited today than nervous. It certainly helped that HE was here.

I saw Thom back behind the candy storeroom counter, so I headed over to replace broken wrappings and dead batteries. I had seen girls trading things off their trays both nights I'd been here, which was a high ratio of broken stuff, if you asked me.

Thom gave me a scowl, so I knew he had his grump on again.

"Hey, Thom," I said, handing him the broken items. "Who's that guy over there, talking to Susannah?" I asked nonchalantly. Susannah was chatting with The Guy, and he was laughing easily. I felt a stab of envy, but turned back to Thom.

Thom snatched the items from my hands, and turned away, muttering. He responded so quietly, I couldn't hear him.

"What?" I said, frustrated. My façade of cool didn't hold very long.

"I said that's Felix. And don't pester me with the million questions you have, because every girl in here has asked after him. He's driving you tonight, so at least you will be off my back," Thom answered angrily, shoving my replacement items in my hands.

I took a long look at him, and noticed the dark circles under his eyes, the rumpled shirt, and the dirty hands.

"Did you sleep at all last night?" I asked gently.

Thom's face was frozen for a moment, then his defensive stance slipped completely, as he shook his head No and turned away from me. I decided to leave him to his thoughts. Thom didn't seem like a naturally bad guy. He was carrying something around; I just didn't know what it was. Not yet.

I headed back to my tray, and saw several girls shoot me sympathizing glances. I nodded my head in their direction.

Felix had wrapped up his conversation with Susannah — I noticed she was looking very pleased with herself — and stood in the middle of the room. "I am leaving in 2 minutes! Girls who are coming with me, get your asses in gear, the boat is leaving the dock!" He strode outside. There was a small silence as the door slammed shut, and the sunny feeling in the room was gone again.

I heard the sounds of chairs scraping and girls hustling as I scrambled to get my tray secure, grab my purse, and do a last minute check of hair, makeup, shoes and outfit. By the time I had everything on and ready to go, I was one of the last ones out of the office, so I hurried outside.

Felix was waiting impatiently behind the wheel of a minivan. I stood there gaping; this was such a stark contrast with what I thought he would be driving. Felix blew his horn, and gestured behind him for me to get in.

The other two girls had loaded up, leaving me the spot directly behind the driver, the hardest to get into. I hurried awkwardly into the street and had a tricky time getting myself, and then my tray, into the vehicle, all while my door was open to a lane of rushing traffic. Everyone made frustrated noises at me, and finally I slammed the door shut. The van was silent.

Felix said, quite clearly, "If you ever make me wait like that again, I am leaving you at the office, and you can try and make money by staring at a wall."

I flushed with embarrassment, made even worse by Susannah's smug grin to herself. I could see her quite well, since she was in the front passenger seat. I cursed silently that I'd ever found such a brute attractive.

The ride was soon filled with the chatter of the other girls, heavily punctuated with Susannah's transparent flirting. I said nothing.

Felix let Susannah out first, then the other girl. She was a bit more subdued than Susannah, but still happy when she got dropped off. Felix was friendly and warm with each of them as they left, wishing them luck.

I was the last one in the van, and as we pulled away from the curb, he glanced in the rear view mirror at me.

"Look, if you are late like that each time, all the girls will start checking their hair for an extra 20 minutes. I grew up with three sisters, I should know!" he laughed at his own joke, giving me an encouraging grin.

I responded coolly, "What section am I working tonight, Boss?"

Felix's face hardened slightly, but he replied, "I'm taking you to the SoMa run first, then likely the West run again. It's my understanding you did those last night, right?"

I nodded silently, avoiding his gaze.

We drove through crowded streets, and while I saw something funny a time or two, I didn't share it with Felix. I was still upset that he humiliated me; he didn't know that I was rarely late. There was no need to go overboard. Then again, he was right: if one girl were late, the other girls would easily crowd a mirror and stay there for three hours, fussing with every little curl and eyelash.

While I was working through both sides of our tiff, I hadn't noticed that we had slowed down, and were pulling over in a loading zone.

"So, do you always take this long to work through things?" Felix asked playfully, raising his eyebrows at me as I packed my belongings together.

I gave him a sharp look in the mirror. "Shut up!"

He gave a full belly laugh, half laughing with me, half at me. I was furious all over again. I walked to the curb and leaned in through the passenger window. He handed me my list of bars for the night.

"Ok, Miss Daisy, have it your way!" He laughed again. "I'll see you back here in 45 minutes. Try not to be late!" He chuckled to himself. He was terribly handsome when he was laughing, and it didn't help matters.

I gave him another scathing look and said, "Oh, I'll be here! And that's Ms. Daisy, to you."

He was already rolling up the window and driving away. Asshole. Infuriating, arrogant, gorgeous, friendly, deceptive, reasonable asshole!

I stomped towards my first bar, slowing down my pace, and took a breath to find my Zen. Jesus, he was so exasperating!

In truth, my second night was not a whole lot different from my first. I was still nervous yet thrilled, and still anxious about sales and obsessed with doing a good job and time management, if only to prove Felix wrong. Tonight, though, I was also distracted by thinking about him: his smile, his laughter, and his easy manner.

I continued to play the 'I'm new, it's my first night' card, as Meredith had suggested. From what I could tell, that card got played for the first couple of months. It seemed weird to me that I wouldn't run into regulars that would know that was bullshit, but I guessed the regulars played along as well.

I was still figuring out how this all worked, trying to find the web of design in the pattern of being out Here, on the Street. You couldn't lose sight of the danger, but there were people who looked after you: bartenders, bouncers, security guards, taxi drivers, regulars.

There were also those who were not looking after you: drunks, insanely jealous girls, crack heads, pot heads, thieves, and just run-of-the-mill troublemakers. I had certainly caught glimpses of both in the last two days.

I thought about how old the tradition of hard sales was. From carnivals to traveling salesmen, from fortunetellers to Vegas, there were a hundred, a thousand tricks to get someone to be interested in what you had. The best I could hope for was to use my honest face to my advantage.

I was standing outside Cat Club getting some fresh air. The stuffy, hot atmosphere of the bars kept me plenty warm, making the chill of the night air a relief. The silk top I wore was not only long-sleeved, but padded, so warmth wasn't an issue. I made a mental note to check for a cooler outfit as the weather got warmer.

A man in a hat broke me out of another daydream about Felix by shouting, "Hey, Gum girl! Gum girl! Come over here!"

I walked hesitantly towards someone who looked like a celebrity, but I could hardly believe it. There was just no way, no way that Jack Black was talking to me! Jack Black was one of my favorite comedians; raunchy, self-obsessed, and totally unapologetic about his sloppy appearance and disdain towards anyone who didn't love rock n' roll like he did. He got me in touch with my inner 13-year-old boy, and I adored him for it. My heart jumped even further up my throat, but I walked calmly over to him and his entourage.

As I got closer, something seemed off about Jack's face. His eyes were too beady; his hair was too wavy and styled. He was pudgier than Jack in the waist, and he was shorter as well. His hat read, "Anti-Hero." He sidled up to me, very oily in his movement.

"Well, Hell-o, there! I'm Jack Stack, a look-a-like for Jack Black in every way, baby, EV-E-RY way. Right down to the see-through boxers, if you know what I mean. Want to see my power stance? Of course you do."

He pulled back from me in a surprisingly fast motion, jumping in the air slightly, landing with his legs spread and holding an imaginary guitar in front of him. He looked so triumphant as he let go of the "guitar" and thrust both hands up in a #1 symbol, I broke out laughing, my disappointment vanishing at the cartoonish display in front of me.

Jack Stack took this, sadly, as a compliment, and slithered up next to me again.

"So, what have you got for sale tonight?" he asked me, eyebrows raised.

"Only what's on the tray, Mr. Big Shot," I told him firmly, moving away slightly so I could face him. If I knew this type, he'd be in my cash box before I could even blink.

"That's cool, that's cool. I just wanted some gum anyway. But you looked so beautiful over there, I couldn't leave you by yourself," he said, winking.

We wrapped up the sale, and I had to give it to him, several other people had wandered over to see if he really was Jack Black. I walked towards the intersection to meet Felix, shaking my head.

I thought this job and I were going to get along just fine.

Chapter 8

I was ready and waiting when Felix pulled up at our meeting point. There was no one else in the van, so I slid in the front seat, determined to patch things up.

"How's the night so far?" he questioned, flashing me an absent-minded smile as he checked his mirrors to rejoin traffic. I told him all about Jack Stack, and we chuckled together over his antics. After a pause, I asked him, "Is Rehka out tonight?"

"Yeah, she's on the North run with Thom."

"Oh, I was just wondering how the bet was going tonight."

Felix stiffened, and didn't reply. The air in the van got distinctly icy, and I was confused. Apparently I'd said something wrong. Again.

The silence after that was so pronounced, I was afraid to say anything else. Watching the emotions play across Felix was like watching an emotional-weather forecast: mostly stony with occasional flashes of anger, followed by resignation. Then disappointment. Then back to stony. We drove a long time in silence.

We were nearly to my drop-off point when Felix said, "I don't know anything about that."

That was so laughably untrue that I just stared at him in disbelief. He pulled the van over and silently handed me my list for the run.

"Ok, well I guess I'll see you later then," I mumbled.

"Yeah, I'll see you back here in an hour fifteen," he said, quietly.

I got out of the van, and he pulled away. I couldn't believe how fast I'd managed to ruin the good vibe between us. I don't know what it was about the bet that had triggered him, but it was really, really bad. And I felt guilty for asking him; I just thought all the drivers were in on that, like Thom said. I made a mental note to ask Meredith about it, when I saw her next.

¤ ¤ ¤

I was standing outside the Blue Saloon. It was my third-to-last bar of the run, and it was right next to a bar with a white neon sign with the P blown out; apparently it was now a "Sorts Bar."

I felt pleasantly light-headed. My outfit had sparked several flirtations and offers of free drinks, but each time I demurred as elegantly as possible. At my last stop, however, I'd snuck in a shot. It had given me a few moments of liquid courage, but I felt a bit guilty for drinking on the job. Sure, this job entailed strutting, sex appeal, swindling, haggling, late nights, and other dangers. But still, it was a job. And I would've hated disappointing Selene.

I thought of Selene's chocolate brown eyes, and her classy but playful manner. I dreamed briefly if I could ever hope to be that cool and desirable. I guessed that was why Envy was one of the seven deadly sins; it had certainly wormed into my heart at that moment. And Lust, can't forget Lust, I thought, as I felt a swift tightening of arousal at the quick thought of Selene, then Felix. Damn, that whisky shot was stronger than I'd realized. I put them both out of my mind and got back to work.

The Blue Saloon had a cramped interior, but was draped with thick red curtains at the door, and everything was antique and old-timey: the bar, the furniture, even the bartenders, who wore suspenders and jaunty hats. I liked it immediately.

After a nod from the bouncer, I started my circuit around the room. Off to my left I heard an excited, "Look honey, look! It's a Tart! It's one of Tawny's Tarts!" This statement was punctuated with a cry of delight.

I turned in the direction of the noise after selling a candy bar, and flashed my new customer a huge smile. She clapped her hands and beckoned me over, through the increasing noise.

"Oh, dear, doesn't she look absolutely delicious?" She put her hand on her boyfriend's leg and gave me a mischievous look. They were both looking at me in the way that people look at you when they want to do something reckless and R-rated.

I forgot for a moment to be flustered, basking in the obvious appeal they both had for me, and I had for them. For a few heartbeats, my head raced wildly to the possibility of what this job could do for my sex life.

With great effort, I wrenched my thoughts back to the damn albatross around my neck. Damn fine whiskey, that was.

"Hey there, Tart fans. Seems like you know all about me, so you have me at a...disadvantage." Oops. That was a bit obvious.

"Oh, sweetheart, we so wish we did have you at a disadvantage," the man drawled in a southern accent, his gaze sliding briefly to his wicked companion," but really, you are the one holding all the... goodies." He finished by ignoring my tray completely, but lingering his gaze hungrily upon my legs.

"Well, that's a relief. Because I have all KINDS of goodies to sell. I might even gift you with something, if you are nice."

They conferred amongst themselves for a few moments, while I made eye contact with a few other patrons at the bar who were obviously waiting for me to go over and offer them something. I swiveled back, just as the girl stood to whisper in my ear.

"How about $50 for a cigar, a kiss with me, and your phone number?" she floated in my ear, not even shouting. Damn, that was hot.

"Everything but the number," I shot back.

Mr. Charming pulled out a $50 bill and laid it on top of my cigarettes. I pulled off the tray and set it on their large oval table. They were both watching me, eager and impatient. She leaned toward me, and I mirrored her. Her face showed confusion as I broke from our dance to bend slightly and reach for her hand. Keeping my eyes on hers, I drew the top of her wrist level to my mouth, then left a long, sensuous kiss on her wrist, followed by a quick peck. Her lover howled with laughter at the look of defeat on her face. He slapped his knee and wiped a fake tear from his eye. I put the tray back on, picked out a cigar and clipped it for him, and tucked the $50 bill into my stash.

"That's not what I meant," she said coquettishly, crossing her arms.

"I'm such a Tart," I said, winking and walking away.

He called out to me as I made my way across the room, "Worth every penny, dear! I will smoke this and think very juicy thoughts of you tonight!"

I worked through the rest of the folks at the bar, but I was getting a prickly feeling like I was running late again, and I could feel their eyes on me everywhere I went. I hurried towards the door, ready for some fresh air, when the bouncer caught me.

"I don't usually let you girls in here, you know. But the patrons like you, so tell your boss to give the manager a call." I was confused by his remark, as this bar was definitely on my list of places approved to go. I shrugged it off and made a note on my post-it to talk to Ransom later in the night.

The sports bar with the funny sign out front was quieter inside, but friendly. I had to switch gears to meet the drinkers on their playing field, shoving away the erotic rush I'd been riding at the Blue Saloon. Though they were mostly distracted with games on the giant TV, most of the patrons threw me an extra buck or two for smokes or gum.

So far, in sales, so good. But then I was really running late, so I hustled out and headed up the street to meet Felix at Evergreen. He was pulling up before I had time to begin at Evergreen — oops, I guess suggestive banter takes up more time than I'd realized. I didn't feel too badly, though, as I'd made really good money off that exchange. Whew.

Felix seemed to have shaken off the awkwardness from when he'd dropped me off, and from his demeanor I could tell he didn't want me to mention it —I was getting a distinct that-never-happened vibe — so we chatted about other things on our drive across town to the Haight district. I was feeling more confident now that I was returning to the same places from last night, and the excitement helped keep my sales personality alive while the boring transit parts were going on. Maybe that was why I liked it so much; you just never knew what was going to happen next.

Felix regaled me with a funny story about the original owner, Tawny, a gorgeous woman from New York with the coloring of a tabby cat: bright golden eyes, strawberry blond/curly hair, along with a sassy, loud personality. I realized while he was talking that I had seen Tawny on the training videos on my first night, and could picture her as he described one of the most famous stories.

"So Tawny had this huge van, right? It was painted kind of glittery gold, just like her coloring, and it had a big logo from the 80's with the company name on it, TAWNY'S TARTS, in big letters. I mean, this van was ugly as all get out, and everyone knew exactly what it was about; she used to drive this van all over the place. It was always gasping and rattling— total piece of shit.

"She used to park it overnight, and always got parking tickets in the morning, because she would forget to move it, or some such thing. Who knows if she was passed out in the back, or slept in the office; things were different, it was more casual back then.

"She got so many parking tickets the van would regularly get impounded and sold. And instead of paying the parking tickets, which were a small fortune by then, she would go to the sale and buy back the van for less than the total of the tickets! I mean dirt-cheap! NO ONE wanted that van; they couldn't sell it to anyone else. And Tawny, she would just flounce in there, scoop it back up, and be on her merry way. She did that more than a few times, I hear," he finished, shaking his head and chuckling. He was totally amused at his own story, and I couldn't help but smile at his energy, and at that gorgeous, easy grin.

Felix dropped me in front of Milk and handed me a longer list than I'd had last night.

"This is the Extended Haight run. It's different from last night. You have a lot more time, but you are visiting almost double the places, and the distance between them is further. Most of them are here on Haight Street, but you will have to take a few detours to get to the others. I will meet you down the road at Masonic, in front of the Ben 'n Jerry's. You've got about 6-8 blocks to cover, so you better get moving. I'll see you in 1 hour and 45. Good Luck, Miss Daisy!" he said, tipping an imaginary hat at me and emphasizing the 'miss.' As soon as I was out of the van, he sped off.

I had no idea how I was supposed to manage flirting and interacting with other people when Felix was taking up so much space in my brain.

The run went very quickly, as Felix predicted, because I had to keep moving. After hitting all the bars from last night's list, I moved further on up Haight to Trax.

Trax was a strange experience. One man lamented to me for 5 minutes how he couldn't buy a vintage Harley motorcycle because he had to make repairs for his tenants on his run-down apartment building; apparently he considered electricity and heat to be luxuries. If he thought he was going to get sympathy from me, he was mistaken. Disgusted, I headed out.

At Magnolia, a man spoke to me in a slow, barely audible fashion. When I leaned closer to hear him, he reached out and started stroking my hair. Creeped out, I cut my circuit of the place short and left.

Sunshine Coast, the last place on my list, was smoky from all the hookah tobacco. I didn't make any sales, but I wasn't groped either, so I decided it was an okay place. It was amazing how fast your expectations could change.

A really nice girl from Texas came up to me to tell me I was "incredible, simply incredible." I thanked her, and headed out to meet Felix.

Felix pulled up on time, and I climbed into his van, blowing a curl out of my face as I sighed and settled in.

"How did it go?" he asked, checking his mirrors for traffic before he pulled away from the curb.

"Sales were no good, but it went fine, though I got groped by this — hey!" I said, startled, as Felix slammed on the brakes.

"What!? Tell me who groped you," he commanded, looking angry.

"It was nothing. It was this guy in Magnolia, and he was stroking my hair. He was all weird and slimy, and I left right away. No big deal," I said, thinking Felix was acting strangely. I looked over and saw he was taking deep breaths with his eyes closed.

Felix muttered to himself, "I have half a mind to have that guy thrown out."

Assessing me, he took another breath. "Would you say that this was something I need to reach out to Ransom and the owner of the bar over?" he asked, giving me an intense look.

I was flustered that Felix was so protective of me, and confused by how something so common — it'd happened to me in bars plenty of times — became such a big deal in that moment. I mean, this kind of thing happened to women all the time. I'd gotten out of the situation quickly, and it hadn't escalated. I struggled to interpret whether that was a personal or a professional response. His speech was all professional, but his eyes were showing me something more.

I made a quick judgment call and said, "No, really. It was no big deal."

Felix took another deep breath. "Pale, listen to me carefully. First of all, the bouncers are there to help you. We have contracts with the bars that include situations like this. Anyone touches you, or bothers you in a way that interferes with you doing your job, you tell the bouncer, or you tell me. We will have a discussion with the owner, and maybe drop them from the list, depending on what happened. Do you understand?"

"Yeah. I'm glad to know there are some general rules in place when I'm in these places by myself. I had no idea."

"Selene should've covered it with you," he said, frustrated. "And while we are on the subject, if you ever get taken somewhere by a driver to 'try a place out,' make sure you are with a good driver that has got your back, ok? I always look out for the girls in my care, but... well, not every driver is like that. " He looked uncomfortable. “Just know that I’m here, and all you have to do is call, or text, ok?”

I stared at Felix, trying to get a handle on the conflicting signals he was sending. At the heart of it, I could tell he wanted me to do well on the job, to feel safe, and to choose my resources wisely. I felt warm at the thought of Felix feeling so strongly about me.

“Thank you,” I said. "I understand what you are saying. Truly, this was a minor thing. But I will be careful in the future.”

He smiled, relaxing his shoulders. We pulled into traffic in a comfortable silence, each of us lost in our own thoughts.

Chapter 9

Felix stopped the car, and it took me several moments to get my bearings. We were in Nob Hill, on a side street just off of Polk.

"This is going to go well for you, I think." Felix looked down, correcting one of his entries on the Post-It in his hand. "It's better sales than the Castro, but not as good as the Haight. Though the Haight may not be for you, time will tell on that one. "

He frowned for a second.

"This run is not full of high rollers, but they do have money to burn. They are easy to talk to, easy to flatter, and they love Tawny's Tarts. Don't be sarcastic, but don't play dumb, either.

"Just try it out. We throw lots of situations at you, to test your flexibility, and see where you thrive. If it feels disorienting, then we are doing it right. We will find the right routine for you, and the money will be more consistent." He concluded all this by handing me my list and waving me out.

Felix had just given me more information than Thom ever had about a run; furthermore, he'd given me more information about this particular run than he had for the two beforehand. Something about that guy touching me must've really set him off. I stepped out of the car, leaning back through the passenger window.

"Okay, thanks. What time and where are we meeting?"

"Right. We're meeting in 50 minutes, at Gold Star Bar. It's just off Polk. Ask around if you can't find it; it's down about 4 blocks. I'll pick you up and take you to the second half of this run." He gestured me back, rolled up the window, and drove off.

The first bar on my list, Big Foot, was all wood and iron fixtures. It looked more like a hunting lodge than anything urban or modern. The bartender shot me a friendly smile as I worked the expanding crowd. It was getting late, and people were growing animated after several hours of drinking and carousing.

I met a young college boy who thought I was devastating. He asked for my number, and I told him it was the same cost as my whole tray, $1000. He mimed being stabbed in the heart, and his friends fanned him comically, while others mock-threatened me with revenge for his untimely demise. I laughed them off, and they threw me a few bucks for being a good sport.

As I hustled my way through the nightlife of Polk Street, I reflected that Felix was right: these were my kind of people. I flitted in and out of each location, swapping stories, telling jokes, hitting a good stride as the energy of the night lifted me up like a wave. I could see above the chatter — I saw strangers forming connections, old enemies burying the ax, even career opportunities blossoming in a friendly way. Everything felt lucky.

At one point, I panicked when I thought I'd lost $100, but I had tucked it into my panty line when I was taking three transactions at once. Other than that scary blip, I glided in and around, up and down, only pausing to take a breath and a drink of soda before heading to my meet-up point.

I arrived early, and spent that time rearranging my tray so that everything would fit and not fall over. My sales had been excellent, though the tips were only modest.

Felix pulled up, saw my face, and burst into a grin.

"Looks like Miss Daisy is finally happy!" he said jokingly.

I grinned back at him and replied, "That was great! I had so much fun! I made money, but mostly I had such a blast. I met this one guy who...." I launched into the story of the guy and the phone number.

Felix listened as he drove me a short distance down the road to the second half of the Polk run. "I'm glad you are having fun. Why else do it, right?"

"You mean, besides the bucket of cash?" I shot back at him.

"You got a bucket? I never got a bucket! What color is it? Does it have your name on it?" Felix was indignant.

"Well, mine was more of a champagne bucket, so it doubles for drinks or cash, but you get the idea. Yeah, my name is engraved on it. It's too bad you never got one." I gave him a pitying look.

"OH, I'm getting my bucket. You girls aren't going to have ALL the fun."

He pounded his fist in his palm in a pretend gesture of determination, which was so ridiculous, we both started laughing. I got my new list, and slid out of the van easily. Still radiating, I glided into my new micro-universe.

¤ ¤ ¤

Felix was waiting for me at the end of the Polk run. That hour had gone as great as the last, maybe even better, and our previous good mood seemed to have prevailed.

"Where to next, Boss?" I asked as soon as I was settled in the van.

"We are going to wrap up at Pier 23. Just one bar. You've got 40 minutes."

"Rehka did that one last night, and I've gotta ask: 40 minutes? For one bar? What is it, the size of a football field?"

"It's spacious, yes, but we've found that you can still get good sales by rotating through this one a few times. They serve food, so customers' tastes are different. This is technically a satellite of the North Beach run, which is highly coveted, but I checked in with Ransom, and he approved if I felt you could do it. If this goes well, then we might try you out on North in a month or two."

"Lucky me," I said sarcastically.

"No, that's me. Felix means lucky," he shot back, grinning and winking at me. My heart jumped a little.

"Any tips?" I pleaded. My nerves were back. I mean, work one bar for 40 minutes? These people were going to be sick of me in about 10. I reluctantly climbed out of the van.

"Sell everything!" he yelled, pulling away.

I squared my shoulders and headed into the bar.

The front was quite tiny, but friendly. It was right on the Bay, so it felt very fishermanly. The lights and TVs were buzzing, and there was loud chatter all around me. I circulated through the bar tables, and sold a few pez, cigarettes, and even a cigar. I didn't have the best-selling candy bars anymore — they got wiped out on the Polk run — but I still had a few good pieces left.

I was standing to the side, rearranging my stuff, when a girl approached to ask for playing cards. I looked at her blankly.

"Well, I don't have any playing cards, sadly, but even if I did, where would you play them?" I looked around, laughing. The place was completely cramped, and the tables were tiny.

She giggled at me, and pointed to a small door, leading to what I thought was the kitchen.

"You've never been back there? It's amazing! Come check it out. And let your boss know we want playing cards," she urged, and walked through the door.

I followed her through a narrow hall, which led to a gigantic outdoor patio. I saw why Felix thought I could easily spend 40 minutes there. The only problem was the fact that it was bitingly cold on the water, despite my uniform's padding.

I ran a circuit around the triangle of tables, and had a great time chatting up hedge fund managers, attorneys, businesswomen, and the occasional group of out-of-towners. The roses and gum were selling well (romance and sex planning, I assumed) but I only made a few cigarette sales, even though we were outside. After selling another cigar, I decided it was time to take a break and sit down for a moment in the bathroom.

When you are in a cramped, beer-stained, single bathroom stall, dressed to the nines, getting in and out of a 25-pound tray that's strapped around your neck was not something you did quickly. Doing this with people pounding, or even falling, against the bathroom door, was far from ideal, but you did what you could when you needed to get off your feet for a few minutes.

By the time I wrestled my tray back around my neck, it was time to meet Felix outside. I wrenched open the door, and hurried out to the street. I saw his van, idling at the curb.

I climbed in and lifted the tray from my neck.

"How was it?" he asked.

"It was fine. Nothing spectacular, no bombing out either. It was cold, though. Sheesh!"

"Glad to hear it. We are going to get the other girls and head back."

"How did they do?" I asked, curious.

"Susannah always does well; she's a natural." The admiration in his voice was nauseating. "The other girl...well, frankly, she cried."

"Cried?" I asked, confused.

"Yes, cried. As in, the whole time. As in, the whole night. There's no way Ransom is going to give her a week. Maybe one more day. She's a mess. And I don't mean a hot mess like you," he jibed.

"Shut up," I said, stung by his praise of Susannah followed so quickly by his insult of me.

"Oh, you are just tired. You did well tonight," he said, sincerely.

"Thanks," I muttered. He was right; I was coming down off my adrenaline now, and worn out.

We drove to SoMa and picked up the new girl, who was sullen and puffy-eyed. Susannah was bright-eyed and fevered, coming off of the Castro run. Apparently that was her best turf, and she must've done exceedingly well because she was very animated all the way back to the office. Some of my gloss had worn off, but in general I was very pleased with my night. The energy was great, I felt more confident, and Felix and I had a great time together.

I settled in to count out my tray, and was happy to notice most of my product was gone. Meredith and I caught up on the details of our evening, and she was delighted to hear that Felix and I had been joking and bonding. She was supportive of the crush, and delighted in my new nickname, Miss Daisy.

A few of the girls standing in line and around the room were swapping stories of the night, and I listened in as I was doing my inventory.

"This one guy wanted me to dance with him so I told him if he bought $40 worth, I'd do it. He actually paid me! He looked like one of those Silicon Valley nerds who has trouble getting a date..." Rehka cackled.

"...I was so floored, turns out this girl went to college with my sister in this tiny town in Vermont," I heard the crying girl say.

"Of course they asked for marijuana! They assume since I'm a love child that I've got the best drugs. I'm not saying they are wrong," Susannah winked in Ransom's direction, and he scowled at her.

As I got in line and made my way up to Ransom, I felt a sense of accomplishment and satisfaction that I'd made it through an interesting couple of nights. Like last night, the girls were more subdued after being On. There was something really tiring and raw for each of us when the illusions came down, and were folded into bags and hung back on closet rods.

Ransom took my inventory sheet without a word, and started stabbing keys and muttering to himself. "You did really well tonight, but not as well as you could have," he said, handing me back my list. "You are underselling your cigarettes at $7; sell them for $8 and ask for a $1 tip. Don't OVERsell, like SOME girls do," he shot a scowl across the room, "for $10, it's too much." He gave me his owlish stare, and handed me a respectable wad of cash.

"Have you got a champagne bucket?" I asked loudly.

"What?" Ransom asked, confused.

"Never mind. I'll get it engraved myself!" I said cheerfully, and burst out laughing. Meredith and Felix, both in on the joke, joined me in laughter.

Sometimes, it was good to be a Tart.

SPRING

Chapter 10

The weeks passed quickly into March. Though the spring had turned foggy in the mornings, it was typical Bay Area weather. The fog burned off by mid-day, leaving it remarkably warm and pleasant, but then the fog doubled back in the evening, leaving it chilly again.

I talked with Jana once a week and with my dad once every few weeks. My dad continued to cluck his tongue and disapprove of the new job; no surprise there. Jana took the stance of an older sister: mildly concerned for my safety, but supportive of my judgment. Besides, she wanted all the gory details, so she made sure I called her regularly to share my exploits. She knew about the restlessness I felt sometimes, and understood the appeal this job held for me.

Dad was raised on a farm by his German parents. He didn't want to be a farmer, so he moved to the "big city" of Modesto to find a wife and a steady job. He'd worked behind a desk ever since, and was closing in on the last few years before retirement.

Whenever he started bugging me about getting a "real" job, I changed the subject to his model airplanes, his obsession being all things Aviation. Dad had planes everywhere in the house — photos, paintings, mugs, models, rugs, blankets — and was always tinkering away in the garage on his latest toy.

From the little bit my dad had told me about her, my adoptive mother was sweet, a good cook, and kept a good home, though he'd also hinted that she was unfaithful. I think that started after they found out she couldn't have children. I don't know how that made sense to her, but she blamed Dad for their inability to conceive. I hated her a little for that, sometimes.

I guess that was one of the reasons I got along with boys so much better than girls, not being around any women when I was younger. It kept my social circle pretty small. I had a few close male friends leading up to junior high, but once the whole 'you are now becoming a Woman' thing hit, being around boys constantly became pretty isolating. Either the boys wanted to play doctor, or only saw me as a buddy and ignored me. Even losing my virginity was fairly anti-climactic, after a drunken night in high school. A few attempts at drugs in college didn't turn out as life-altering as it did for others around me.

As for my birth mother, well, sometimes I wondered about her. When I turned eighteen, Dad and I wrote to the adoption agency for the information. He was really great about it when I asked, and even as I waffled back and forth, he was very encouraging. When we got back a letter with "non-identifying" information about her, I chickened out. I still couldn't bring myself to read it. I mean, the important part, I already know. She was young, got pregnant, didn't know who the father was, etc, etc.

There were times when I wished my mom were around. My adoptive mom, I mean. At least she committed to getting me and stuck around for a year.

Sometimes I felt the absence of a mother figure keenly, and Dad wasn't exactly the talk-about-our-feelings type. He tried hard, though, and I loved him for that.

I think that was something I could appreciate in the people I met on my night job. Everyone was putting themselves out there, navigating through their own wounds and broken hearts, trying so hard to be noticed, to have a special relationship, even if it was in the bullshit of broken pasts and stale dreams. How do you create something fantastic, when you don't feel you are worthy of it? I could relate to those sad bastards because I was one of them, too.

As a Tart, I used courtesy, flattery, manipulation, deception, sometimes even the truth came out to play, all in the name of the score. The Sale. Doing my part for Capitalism. It started long before me, and would end long after me. It wasn't as bad as the oldest Profession, although sometimes I wondered how far apart the line was between being a Tart and, well, a tart.

I didn't like to think about how bad things would have to be for me to actually do that, but it was all around me, at night, and I couldn't help when my mind drifted there. And of course, I wondered about the other girls in the office. Had any of them ever done anything like that? Worked as a stripper, or a prostitute?

I asked Selene about it one night.

"Sure. This job attracts all kinds of girls. Susannah was a stripper briefly, but she didn't care for it. She was very good, I hear. And of course, Lisbet." She winked at me. "I would never do that, though, no. I enjoy being in management, it's less...physical." She laughed and gave me a shove.

I couldn't help it; she was so hypnotic to me, with her beautiful accent. I knew she'd told me she'd been in the States for a few years, but it sounded like she had just stepped off the boat. It was wonderful.

¤ ¤ ¤

I loved the peaks and valleys of the nightlife. I didn't work every night, but when I did, my sales were strong, and I had begun to know the cast of regulars on the West, Polk, and Haight runs who greeted me cheerfully when I worked their bars. Although the gay boys in the Castro were so nice to me and demonstrated their support by occasionally buying a lolli, I didn't usually turn a profit there. The sex appeal of a cigarette and candy girl was powerful — I mean, what's not to love about a girl who serves you, and looks like a cross between a flight attendant and a stripper? — but I just wasn't a real brief-snapping turn-on for those flamboyants.

I was getting to know several of my fellow Tarts better. Selene and Meredith were by far my favorites, and we chatted easily together about everything and nothing.

Selene was a bit of a mystery, but I had learned a little more about her. Although she dated frequently, it was always monogamously. She enjoyed the nightlife industry and wanted to own her own company. Her presence was very reassuring and her movements always graceful.

Meredith was young, but old at heart. I watched and laughed as men from every culture were drawn to her size and sassy nature, though she was adorably clueless about what to do with them. They couldn't resist her piggy-tail shaped, corkscrew hair, her sly smile and her infectious laugh. She was single and, though I didn't know for sure, I thought she might've been a virgin. She was pretty conservative, surprisingly, and maybe with all those brothers...well, I think she might have been waiting for marriage. One of my favorite things about Meredith was how hard it was to make her angry.

Susannah, I had learned, was a real love child of some seriously hippie parents. From what I gathered, she had seen it ALL. She knew all the tricks to hard selling, and was happy to share them with me, but nothing fooled her either. I heard her talk of her lovers, but she never mentioned any steady relationship. When I'd asked her about her family, she clammed up and changed the subject back to her favorite philosophy, Toujours gai! I liked Susannah, but she intimidated me, and seemed a bit sad.

The weepy girl from my first week didn't last one night. Two other girls came in together the following week, but got fired on their first night after getting outrageously drunk and making no sales. Selene was furious.

Rehka was another handful. She carried off the sweet and shy act on the job, but in the office she was bratty and privileged, always complaining and wanting special treatment. She didn't take the job very seriously; for her it was more of a lark, a means to an end. Her parents mostly paid for her college, but a little extra cash helped keep her in designer clothes. She was constantly, maddeningly, always on the phone to her boyfriend. She almost got kicked off the job in my second week due to her cell phone drama, but she sweet-talked her way back in. She hadn't been doing really well at sales.

Thom's bakery job had some brutal hours, which explained why he was always exhausted, smelled amazing, and was grumpy about it. The scrumptious aroma that permeated Thom's car was from his signature blackberry-date madeleines. He wouldn't bring any to the office, nor would he tell us which bakery he worked at, so his torment was absolute. Thom lived with and cared for his mom, and he had an older sister who had a big shot job. I think his mom had some sort of degenerative disease, but I wasn't sure about that. He was also pretty tight-lipped about family.

My favorite distraction, though, as well as my daydream superstar and focus of my lust, was Felix. Felix was very open about some details of his life. He wasn't shy to say that he had three sisters, and happily shared that his oldest and favorite sister was 40-year-old Sam (short for Samantha, I assumed), who lived back in his home state of Texas. Audrey, the middle sister, lived in Santa Barbara, and was clearly the troublemaker in the family. The youngest sister, Nicole, was just a year older than Felix. They didn't talk often, but they seemed to get along okay. Felix was 32, and as the youngest he was clearly doted on and spoiled by his older sisters. I suspected this was why he was so arrogant.

I'd done a little more digging into his life, so I knew that he'd studied electrical engineering at a college in Texas and then moved to Las Vegas. From there, though, the well of information dried up. Felix wouldn't talk about Vegas, and nobody in the office knew anything either.

Still, it was enough information to keep my fevered crush alive, every time I walked in through the door.

¤ ¤ ¤

One night in early April, I arrived to find that a tall, gorgeous Bettie Page doppelganger was storming throughout the office, muttering angrily. The girls and I watched in awe and a little fear as she grabbed tops, skirts, accessories, and even helped herself to the storage closet. Selene, sitting calmly behind the front desk with her legs elegantly crossed in front of her, gently scolded her for scaring the rest of us. The force of nature stopped abruptly and glanced up, and her face went from angry to stony in a heartbeat. Dropping her assorted booty on the nearest counter, she continued to ignore us as she started working on her makeup and hair.

"Fine," she said flatly to Selene, fixing her with a blue-eyed stare. "I'll stay out of their way, if they stay out of mine."

I wandered over to Selene, and leaned in. "What's the deal? Seems like she would be a scary Tart! " I whispered. I mean, I felt bold, but not THAT bold. I glanced back to make sure Tall, Gorgeous and Pissed

Off didn't hear that, but she was oblivious as she concentrated intensely on her makeup.

"Oh, Lisbet is a very special case. She makes a ridiculous amount when she's here, but her time is extremely limited. She works a few other jobs, and she's talented and gifted at so many things, she uses this job as a kind of...how would you say? Tension release?" She searched for the right term in her halting accent. I never got tired of listening to her search for words in English.

"Pressure release," I said absently, as I watched Thom and Felix stare raptly at Lisbet, following her every move. "So, the boys are...quite fond of her, I take it?" I asked, tentatively.

"Oh! Look at you, so discreet! Yes, they are, as you say, quite fond of her." She winked at me and gave my arm a squeeze. "But you have nothing to worry over. She does not like men as much as she likes women. Even I considered; she is so beautiful and magnificent when she is angry, like today." Selene admired Lisbet as she got dressed openly in the front room, no trace of self-consciousness in her movements. Her thick black hair fell in front of her silhouette as she bent down to pull on her stockings.

I looked back at the guys and saw their eyes were glazed over. I sighed heavily.

Selene laughed and gave me another shake.

"I told you, she's a special case! Because she does so well here, we give her the best run, the North Beach run, whenever her schedule brings her in. She's very valuable to us."

"North Beach? When will I get to do that one?" I asked Selene, turning back to her.

"Soon, *ma cherie*. You are doing very well; I'm hoping to move you there within the next couple of weeks. Now, shoo, you pest! Go get ready." She gave me a little push, and laughed softly.

I headed back to my own station and got to work. I considered getting dressed in the front office like Lisbet, but decided against it. Following up after that display would just seem desperate. I wanted Felix to think of me in a romantic way, but that was not the way to go about it. I headed to the back room and gossiped with Meredith about Lisbet while we got dressed.

I brought in an outfit of my own that night. It was a sleeveless black and pink cocktail dress, with low cut cleavage, but it hung long, near my knees. I topped off the dress with a cropped jacket, buttoned low. We're allowed to do this, but Selene had to clear it first. I was feeling better about myself by the time I walked out.

"Wow, Pale! You are going to sweep the floor in money tonight!" Selene exclaimed, admiring.

"You like the dress?" I asked, beaming.

"*Absolutment*!" she said firmly, coming out from behind the desk and giving my hip a push with her hand, encouraging me to spin around.

I twirled obediently, smiling. I caught Felix looking at me and flashed him a wink. He smiled at me, but there was a hesitation there, and he turned away, muttering to Thom. The other girls in the office looked me up and down, and were obviously taking mental notes in order to put together something on their own. I was pleased that I had put together an outfit that was classy enough for the company, but original enough that I could feel more like myself when I went out.

"So I'm cleared to go, Boss?" I asked her jokingly.

"Pale, if you do not come back here with $1000, then I'm firing you for not learning anything!" She gave my shoulder a playful bump to let me know she wasn't serious.

I left the office feeling confident about the night, and decided that I was going to take Selene's dare seriously. I'd never brought in that kind of money before, but why not? I didn't really know what I was capable of. The worst that could happen was that I'd be just an average seller. I didn't want to be average, though. For a long moment, I missed Jana, and wanted to call her and share the high I was on, but I took a deep breath and decided to concentrate on my evening.

Lisbet and a girl I didn't recognize climbed into the backseat of Thom's blight-on-humanity of a car. Gods, if the aliens ever did land, I hoped they wouldn't judge us all, based on that Flintstone-mobile. I shook my head and settled into the front seat, wrapped in the heavenly smell of fresh baked goods. We drove up Market Street toward the Castro to drop off the new girl. She mentioned her name in a clipped tone, but I missed it over the blare of the car radio. Something like Kelly? Sally? Nelly?

Just as we passed the Mission district, the turd-car started to gasp and jerk. Thom looked alarmed, and started pumping the clutch and gas alternately.

"Oh great!" shouted the new girl, stomping her foot.

Before I could register the ridiculous overreaction she was having, Lisbet calmly but firmly began to instruct Thom.

"Drop the car to second gear, and turn on your hazards. There's a gas station a few blocks up the street; can you make it?"

Thom seemed relieved to have someone tell him what to do. I sat quietly, tense, hoping no one rear-ended us as we crawled up one of the busiest streets in San Francisco on a Saturday night. We inched along like a Sunday driver as BMWs, Mercedes, and Jettas honked and swerved around us. Though it seemed to take several hours, we limped into the gas station in short order. I hopped out of the car, and unlatched the passenger seat so Lisbet could get out, since she seemed to be in charge of the situation.

She got out without a word, and immediately commanded Thom to pop the hood. I decided to go use the bathroom, since I didn't do that before we left. Using a bathroom without the tray was a luxury when your night has started already, so I settled my tray into the passenger seat and took advantage of the chance to stretch my legs. When I came back, I was hesitant to get back into the stuffy, sweet-smelling car, especially with Ms. Anger Management in the back, looking daggers at everyone. I swear, sometimes I thought Selene would take just any girl who walked in the door.

I moved to stand near Lisbet, who glanced up at me and said, "Here, hold this." She handed me a bottle of oil she'd sent Thom to buy while I was taking my bathroom break, and I took it from her, glad to be helping.

Lisbet peered at the engine, fiddled with a few valves, and told Thom to run the engine for a few seconds. It made pathetic sounds, so she fiddled some more. I stood there enjoying the fresh air — as fresh as you can get in a metropolitan gas station — and decided to strike up a conversation.

"So, how do you know so much about cars? If that IS what this heap of junk is," I said wryly.

For the first time, Lisbet smiled from the corner of her mouth. "Yeah, right? This is a sad excuse. I'm a mechanic, actually," she said, hesitantly.

"Wow, that's cool. That can't be easy, being a woman," I said.

"Yeah, it's no picnic, but that's why I'm going to school too. I'm working on getting my master's degree." She pulled hard on what I thought was the carburetor cap, but I couldn't be sure.

"Holy shit. That's a lot to have going on," I said feebly. "You must either never sleep, or have a passion for coffee,"

Lisbet glanced up at me, and her guard seemed to soften a bit. For some reason, it felt like she was checking me out, and I blushed, looking down.

"I do a few other things too, but yeah, I do love my coffee."

"What are you getting your degree in?" I asked, curious.

"I'm studying to be a mortician. Thanks for the help."

She slammed the hood down, and walked around to Thom's driver window. He looked like he was anxious to hear the news, and dreading it as well.

Lisbet already had her phone out, and she gave her report to Selene while Thom listened.

"Yeah, his engine is shot. No...no...even if we could get it to the office, we are going to need another car, right away. Yeah....Yeah, I hear you. Will he do it? He's not exactly easy to...okay. Ten minutes."

Lisbet hung up the phone, and leaned in to Thom.

"Basically, this car is dead. You could get the transmission replaced, but it's not worth the price of the car. Ransom is on his way to get us; you two are going to switch for the night. He'll give you a ride back to the office in between drop-offs. Selene's orders."

Thom looked angry, but he said nothing. The nameless girl gave him a shove on his seat, and said, "Let me OUT! I'm cramped back here." Thom's face was stony as he deliberately and carefully stepped out of the car, letting Tantrum Pants get some air.

As we stood around waiting for Ransom, no one was talking. Though the night had gotten off to a bad start, I was still riding the combined highs of Selene's dare and my talk with Lisbet, and was secretly happy that Thom's car had finally died. I would never tell him this, but that car was a monkey on his back.

Ransom pulled up in a sedan; of course it was black. As we pulled away, Thom glanced back at his sad, yellow wreck, pushed to the side for later retrieval. He looked so worn out. I leaned over to him, and gave his shoulder a little bump. He glanced up and gave me a resigned smile. I held his smile, and soon we were both grinning at absolutely nothing.

Chapter 11

Ransom drove to South of Market, where we dropped off Ms. Angry in short order. I felt morbidly curious how she was going to do, as I watched her slam the door and head into her first bar without a second's hesitation.

Next, Ransom headed to North Beach, to drop off Lisbet. He stared at her longingly as she stepped out of the car. She waved off the list he had ready for her.

"Don't you think I know them by now, Ran?" she asked, laughing.

As Lisbet walked away, Thom and Ransom stared at her like she was Aphrodite incarnate, bursting forth from the foam. I shook my head, waiting for them to pull themselves together. Ransom faced forward, and lurched the sedan back into traffic.

As soon as we were a safe distance from Lisbet, both men started talking about the Hothead we dropped off first. They placed bets on how long she would last.

"Won't Felix want in on this wager? Don't you want to call him?" I asked Thom, who had since popped out of the back and into the front seat, presumably so they could keep the invisible wall up between drivers and girls.

"Um. Felix doesn't bet," Thom said uncomfortably.

Ransom said nothing, as usual, but had a gleam of satisfaction in his eye. They were both acting weird, so I dropped the subject.

"So, where am I headed tonight?" I asked, curious.

"We are taking you to Pier 23 as a starter, then you'll do the Polk run," Ransom said curtly. "I will be taking you around. Thom is headed back to the office, so don't expect any special favors. Thom is too soft on you girls." Thom said nothing, just looked tired.

"Thom's all right," I said, weakly.

Ransom cruised up Broadway, turning left onto the famous Embarcadero. Even at that time of night, there was a steady stream of runners, bicyclists, tourists, and street performers, all hoping to catch a few nighttime bucks for their performances. As we got closer to Pier 23, the telltale round neon sign in view, the crowd thinned out, and in a blink we were there, the sidewalks empty. Pier 23 had the feeling of the Bar at the End of the Universe, from Douglas Adams' *Hitchhiker's Guide to the Galaxy* — I loved that book.

I briskly stepped out of the car, and Ransom called out "25 minutes." I waved in acknowledgment, and he sped away. Ransom didn't seem too bad, but we were never going to be buddies; that much I could see.

Although the whole only-working-one-location thing could be a bit weird, it could also be really fun. I went in and greeted the staff, and made my way to the chilly back patio. The sun had gone down, but the sky was still light, so I took advantage of the relaxed atmosphere, and talked a few folks into lollipops and cigarettes. People took their evening drinking so seriously, almost as if they were getting down to business, making an event of it.

My sales on the back patio were a little thin, so I decided to head into the back kitchen office to re-arrange my stock and take a small breather. I still got a little nervous on my first circuit of the night, even after the time I'd put in.

While I was taking a few breaths, one of the wait staff popped her head in. "You know about our side patio, right? I've seen you here before, but you haven't worked it over there, and there're definitely some folks hanging out." She gave me a warm smile.

"Oh! Yeah, thank you. That's great. I will get out there in a second," I said, starting to rise.

I turned to the right and saw yet another door I had missed the first time I worked this place, and peeked through it. There was a plain, undecorated area with two large plastic round tables, which would easily hold eight people. I was startled to see a group of men at one of the tables beckon me over.

"Hey darlin'! What you got for us tonight? We're celebrating!" A well-built, exuberant Latino man startled me, gave me a quick side hug and then let me go. The other men whooped briefly, then settled down to stare intently into my tray, pawing through it, carefully pulling out items they wanted and setting them into piles. They all started waving money and talking to me at the same time. Laughing, I threw up a hand to fend them off.

"Okay! What's this all about? You guys aren't trying to stiff me, are you?" I asked smiling, looking at each of them in turn.

They were all fit, friendly, and had that sense of being close, like a tight knit family. They didn't strike me as men who just worked together, but more like a team. Some of them were awfully cute. Some of the faces were a bit guarded, but they all just looked like really good guys. Motherload!

"No, no! We're not like that. We just like pretty girls who've got lots of goodies," said the one on my left, a blond-haired, blue-eyed Adonis.

"Don't worry, we're all firefighters," one of the shorter, huskier ones reassured me. "We just got an award, and we are out to Cel-e-brate!" he said, punctuating his words by pumping his beer in the air.

They all started their deep "Whoop! Whoop!" and I couldn't help it, I started laughing again. I spent the next 15 minutes with them, swapping jokes and stories. I took six sales, getting generous tips from each. They were a belligerent bunch, but they meant well, and my first instinct was right, they were a tight knit group.

With regret, I waved goodbye, and they catcalled my legs and butt. They meant it to be flattering, so I gave them a little shake on my way out to the main patio. They hollered and stomped their approval.

After that, I only really had time for one quick circuit of the bar. My time outside had led many people to think I had left, so they were grateful to discover I was still there. This led to brisk sales, and I ended up making more than I had expected from this run.

I hurried out to the street to meet Ransom, who had just pulled up in his oily sedan. It barely showed up in the dark of the night. I wondered briefly if he had managed to find a special kind of black paint. It would be like him.

"Hi there!" I said, cheerfully.

Ransom said nothing, just pulled into traffic. After a few minutes with no response, I sat back and decided to keep my good mood to myself.

We drove silently along the Embarcadero, turned left onto Hyde, and headed toward California Street. Ransom dropped me in front of Big Foot, and wordlessly handed me a slip of paper.

"I'm familiar with this route, you know," I said mildly. He was still holding out the paper, so I took it, and glanced down. Sure enough, it was the usual route.

"Ok, well, thanks for the ride. See you at?" I asked.

"See you in an hour," he said flatly. He drove away without another word.

I wasn't sure that Ransom hadn't killed a man in the past, and those were some hidden depths that I didn't want to know about. He scared me, no doubt. I certainly tried not to let him know that, but I was pretty sure he sensed it. Like a dog. Or a shark.

With a shudder, I headed into my new circuit, and lost myself in the waves of the night.

The Polk run went well, though it did have a few low points. In Amelie, a guy reached down my back and tried to unzip my skirt. That pissed me off, and I slapped his hand away. His buddy reprimanded him and dragged him off, shooting me an apologetic look.

There must have been something in the air, because at Kozy Kar while I was making change for a customer, a rat-faced guy came up and placed his hand flat up against the bottom of my tray. He jerked up on the tray hard, sending several items flying through the air, and spreading all over the floor.

The next few seconds were unreal, as a bouncer leapt forward and bodily threw that guy out of the bar, shouting at him. Several patrons picked up every single item I'd lost from my tray, bringing them back to me with apologies. I even made a few sales that way; some of the girls felt sorry for me.

I was so shaken that I hardly had time to feel angry. Actually, I felt protected. A few weeks ago I would have been so anxious that I wouldn't have been able to handle what just happened.

As I got settled into the car, Ransom shared some startling news.

"Change of plans," he barked. "Lisbet got her tray bought, and has decided to go back out for a second run. Which is good for us, because Sally--," right, that was her name, "--got into a fistfight, and has been taken off the SoMa run. She's back at the office, counting out." He scowled, and looked thunderous.

"Wait, go back; I don't understand. Got her tray bought?" I said, hesitating.

"Yeah, a customer bought her entire tray. It's rare, but it's happened to Lisbet, like, three times. Basically, they pay $1000 for the entire thing: candy, cigars, cigarettes, even the physical tray. A girl can decide at that point to cash out for the night and go home, or she can come back to the office for another tray. Selene is the only other girl who's had that happen, and she always went back out. Lisbet's in a good mood, so she decided to take the rest of the SoMa run for that Fighter. This means we are putting you on North Beach."

"Wait, so I'm going to North Beach? I thought Selene said I wasn't ready for a few more weeks," I said, trying to take it all in. What's-her-name got in a fistfight? Holy crap!

Ransom glanced at me with disdain. "Selene left an hour ago. She only comes in for the early shift; I'm always the night manager," he said curtly. "She's not here right now, and I need you to go out, ready or not. Now stop asking questions."

We drove back over to Columbus Ave, and Ransom pulled into a red zone.

"Lisbet's already worked the first shift, so the hard part is done. The reason this run is such good money is that the wealthy folks love to party over here. Keep your head, and don't call me unless it's an emergency." He handed me a list I'd never seen before. We both jumped suddenly at the knock on his driver's door window, and he rolled it down halfway.

"Ransom! Oh my god, I haven't seen you in so long!"

A black-haired beauty reached in a hand, and oh my goodness, Ransom automatically lifted it to his mouth for an old fashioned gentleman's kiss! I was entranced by her, and took in Ransom's total lack of composure with silent glee. He released her hand, quickly rolled up the car window, and stepped out in a blink. They talked for a few minutes beside the car, and I craned in my seat to get a better look at her. Damn him and his tinted windows!

After a short time, Ransom got back in the car, and the mystery lady walked away. He looked distracted and deep in thought.

"Anything else I need to know?" I asked him finally.

"Get out! Stop asking me questions!" he said, deeply irritated.

I didn't take it personally, as it was obvious that the woman had unsettled him. I would have to ask Selene about her later. I could hear her now, "Oh, la, la!"

I smiled to myself. I would have to ask about Sally's fistfight on the SoMa run as well; I couldn't wait to hear about that!

I glanced down at the list, and made a mental note of which places were nearby. Then I looked up Columbus Avenue, entranced by a lightshow worthy of Vegas: flashing neon-dancer legs waved jauntily back and forth, while a warm glow spilled from late night restaurant windows, and a steady stream of headlights poured from the river of taxis and tourists' cars.

According to my list, I started on Broadway with Kells, and then headed to Mr. Bing's, Vesuvio, and Tosca. After that, it was on to Specs' and the Basque Hotel. There must have been twenty locations on that list, and for a moment I felt overwhelmed. I could hardly believe Lisbet was already done; she had only been out for a little while, and didn't come out that often at all, from what I could tell. I guess she had that It Factor.

I checked my watch, and saw I had a little less than two hours to get through the entire list. It was going to be insane, but here was my chance to make some real money tonight.

I headed into Kells Irish Restaurant & Bar, and started working my way through a packed crowd. I made good money, but was beginning to lag behind schedule, so I hustled quickly through the downstairs. As I rushed back up to street level, I felt a strange coolness. Reaching back to smooth my skirt, I discovered someone had unzipped it! As I frantically tried to fix it, a guy stumbled up to me and breathed booze straight into my face. He was enthusiastically telling me his life story, and begging me for my phone number. I ignored him and headed down the street to my next bar.

North Beach was unlike any of the other neighborhoods in San Francisco; it boasted an opulence born from its history, always reaching past good enough to truly take your breath away, and evoking a real "Wow!" reaction. The entire district had an assumed sense of privilege, much like royalty. The people were more aggressive, but they expected to pay more for their night's entertainment. I quickly learned that frat boys and male financial managers made lucrative customers. The women — so gorgeous, it felt like I was surrounded by models — hated me as a rule, didn't tend to buy anything, and they tipped poorly even when they did. I made a point to politely say "Hello," "Good night," "Please" and "Thank you" to the patrons, as they seemed to appreciate the good manners.

The hour flew by, and I kept up the pace, hurrying on to the intersection of Grant Avenue and Green Street, which started me at The Saloon, followed in quick succession by Blue Royal, Grant & Green Saloon, Lost and Found Saloon, and Savoy Tivoli. The feel of old-world Italian, coupled with modern conversation and attitude provided a strange but warm backdrop. I was generally welcomed as "part of the landscape".

At Savoy Tivoli I had a great interaction with Aziz, an Arabic and French translator from Washington, D.C. At Magnet I met a newly married couple wearing fake crowns; his read, "You can run..." and hers finished, "But you can't hide." They were happy to buy roses, cigars and gum off of me, and tipped me an outrageous $20.

My favorite part of the run started somewhere around Gino and Carlos, where I met three boys I soon dubbed the Musketeers. They purchased a few packs of cigarettes and then declared that I surely must know the best spots in town. They wanted to see what it was like, the nightlife of a Tawny Tart.

"Is it ok that we follow you for a bit? We are celebrating my buddy's birthday, and we want to jazz up the night."

"Sure, just don't crowd me."

"How much time do we have to order drinks where we are going?" they asked.

"Get ready to down those drinks; I move fast," I said, grinning, as we made our way into Columbus Café.

As I was working a tough section of a bachelorette party, the boys decided to "help" me by coming over and charming the pants off those jealous bitches. With the boys crowding around me, the ladies' faces transformed and they leaned into my tray in a subtle fight to coquettishly impress the guys. I turned slightly and caught one of the boys winking at me.

"That ought to buy us a few more minutes of drinking, right?" he asked me enthusiastically.

"Yes," I laughed and nodded.

Soon I was ready to move on, and I began briskly maneuvering towards the door. I heard a shout, and the guys were rapidly downing shots, shaking heads, and grabbing coats to follow me.

"You can't leave without us! You are our Muse!" they cried.

"I didn't think you guys were serious."

"Of course we are! Look what we just did for you! Those Marina bitches never would've looked twice!" They started punching each other in the arm in a congratulatory way.

"That's true," I said, mockingly thoughtful. "How about I call you my Musketeers?" I asked. Much whooping and jumping ensued, and they sprinted ahead, thinking they knew where they were going. I laughed and trailed after them.

Our next stop was Amante, and the guys were true to their word. They went immediately to the bar to order shots (smart) and only came over to "rescue" me if it looked like my sales weren't going well. One would come and buy something, acting as if he didn't know me at all, stimulating sales in the group around me. They were brilliant, and I rode their success high with them. They acted as if leaving each bar broke their hearts, and complained how hard this job was on their feet, and powers of concentration.

"Well, typically I don't drink heavily while working," I chided mildly.

This resulted in a rousing speech over the injustice of management everywhere in the world, which kept them entertained on the way to North Star Café.

The boys charmed their way around the room, and my tray grew lighter. The ringleader asked what I'd like to sell the most of, and I told him the roses. He promptly bet a big burly guy the last two roses I had, and got into an arm-wrestling contest over them. He was a lanky guy who looked like he spent more time in libraries as a kid than playing football, and the contest was over in just a few minutes. They both bought the flowers off of me and, while pounding each other on the back for being such good sports, immediately gave the flowers away to a beautiful girl, each getting a phone number out of the deal. I was amazed at the manipulation that came naturally to these men; getting a prop to seal a deal with a girl was second nature to both.

I called out loudly with our prearranged signal – "Musketeers!" – then waited outside for the rush stampede. As they came out, they asked me where we were headed next. I told them I had to backtrack down Grant to the Beat Lounge. They muttered amongst themselves, and decided to follow me there.

My little gang sang songs along the way, greeting strangers and joking with me about splitting proceeds. They continued to implore me to speak to management about being allowed to drink heavily on the job, as it had obviously created more profit. I agreed solemnly, and promised to mention it. While I did appreciate them, I was getting a bit tired of the entourage.

Beat Lounge was right on the corner of Broadway and Columbus. It marked the beginning of the cusp of the strip joints. The bar was all cold modern glass, black curtains, and muted neon strip lights. While we were technically still in North Beach, the warmth of the rest of the strip was gone. The music was so loud, I couldn't even talk to customers; I just used gestures to communicate. No one was dancing; everyone was pressed into small tables, looking miserable.

The guys' enthusiasm totally deflated, and it wasn't long before they decided to separate and jump back on the wave of their night. They wished me luck and promised to always tip a Tart in the future. I gave them a smile and a wave, and was relieved when they hopped into a cab.

I was running late, and still had to get through seven more bars in the next 25 minutes. I breezed through Sake Lab and Fuse, skipped Bamboo Hut, and opted to try for Dragon Bar, Velvet and Dolce before finishing up at Crow Bar. They all went pretty fast, as my transactions were more about the sales themselves than the presentation or the flattery. The door guys were all consummate gentlemen, waving me through immediately, smiling, and holding open doors or heavy curtains for me. I made sure to thank each of them, and they smiled back.

By the time I got to Crow Bar, I was presumably rich, moderately happy, and definitely tired. It was pitch black inside, and I did a cursory tour past the air hockey table, selling a last candy bar and pack of smokes.

As I came outside, there were people on the sidewalk everywhere, and Ransom's black sedan was right in front. I climbed in tiredly, and closed the door, heaving a sigh. He glanced at me, saying nothing, and honked to clear the road, which had spilled over with people.

We cruised silently back to the office, and for once I was too tired to ask questions, though I still wanted to know what happened with Lisbet and the new girl's fistfight.

Back at the office, Thom had left and Felix was putting away the goods that girls were turning in to him on their trays. Susannah was in a good mood; both she and Lisbet were laughing away, occasionally dancing to the music on the cheap cracked plastic radio.

Meredith filled me in on the details about the fistfight. Apparently, some girl had tried to sneak her hand in and grab a couple of twenties from Ms. Anger Management's tray, and got clocked in the face. The would-be thief's boyfriend joined in and shoved Sally. When a bouncer came over to get things under control, Sally kept punching and kicking out, and needed to be bodily removed. Needless to say, she wouldn't be back.

Lisbet's coup de gras of the night had come from a filthy rich businessman from Japan who'd gotten even more filthy rich from a successful investment and flew to San Francisco for the night to celebrate. He had wanted Lisbet to join him in the festivities, but she was apparently so charming that when she refused, he still bought the tray outright.

I took my time cashing out, mostly so I could talk with Felix afterwards, even though I was dying to know how well I did. I certainly had more cash than I'd ever seen in my life; I could barely get my hands around it.

I took my bounty up to Ransom, and tapped my fingers impatiently on the counter. He glared at me, finished a few entries on the screen, and then added up my take.

"You did well," he said finally. "I think you did well enough that we can put you back on this run. This is no guarantee that you will keep it. Girls get put on that run all the time; the best ones do."

I started to open my mouth to ask what it takes to be the best, and then closed it when I realized I was too tired to care. I took my earnings and stuffed them deep inside my bag.

My stomach was in knots from trying to get up the nerve to strike up a conversation with Felix that wasn't work-related. I saw he was still chatting up Lisbet, so I took those few minutes to hurriedly put my stuff away. As he headed towards the door, I called out, "Hey, Felix, wait up."

He hesitated, and then held open the door for me. We walked outside to the now chilly early morning spring air.

"Hey...um. Listen. I have a question for you, but..." I said tentatively, not looking him in the eye.

"Spit it out, Pale, it's damn cold out here," he said impatiently.

I froze, chickening out of asking him to go out with me. I frantically tried to think of something else to ask, while he stamped his feet trying to keep the circulation moving.

"It's just...I noticed you really have a hard time with the bets around here...are you, ha, like an addict or something?" I stammered.

Instantly I could see I had said the wrong thing. Felix was holding very still, and looked as if someone had just peed on his steak dinner, right in front of him.

"Or something. Are we done here?" he asked.

I blanched, and Felix glanced down at me.

"Shit. Look. You are a cute kid, and I can see you don't mean harm, though your priorities are a bit out of whack. Not that I'm one to lecture anyone on what they do with their life. Hell, I'm not even sure this is for me," he gestured back at the office.

"But if this is about my private life, and the stuff I'm dealing with, it's none of your business. I don't want to get involved with anyone here at work. Understand?"

I nodded silently, feeling confused and rejected.

"Look, I'll see you later, ok? We are friends, and lucky for you, I'm a damn good one of those." He laughed darkly, and then waved good night.

I certainly didn't feel like I'd made out well that night, despite the wad of cash in my bag. I was not certain I did understand, but I was hoping to at least find out what was bothering him. A small relief was that he didn't want to date anyone at work. But it was a very small comfort.

I headed home and tried to console myself with my money, reviewing my techniques of the night in my head. I made $185 in 6 hours, which wasn't bad at all. Not one little bit.

Chapter 12

My days had developed a predictable rhythm, shaped around the contours of being a Tart: I slept in until around noon, then spent my afternoons exploring the City, although I also did some deliveries or an odd job in an office to help pay for the cost of living here. I ate dinner at an earlier hour so I could be in the office by 6:30 pm. When I got to the office, I spent as much time as possible with Felix, cracking jokes, horsing around, all while getting my makeup on and picking out clothes.

I headed out on several runs each night. Honestly, I didn't mind any of them. They all had different personalities; each required its own level and type of energy. The run that took the most effort for the least payoff was the Castro. I only made money if I was totally loud and ostentatious, almost cartoonish. It was a huge amount of work, since I was not that extroverted, and my mediocre sales brought down what was otherwise a steady climb in profit. Still, Selene insisted it was good practice.

After going out on my runs with either Felix or Thom driving, I cashed out, went home, and collapsed into bed.

Tonight I was out with Thom, who was even grouchier than usual for having had to fix his lemon of a car. We had just dropped off Meredith and a new British girl named Beth, but Thom was just sitting there, silent. Since it looked like he wanted to say something, I gave him a moment.

"Listen. There's a place that Selene's been wanting to get our foot in the door, and they told us we could stop by anytime. But it's not a typical place, and not every girl would be up for it. As a matter of fact, I'm not even sure how it would go, and I wouldn't be with you, so if anything goes wrong, you have to bail and wait outside while I come and get you."

I was so perplexed by this speech, and the idea of Thom being with me while I did sales. I had no idea what he was talking about.

"How bad could it be? Is it some sort of kinky leather bar?" I joked, laughing. "Because sign me up, baby! Ha-ha."

I waited for him to laugh with me. He didn't laugh.

"Oh. So it is a kinky leather bar?" I said uncomfortably. I mean sure, I was a progressive woman, getting more open all the time, but I was still just a girl from Modesto. I got a thrill when I thought of what I'd tell Jana. I got a sense of dread when I thought how I'd have to keep this from my dad. For the rest of my life.

Thom had never looked so uneasy, and that's saying something. In two months of working with him, he'd never stopped being grumpy, closed-off at best.

"Noo-o, it's not a leather bar, exactly." He sighed heavily. "Actually, I don't really know. It's called the Power Exchange, and it's a kink and fetish place. They have different floors for different things. Like I said, Selene wants us to check it out, but most of the girls don't want to go in there. If you don't want to... I'll just tell Selene...." he trailed off again.

"No, it's fine. I'll do it. I mean, if it's for Selene, then no problem. Any chance I would win points with you over this?" I asked, trying to improve his mood.

"Well, it's one less thing for me to do I guess," he muttered. Great. Thanks for the big props there. Don't strain yourself.

Thom parked us in front of an imposing black façade, not far from Mission. He dug through the glove box, retrieving a wadded-up scrap of paper with a code on it. He pointed out the entrance, and reminded me to call him if I needed anything.

"Remember, we have no idea what kind of sales you'll do, how long it will take, or anything. Just go slowly, and we'll meet back here in 30. Don't be late."

I headed through the door and immediately climbed a long set of wide black stairs, lit at the top by a cheap, dingy light fixture. I heard distant music.

I didn't see a bouncer, so I stepped through the door that opened to my left. The walls were wood-paneled, and cheap neon lights flickered. A long pool table sat in the middle of a large, open room. There was no bar, no staff, and no food served either. Not even a jukebox. An adjacent room seemed to have dark corners where customers were making out. I didn't see anything that wouldn't be seen in a regular bar, but the energy was so different that all the hair on my arms stood up.

I saw a hallway in the far corner of the room, where I discovered a staircase leading to an upper floor. A woman at a small podium stopped me with a sweet smile. She was the first person I saw who seemed to actually work there.

"Men only upstairs, honey."

"Oh. I can't even do a walk-through?" She shook her head no.

I was at a loss as to what to do next. Thom had seemed scared to have me go in there, but other than the willies, it was sort of a letdown. If this was the only floor I could work, I wouldn't be there more than 10 minutes, much less 30.

"Of course, you could always wander downstairs." She gave me a knowing smile. I smiled back uncomfortably. I'd be damned if I was going to be intimidated now. I was in there already, wasn't I?

"How do I get there?"

She gestured behind me, and I saw another wide, black staircase leading down into utter darkness.

I took a breath and walked down the stairs. I reached the bottom, went through the open doorway on my left, and paused a moment so my eyes could adjust to the blackness.

I followed a wandering path past small, open stage areas. Most of the stages were empty, but on some of them I saw...performances going on. The air was thick with sexual tension, both withheld and enjoyed. Most of what I saw was only surprising because it was happening outside of the private bedroom: a couple was engaging in missionary sex on a bed, and a threesome between two women and one man began by making out, though it looked like the second woman wasn't very into it.

I was baffled as to how to work this area for sales. The people on stage were very...in the zone of what they were doing. The few people watching were also totally entranced, and I certainly couldn't interrupt them. I tried to discreetly offer some cigarettes to a few couples, but everyone turned me down.

Further along my wandering, adult-Disneyland-like path, I came across something else entirely. Women were on their knees, ball gags in their mouths, getting spanked on the ass. A couple of guys demanded their slaves come over, so they could sit and prop their leather-booted feet up on their backs.

As I approached, one of the dominant men glanced up and saw me. His eyes took in everything about me, and I felt strangely naked, despite my clothes and the distance between us. He nodded for me to come over, and I walked closer, cautiously. He snapped his fingers, and the slave he had his boots on jumped up. I was nervous about what was going to happen, but determined that since I had his attention, I might as well try to make the best of it.

He gestured for his slave to approach me, never taking his eyes off mine. I boldly stared back. His slave started caressing my hair, running his hands up and down the straps of my tray, tugging on it for me to take it off. I shook my head No, and the leader stood up, and leaned into my ear. He whispered, "Take that off." I shook my head again, No. He slowly pulled a whip from his waist belt, and started snapping it against the floor, lifting his head in a nod, beckoning his slaves to circle me and draw me in. I took a staggering step back, and fled down the corridor. I could hear laughter echo in the dark hallway behind me.

I was starting to get really freaked out. I didn't really see how my being there was going to help Selene, so I went back up the stairs, and was relieved when I saw the pool table, and a handful of patrons calmly having a game. I hurried across the room to the original staircase I had come up, and sat down on the stairs.

I didn't really understand how people could find a way to connect through those... games. From the outside it looked so contrived, so expressionless. I didn't see any tenderness, any love. I wasn't sure that I got it, but maybe it just wasn't for me. And I couldn't imagine doing anything like that publicly. Even if I wanted to try a few new things, it would be at home, never where other people were watching, judging, leeching off the energy of what I was experiencing.

"I can't believe I just walked through there! I can't believe I agreed to that!" I thought to myself. I was thrilled I did something new, but it was a bit more of a diving-in than I was comfortable with. I decided to blow off the last ten minutes so I could compose myself.

I checked my phone, and saw that it was close enough to the time to go downstairs to meet Thom. He pulled up a few minutes later and looked at me anxiously.

"Well?"

"It was definitely an experience. I don't think I'm up for going back. I am not sure we would do well in sales there, either. Everyone was pretty... focused on why they are there."

"Anything else?"

"Not unless you want to talk about ball gags and slaves," I said, laughing nervously. Thom was silent on the way to Fiddler's Green.

Fiddler's Green was a refreshing change after the Power Exchange. A classic Irish pub, the downstairs was bright, cozy and cramped. Several of the older patrons beamed when I walked in the door, and started playing with my various lights, toys, and Pez dispensers. They were all good sports, laughing, telling jokes, and even buying a few things just to help me out.

In a much better mood, I walked up the back stairs to a large, dark, mostly open dance floor. There was a second bar up there, and two older ladies sitting in front of a bored bartender immediately waved me over. Two older gentlemen sat at a table nearby, but they were intent on their conversation. Two younger men stood out on the breezeway, laughing and clinking their beer bottles over some personal triumph.

The two ladies tittered and giggled, slightly tipsy. The elegant, chignon-wearing one on my right pulled out a flower, a pack of cigarettes, and a pack of gum. "Dear, I will buy these from you, and will even tip you well, but you must do something for me."

I nodded yes enthusiastically. She was so adorably cheerful, and the thought of doing something for this sweet older lady was washing away all traces of my lingering apprehension.

"Take this rose over to the gentleman in the hat at that table. Tell him it's from his lighthouse love. Will you do that, dear?" She looked up at me, smiling.

"Of course. Any other message?"

“No, dear, that’ll do quite nicely.” She cackled with her girlfriend, slapping her knee and waving her victory fist in the air, as if my doing this would make her evening complete.

I made my way over to the two older gentlemen and waited patiently for them to pause in their conversation. They barely noticed me, but when they did look up, they both looked astonished; their jaws hinged open and they sat there, gaping.

“Hi there. Sorry to interrupt. I’m not here to sell you anything. Unless, of course, you need something. But mostly I’m here because I have a gift and a message for one of you.”

They looked back and forth to each other, gesturing with their fingers as if to say, "Who, me?"

I didn’t want to draw out the suspense, so I said, “This rose is from your lighthouse love.” I handed the rose to the man in the hat, and even gave a small curtsy. I wasn’t sure why I added that. It just felt right.

His face froze for a moment, and then softened, as he got lost in a memory. His friend looked totally puzzled, so he must not have known what the reference meant.

The man with the rose looked up at me, his eyes gleaming. “That rascal of a woman. I thank you, love. I know exactly what to do about this.” His face crinkled up into a smile, and he pushed back his chair, and stood staring past me to the woman at the bar.

I stepped back, not wanting to interrupt their moment. He did a little jig across the floor, finishing with a flourish in front of her and her friend. Both ladies clapped their hands in encouragement. He held out his hand, which she took, and despite the modern music playing, they started a slow waltz. He caressed her cheek with the rose; she gave his jacket's pocket handkerchief a tug, freeing it into the air. He handed her the rose; she tore off the bottom, placing the bloom in his top pocket.

I smiled and headed towards the breezeway. The boys on the balcony, who caught the whole thing from outside, purchased a few items quietly. They too were blown away by the romance and grace they had just witnessed. We shared a moment of appreciation. Light-hearted, I floated downstairs and stepped back into the night.

Chapter 13

Thom came to retrieve me in his car-bomination, and was showing some strange behavior: he was tapping the wheel to the music, he was humming along, and I think I even saw the faint trace of a smile at the edges of his mouth.

"Do my eyes play tricks on me? Are you actually in a good mood?" I asked incredulously.

He paused in his little musical break while he rejoined traffic, but went back to tapping the wheel after a moment. "Yeah, I guess so. My sister and I talked today. It's hard to reach her; she's really busy at her job, lots of stress."

"What does she do?" I prompted. I wouldn't miss this opportunity to get Thom talking. All the girls in the office were dying to butter him up, in hopes he'd bring us some of those heavenly pastries. I was doing my part, for the team.

"She's a CFO, you know, a chief financial officer for some big financial company. My mom and I don't see her often, and Mom asks after her a lot. She's promised to come visit this next weekend so I can take a break."

He looked lost in thought for a moment. "Take a break?" I asked gently.

"Yeah, my mom is kind of ... not all there. She needs help. She has Alzheimer's. It's not too bad yet ...

she still does *some* stuff on her own just fine." He said this last bit defensively.

Wow, I had no idea. No wonder he was always under so much strain.

"I'm sure she does. She's lucky you are there for her. Still, Thom, that's rough. So your sister is coming to relieve you? What are you going to do with the downtime?"

He barked a laugh, saying nothing for a moment. I waited, letting the silence stretch.

After a minute of daydreaming again, Thom muttered quietly, "I have something I may finally get to do."

"What's that?" I asked.

Thom didn't respond right away, and after several minutes, I could see that the conversation was closed. He wasn't going to tell me any more than he already had, and I wasn't going to push him. But Jesus — two jobs, a sick mom, and an absent sister? That's a heavy burden. Thom must really love his mom, to care for her personally. Of course, he might have to; in-home nurses are expensive. But with a sister who's an executive, I thought she would at least pitch in.

While I felt a bit closer to Thom, I certainly couldn't talk to him further about it, as these conversations seemed to be more of a one-sided-confessional in nature. I didn't mind, actually. I liked that Thom worked so hard, and he didn't chase after the girls in the office. Of course, he probably would if he had the energy, but now I could see he was too exhausted.

We pulled up to Polk Street, where I would be starting at Shanghai Kelly's. I was halfway out the door, tray propped and door open to the sidewalk, when Thom stopped me.

"Hey, Pale," he said tentatively, with a small smile.

His hazard lights were on, cars were honking, and I could feel the tug of a few sales smoking in front of Blue Light, waiting for my act to start. "Yeah?"

"Thanks. You know. For letting me..." he trailed off, looking down and playing with some ripped-up part of the upholstery. This car was such a piece of shit, he had his pick of spots for continued destruction.

"Hey, no problem."

I gave him a big smile, and he actually grinned back a bit.

The rest of my night was a typical mosaic of good and crappy experiences. One guy followed me out of a bar, screaming, "I'm prettier than you! I'm prettier than YOU!" which I ignored. But later on, I got an amazing neck massage from David, one of the cuter bouncers I'd gotten to know. The tray was pretty heavy, and I'd developed a constant ache in my feet and shoulders from the weight combined with walking and climbing, so this was a little slice of heaven.

I met a guy everyone called Coach Bill, and had a great talk with him. I also met Lydia Kim, who was famous among Tawny's Tarts because she had been collecting pez dispensers from us for years. She was a big fan of us Tarts, and Susannah had told me that she would always leave a tip, but it would be an especially big one if one of us was carrying a pez she didn't have. Sadly, I didn't have anything new for her, but she promised to keep an eye out for me in the future. I was happy to know what she looked like so I could find her again.

When Thom returned to pick me up at the end of the night, he had news for me.

"We're having a little celebration back at the office tonight, by the way. It's Felix's birthday."

"His birthday? I had no idea it was coming up. I can't believe no one told me!" I gasped. Thom smirked.

"What?" I barked, irritated.

"Actually, it was a week ago, but we wanted to wait until his schedule cleared to drink in style." Thom was evil, I decided. Simple, plain old-fashioned evil.

"Oh, well, that's just great. It was a week ago. I had no idea, I didn't even get a chance to say Happy Birthday, and now I have no gift." I stewed, frustrated and embarrassed. This was not going to help my chances.

I tried to think of something special to do for Felix on the way back to the office, and Thom kept up his cheery attitude.

At the office, I could feel the whole energy of the night had shifted. Everyone was pulling out glasses for champagne, lighting joints, and the girls were teasing and flirting with Felix more outrageously than usual.

I hung back, unloading my tray and setting it aside, while I checked my makeup in the mirror. The only one not celebrating was Ransom, who was sitting and pounding on the keyboard, looking disinterested. Selene was even there; it was strange to see her up so late at night. She looked like she just woke up, yet still managed to look completely composed and fresh. She came over to me and gave me a hug.

"Hello, darling! How were the sales tonight?"

"They were fine. Nothing special," I said, absent-mindedly. Selene laughed angelically, and I turned back to her from staring at Felix.

"I'm sorry. Long night. Thom told me about his mom, and I feel embarrassed I didn't get to wish Felix happy birthday. You know, on the day." The party was in full swing then. A couple of girls were dancing, and shoving Felix around like a croquet ball. He seemed to be fully enjoying himself, getting lit and basking in being King of the Party.

"Well, you could go say happy birthday now," Selene said slyly.

"Yeah, I guess I should." I casually walked over to the makeshift dance area, and Felix finally spotted me. He pulled himself out from the girls and came over, laughing and sweaty. His eyes were bright and happy, and my heart contracted with jealousy and desire. God, he was just so gorgeous. It was maddening!

"Hey. So, I didn't know... but I guess the word is out. So happy birthday!" I said, faltering.

"Oh, Miss Daisy. Aren't you cute!" He laughed, giving me a punch on the arm. "Getting all flutter-bugged over little ol' me. Don't you know I'm an old man now? I'm no good to anyone."

He laughed again, leaning down close to my face. I could smell a trace of musk and alcohol as he brushed a kiss against my cheek. I held still, astonished.

"Hahahahaa! Oh, priceless. I just love keeping you guessing, Miss Daisy. Don't go thinking too hard now — just enjoy yourself." He gave me a wink and wandered away.

I knew he meant it in a friendly way, but my face was burning. Meredith came over and shook her head at my expression, wordlessly handing me a joint, which I gladly drew from, coughing a bit. I caught Selene giving me a look from across the room.

"Felix has asked me to sing him a song. You okay?" She was looking happy. I could see she'd already cashed out with Ransom, and had a respectable bulge in her hand.

"Yeah, I'm fine. That just threw me. Looks like you did alright, yeah?" I asked, gesturing to the money.

"Yeah! It was a great night. Really fun. And I'm adding another night of singing to my week at the coffee shop, so that's going well."

"Hey, would you mind if I came to hear you sing sometime? I'm really interested in what you do, and would love to show my support," I said shyly.

"Sure, that would be great. I will email you the address and the new night I'm performing on. I better get to Felix." She nodded in his direction.

"Sure. Can't wait to hear you!" I said.

Meredith walked over to Felix, and got his attention by giving him a playful slap on the arm. They shared a private joke for a minute, then Felix asked everyone to quiet down so Meredith could sing. This took a bit of effort, as quite a few girls had gotten rowdy in the corner and weren't paying any attention.

Meredith broke into a sultry version of "Happy Birthday, Mr. President," slinking around Felix, her voice a ribbon of velvet, mesmerizing the whole, drunken, stoned lot of us. Felix was frozen, captivated by this curvy, silky, sexy display. At the end of her song, she finished by tipping up on her toes, pulling his face down to her, and giving him a big smack right on the cheek, which left a huge kiss-shaped mark.

I glanced around the room, and while everyone was amazed at the show, Thom looked completely star-struck.

We all broke into thunderous applause, drowning out her "Thank you" by stomping and yelling. Meredith truly had a gift, and it was wonderful to finally hear it.

Eventually, I staggered home and dropped into bed, my head spinning, grinning over the night's events.

Chapter 14

I decided it was time to pay my dad a visit. I had a couple of days off, so I gave him a quick call to let him know laundry was coming. He was overjoyed and impatient, but reminded me to "drive the maximum speed caution."

When I was home we tended to fall into a predictable routine. During the day I would do chores and little things around the house, while he went and tinkered in the garage with his model airplanes. At night we watched TV together or popped in a *Star Wars* DVD if nothing good was on.

While I was working my way through cleaning the bathroom, I noticed a few prescription bottles I hadn't seen before. From reading the warning on the label, I thought they were blood pressure medications. Worried, I stood in the bathroom, trying to remember if Dad had mentioned anything to me on the phone. I hadn't been paying close attention during our phone calls since he was usually lecturing me.

I was pretty sure he hadn't said anything.

I stormed out to the garage and banged on the door. "Dad!"

I heard a crash and a thump, and he swore loudly, "*Schiesse*!"

"Dad! Are you okay? I'm coming in!"

"No! Wait a moment." Dad was really private about his man cave, even though he had the whole house to himself. He saw it on some TV program years ago and loved the idea. Said it was very American.

He rustled around, and I heard some more banging before he came to the door of the garage.

"What are you doing in there? I thought you were building a model," I said suspiciously. Plus, my birthday wasn't for another couple of months.

"I am. And you startled me, so I hit my leg. Don't shout, Pale. It's rude." He glared at me from the sliding door that he had cracked open. His glasses had slid down his nose, leaving a sweaty line on the bridge, and his normally salt-and-pepper colored hair was now covered in a fine sheen of dust. His blue eyes were curious, though.

"Don't give me the dirty look, Dad. I just found this." I thrust the bottle under his nose.

"Oh, this? This is nothing, just a little something from my doctor at my last check-up. My blood pressure was a little high. Why are you so upset?" he asked, opening the door a little more to allow his hand to reach out, where he grabbed the bottle and hastily stuffed it in his flannel shirt pocket.

I reached into his pocket and pulled the evidence back out.

"Because you didn't tell me about this! You're hiding it, and that means something is wrong. Is something wrong? Are you okay? What happened at the check-up? What did the doctor say? Why didn't you tell me sooner?" I fired off, frustrated. I gave the garage door a little shove in my anger.

"Now Pale, stop it. This is why I don't tell you things, because you get all obsessive. It's always like this, when you care. Nothing is wrong; it was just a little high, so now I take a dumb pill every day, ok? Calm down, and don't get all Wookie on me."

"Dad. Just...don't keep things from me, ok? I couldn't stand it if something were to happen to you." I choked up on this last part. Seeing those pills really scared me. He's only 60 years old, for God's sake!

"Oh, sweetheart." He pulled me into a tight hug, and despite the cascade of dust that fell all over my clothes and face, I hugged him back fiercely.

"I couldn't stand anything to happen to you, either," he whispered. My eyes teared up a little, and we broke apart awkwardly.

"Anything else I'm going to find inside?" I asked, changing the subject to something light. "A zoot suit, maybe a Tommy gun? Are you working for the Modesto mob?" I joked. Only someone who had been to Modesto would have known how laughable this was.

"Zoot suit? No, no mob for me. Clown suit maybe. A red nose, who knows?" He laughed at his terrible pun.

I rewarded this with a deadpan look. "Ok, ok. I'm headed back inside. Love you, Papa."

"I love you too," he said softly, retreating back into the garage.

I returned to the house, and put the bottle back in the medicine cabinet. I stared at it for a long time, feeling vulnerable. I didn't like how casual he was being about this.

I decided to keep a closer eye on him, and to make sure to ask him about it during our phone calls. I wasn't going to move back home just yet, but I was still worried. What could possibly be giving my gentle and steady dad high blood pressure?

¤ ¤ ¤

Back in San Francisco, I took advantage of an afternoon off to visit Washington Square, a mini-park in North Beach that I had always really liked. It wasn't very big and had a quaint, neighborhood feel, even though it was in the middle of a tourist section of town. I sat on a park bench, people-watching.

The spring nights weren't very warm in the Bay Area; the fog rolled over the city in the evening, and stayed until mid-day, only exposing the sun for about five or six hours at a time. It wasn't particularly biting cold either, so there were still some brave souls out in the late afternoon. Two guys were playing Frisbee, a few couples were sitting on blankets, and several kids were running around, squealing and laughing.

My mind drifted to Felix. I thought about his birthday. I wondered what he would've liked, if I'd had time to get him something. I wondered if he had gotten in touch with his sisters and what they might have surprised him with.

As I got to know him better, it became glaringly obvious that he grew up in a house full of women. He never got icked out by talk about PMS and tampons. He never pulled any macho stuff in the office by talking badly about the Tarts. He often walked one of us to our car at night, sometimes holding open doors for no reason at all. He never bet on which girl was going to get drunk. That last one probably had a story behind it, given that he all but bit my head off when I train-wrecked THAT conversation.

Even though he expressly told me there was no romance in the future, I couldn't help it: I had the deepest crush on him. He was a bit weird, but he was my kind of weird.

As the sun dipped below the horizon, the chilly fog rolled in, leading my fellow park-goers to hastily pack up and drift away, off to fulfill their dinner plans. Soon the entire area would be filled with winos and the homeless, while the rest of North Beach would come alive with the pulse of sex, danger, and stolen opportunities.

I'd be back in that river of urban intrigues soon enough, but I had a little bit of me-time left, so I decided to grab a square of pizza at Golden Boy, rumored to be a great local hole to get a perfect, greasy slice.

I heard the tinkle of the doorbell as I walked in, and glanced up at a shockingly beautiful girl, casually dressed in jeans and a tight shirt that showed a hint of voluptuous breasts, peeking out from under a half-open flannel shirt. I stood there, gaping.

She gave me a big grin. "Can I help you?"

"Yeah, I'll have a slice of the pepperoni," I stammered. "Thanks."

"It's $3.50, but for you, on the house." She winked at me, and handed me a square on a sheet of wax paper.

"Why? I've never even been in here before!" I actually blushed.

"Yeah, but you're really cute. My name is Fred." She accepted money from another customer and handed him a cheese slice.

"Your name is Fred? Really? Is that something I should ask about?" I laughed.

"If you want to, but my name really is Fred. And you are?"

"Oh! Sorry, my name is Pale. I also work this area as a Tawny Tart, but have never been in here during the day."

"Well, we are open late, 'til about 2:30 a.m. If I'm working, slices are always free for you." She winked at me again, then moved to take care of a rush of customers that came in. I blushed again, and went eat at the bar.

I enjoyed myself a few more minutes, hearing conversation flow around me, then strolled out the door. As I exited, Fred gave me a wave, and I waved back.

It was time to get my stuff and drive to work. I floated home, feeling content with my day and daydreaming of Felix.

Chapter 15

When I got to the office, I noticed that Beth, the new girl who started a week ago, was still there. I remembered back to when Meredith was so friendly to me, even on my first night, and I felt a little guilty for blowing her off so far. The thing was, you never knew if they were going to make it past the weekend or even a single night. Like Sally, also known as Ms. Anger Management. And the Sobby Girl. I never did learn her name. This one, however, looked like she might stick around.

I walked confidently up to her and said, "Hi Beth! I know you've been here a bit, but I wanted to check in and see how things are going. I'm Pale. We met last week?"

"Yeah, Beth, obviously! No, it's okay. I'm sure there are tons of girls coming through here. Things have been great, just great."

We started exchanging background stories, and I found out she was from Britain on a work visa. She was only in San Francisco for about 6 months. It actually sounded like she'd been here a bit longer, but I couldn't care less about immigration status, so I didn't press the point. She'd been in sales before, but wanted something a bit more exciting. She'd rocketed up to the North run in her first week, and we talked about the finer points of our experiences.

I was certain she would do well – accents usually did – and certainly a British one tended to relax customers. Selene had encouraged me to try out different personas on the job, but I was too chicken to do it. I listened closely to Beth though, and while I was doing makeup I occasionally mouthed certain words quietly to myself.

Felix wandered over while we were each working on our hair and faces and announced, "You two are doing Rock, Paper, Scissors for the North run tonight. I will bear witness, because I think Pale will cheat." He winked at me, and stood with his arms crossed.

"I will not! Besides, Beth might be the cheater." I gave her a suspicious look, but she just laughed.

"Aren't you two a riot! All right, what's this all about?" she asked.

I explained that we had to play a game to win the right to work the best run of the night, and she instantly got a competitive look. "Oh, you are on, darling!"

We threw the first round, and I won. Then we threw the next round, Felix watchful, and Beth won. With our last throw, she had rock, and I had paper.

With a shout, Felix turned and told Thom "Put Pale on the board!"

Thom wrote my name under North run on the dry erase board, and I felt a strange burst of pride, though it really was a game of chance. Plus, any attention from Felix was good attention.

Beth looked slightly put out, but when she saw she was scheduled for the SoMa run, she cheered up a bit. Apparently she liked that run just as much, so that worked out well for both of us. Sometimes the girls in the office got competitive, and I didn't like the bad blood, especially with new recruits.

To my delight, Felix was driving me out to Grant and Green. I asked him a bit more about his sisters, and soon enough he was babbling stories to me about growing up in Texas: getting in and out of trouble with his favorite sister Sam, getting pampered by old ladies, and even chasing storms as a child. I delighted in hearing him ramble. He was a wonderful storyteller, especially when the topic was his youth. I had overheard him a time or two with the guys, waving his hands in the air and toasting drinks while sharing outrageous things from the past. It seemed he had an endless supply of material to draw from, what with all those sisters.

Felix didn't ask me any questions, but I was happy to focus on him while I gathered my thoughts on going out tonight. Something about the air felt off, but I couldn't put my finger on what it was. I cracked my knuckles, stretched my neck and fidgeted with the items in the tray on my lap.

Just as we pulled up next to the Saloon, Felix stopped the car, and stopped talking.

"All right, what is it Miss Daisy? What's going on in that pea-brain of yours?"

I shot him a dirty look.

"I don't know. Something feels off tonight. It's not me, I feel okay, I just mean... never mind."

"You've got the willies?" he asked, curious.

"Yeah, I guess that's what you'd call it." It sounded feeble even to my ears.

"Listen to that voice, Pale. It's your instincts. Guess you better be extra careful out there. And stay in touch if something happens," he reminded me.

"Yeah. Okay... Thanks."

I slid out of the car, and headed inside my first stop. As I was squeezing myself through the packed bar a guy in front of me shot me a dirty look, and turned away from me. I've learned by now that people giving off a really hostile vibe shouldn't be approached, but as I went to move past him, someone bumped me from behind, sending me into Captain Hostility, and knocking beer out of his glass, which sloshed all over his hand.

He turned to me angrily, and as I started to apologize, he growled, "Forget it!" and poured the entire rest of his beer into my tray. I was shouting at him now, and the other patrons around me were so upset, they wrenched him away from me and dragged him to the bouncer at the door. When the bouncer heard what happened, he shoved the guy bodily from the bar. I set my tray on the bar and the bar back passed me several clean, wet towels and a shot of whiskey, which I drank in one gulp. I could see from my vantage point that over half the bar was involved with keeping the asshole out, since he was fighting and shouting to come back in. But the bouncer and the others weren't having it after seeing how vicious he was.

I did my best to clean off the cigarettes, which were the most valuable. One of the packs was ruined, and the candy was a bit worse for wear but still sellable. One of the cigars was also wrecked, and this made me flat out angry. I had to pay for all this stuff! What an asshole!

I wasn't sure how to get out of the bar; I was running behind now, and that jackass was at the only entrance. I gestured to the bouncer that I wanted to leave and he nodded back. I made my way back through the bar, and a path cleared out. At the entrance, they forced the guy back 10 feet so I could leave in peace. I flipped the jerk the bird, and the bar patrons clapped as I was leaving. I really appreciated the people who were helping me, but I was still angry and hurt that this had happened. Maybe this was what my weird vibe was about.

I walked over to Kells, stomping and trying to shake off my mood. I was still trembling a bit as I wedged my way into the bar, but the crowd was unforgiving in letting me by. People around me were shouting in my ear at each other, shoving and scowling. I made my way downstairs, and got stopped by a rugby player who told me he'd buy a candy bar if he could feed it to me. His rugby buddies were watching to see how it was going to go. They were a bit rowdy, but I concentrated on the guy in front of me. His eyes were hard, but I wanted to turn around my night, so I decided to go ahead with a flirty exchange.

He carelessly tossed a fiver on my tray, and I tucked it in my cashbox. He unwrapped the candy bar slowly, and told me to open up. I opened my mouth and tried and give his hand a little flick with my tongue, but suddenly he was shoving the bar down my throat, hard. His buddies all laughed while I was pulling back, shaking my head, choking. They laughed uproariously as I wrenched the bar out of my mouth and smacked him as hard as I could on the arm. I was so upset at their callousness, I went running out of the bar, not even pausing to tell the bouncer what happened.

Back on the street, I was total mess. I couldn't catch my breath, and I was angry. I didn't know how to turn things around, and still had the rest of my night to finish. Impulsively, I called Felix.

"What's wrong? Where are you?" Instantly Felix knew that something wasn't right. He sounded authoritative, all trace of playful teasing gone.

"I'm in front of Kells. I think I'll be okay, but I don't know, this ... thing just ... happened. This guy just shoved ... in my throat ..." I managed to get some of the words out, but I was taking deep, raspy breaths.

Felix waited silently on the phone for me to compose myself, but the silence was so absolute. I could hear the menace rising, and I could practically feel him stalking, gathering the details he needed to make his attack.

"Tell me. Exactly. What. Who. Where," he said, icing me frozen through the phone.

I stammered out a few details: rugby player, candy bar, feeling surrounded. The previous guy and the beer pouring. I insisted that I was feeling better after telling him what happened, and that I would be able to finish the rest of the run. Felix breathed loudly through his nose throughout my speech.

"All right. Tell you what. If you think you can finish, how about you tackle the next three places, and call me back. We'll see how it goes. And if you see those guys out on the circuit, don't go anywhere near them. I mean it," he demanded.

"Well, duh! I don't want those jerks near me," I said, exasperated. I felt better now that he was back to just bossing me around, instead of that scary calm. I probably over-reacted by calling him, but it was too late now.

"What is your next stop?" he asked.

"Vesuvio, then Tosca, then Specs," I told him, as I waited at the pedestrian crosswalk.

"Okay, be careful. Talk to you soon." He hung up abruptly.

When the light changed for me to walk, I saw a guy directly across from me drop his pants to his ankles and hobble, penguin-style, across the crosswalk. As if that weren't enough exposure of him through his paper-thin boxers, he then turned around, and penguin walked back across the street. The light had long since changed to red, but traffic was at a standstill and nobody was honking. People were hanging out their windows and laughing at his antics. His face remained serious the whole time.

"Tonight is CRAZY!" I said out loud to no one in particular. No way was I crossing with that guy; too much freaky stuff had happened already. I waited for the lights to change, and then struggled up the hill to Vesuvio.

The bar was crowded but friendly, and I ran into a few regulars. One girl came up to me and introduced herself as Maria. She bought a pack of smokes, and started to tell me the story of how she was a Tawny Tart for one night and got fired. She went on loudly to her friends that she couldn't understand why she got fired for getting smashing drunk, yelling and pushing customers, ripping the costume, losing product, overcharging, giving stuff away, and--my personal favorite--peeing in the street. I expressed regret that I never got to work with her, but the sarcasm was lost on her.

I crossed the street and doubled back to Specs, where Ben the bartender lifted his shirt in greeting. This was a thing with him, I had learned, which was understandable, since he looked like Adonis, and had the abs to prove it. I made a few good sales, and even shared a shot with Ben, but I was still pretty shaken about the earlier events. It just seemed too volatile out here.

I moved on to Tosca, and it instantly made me feel better: the low lighting, the gentle murmur of conversation, the soft pop of champagne. I felt cloaked in a refinement bubble, away from the urgency and desperation of the rest of North Beach. I considered holing up in here for an hour, and blowing off the rest of the clubs.

The bartender acknowledged me with a head nod, and shot me a thumbs-up, a question in her eyes. I shook my head no, as I had had one drink recently. I would wait a bit before I had another.

I started my circuit around the room, but noticed something strange was happening. People were talking amongst themselves, but they were also craning around to look toward the back. They were distracted, interacting with me almost as an afterthought, casually tossing money at me. Twice I had to check and make sure that they meant to give me a $20 tip, which they didn't realize they were doing, but were fine with when I pointed it out.

Shaking my head, I made my way to the back, housing large leather booths that could fit eight people easily. In the very darkest corner, I noticed a tall, imposing man standing next to the end booth. Definitely a bodyguard. A super hot bodyguard. I gave him a smile, and he looked me up and down, smiling slowly. I turned to look at the booth's occupants, and my jaw fell open. It was the Mayor. The Mayor of San Francisco. Handsome, charismatic, witty, sharp, likeable, lovable, and terrifically powerful Mayor Flint Lucasey. I had heard rumors that he enjoyed hanging out here, but I never thought I would actually get to meet him.

Now I got why all eyes in the room were swiveled to the back.

"Miss, would you spare a moment to help me with my after-dinner breath? I desperately need some gum. I feel like I could slay a dragon, and I'm meeting someone here shortly. Of course, that's the whole point of eating at the Stinking Onion!" He laughed merrily, and his entourage laughed along obligingly. I was grateful he gave me an opening, as I wasn't sure how to break into the conversation, much less make it past that bodyguard.

"Sure thing, Mr. Mayor. Can I call you that?" I asked, giving him a smile but not moving any closer.

He laughed, and pointed at me. "Most people do call me that, but YOU can call me Flint, darling." He laughed again at his own joke, but was watching me keenly.

I decided to play along, and said in return, "Sure thing, Flint Daa-hling." He roared and slapped the table, jolting everyone's drinks.

After he calmed down, I leaned into the table and slid partway into the booth, to give the Mayor a better view of the tray items. While he was deciding, I stole a glance at the bodyguard. He was watching me closely, and gave me another of his drinking-me-in looks. I turned back to the Mayor.

"Yes, these items please." He had pulled out six packs of cigarettes, three cigars, all my gum, and four of my roses. For a moment, I was too stunned to count up the cost properly. He pulled out money, casually tossing a few fifty-dollar bills on my tray and waving me away, bored already. I was confused by this, and looked to the Mayor, but he was already in conversation with one of his female companions.

I felt a gentle tug from the bodyguard, and turned to look at him.

"He's done now. I know he's abrupt, but he's getting ready for a big meeting. Thanks for making him laugh; he appreciates coming here just for that reason." He paused briefly.

"Hey. You want to meet up sometime?" he asked, eyes intent on mine.

"I don't even know your name?" I stammered, blushing under his gaze.

"I'm Michael. What's your name?"

"Pale. Nice to meet you."

He gave a deep chuckle, revealing very white teeth. He handed me a number on a piece of paper, and I tucked it away. He turned to the Mayor, and as I walked towards the front, I heard the Mayor call out "Pale's the highlight of my night, everyone! Barkeep, give her a cocktail!"

The whole bar burst into applause, and I was grinning as I made my way hurriedly towards the front. Gods, tonight was just turning out to be surreal.

Even more freakish, Felix was waiting for me at the bar.

Chapter 16

"What are you doing?!" we both asked, simultaneously.

"Me, what about you?!" we both asked at the same time, again.

I started to respond, but Felix interrupted and talked over me. "Do you have any idea how dangerous this place is? I mean sure, I know you need to work the clientele, but do you have to get so involved? Who's that guy whose number you took?"

He looked thunderstruck and angry, and I got angry in response, my nerves flaring up all over again.

"What are YOU doing in here, skulking around and judging how I work? If you were this worried, why didn't you call me? And what business is it of yours if I go out with a hot bodyguard? TO THE MAYOR?" I threw this in his face. The bartender handed me the Lucasey cocktail, and I downed it in one gulp before Felix could stop me. He looked shocked and didn't respond.

He turned toward the door, watching a group of six men enter. They were impeccably dressed, and five of them were arrayed around one in the middle, the only one wearing a hat. The leader's eyes were strong and sharp, and he reminded me of a hawk. No, not a hawk. A vulture.

The hairs on my arm stood on end again, and my willies were back in full force. Felix was stony-faced as he turned to me. He glanced at the now-empty drink, shook his head and grabbed my hand, pulling me outside. I stumbled with my tray after him, slightly dizzy.

Indignant, I said, "Listen up, Professor Higgins! I'm not your doll and I'm not your little sister. Take your hands off me. I'm going to go work the rest of this God-awful night, and when I'm done, I'm going to sleep with a bodyguard who wants to drink me down like a tall glass of lemonade," I boasted defiantly. Thankfully I had remained upright, with only a touch of woozy.

"Pale, you have no idea what the fuck is going on. You don't see what I see." He stopped, frustrated. "Sleep with whoever you want, but just be careful who you talk to, and try to stay out of trouble. I wasn't judging you, I was worried about you." He walked off, leaving the conversation and draining off the last of my righteous indignation.

Worried about me? See what he sees? What did that even mean? Arrggh!! Men!

The rest of my night was pretty miserable. I had no energy to schmooze with people and dance to their tune, and had no patience for those who wanted to test me; this, of course, drew them to me like magnets. The bouncers had their work cut out for them, as there seemed to be patrons poking and prodding me all night, trying to get a rise out of me.

Two things consoled me. First, even though Felix was upset with me, it was because he was worried about me, which showed that on some level, he cared. My other consolation was on a slip of paper, if I could just work up the courage to call Bodyguard Michael.

Felix picked me up later at Crow Bar. While I was working in there, a former bartender who'd been fired for getting addicted to meth came in threatening to blow up the bar. He was thrown out, and the cops were called. It was a madhouse outside, and as I crawled into Felix's van, he asked me gently how the rest of the night went. I told him about Crow Bar, but nothing about the rest of the night, as it likely would have made him more worried.

"Did you really call me Professor Higgins? As in, *My Fair Lady*?" he joked quietly, and I gave him a tired smile.

"Sorry, but I was feeling pushed around. I don't like that."

"Noted."

Back at the office, I had a quick shot with Meredith and filled her in on the evening. She was shocked, and sympathized with the bad night, but was excited I got to meet the Mayor.

I cashed out, and my sales turned out to have been okay, but it was not because of any effort on my part. Had I not made out well at Tosca, the night would've been a total loss.

As I got ready to leave, I turned to see Felix flirting with Susannah. I joined a couple of the girls who were drinking in the corner, and the rest of my night soon turned into a haze.

Chapter 17

I woke up in a swamp, underwater. No, wait. That was just my mouth. My eyes couldn't open underwater, because they were soaking in vinegar. My nose was clogged full of stale sweat and old dog. My head was a 10 lb. hammer I couldn't lift. I wiggled my toes, just to make sure I could. My toes told me to shut the fuck up and go back to bed.

I winced, focusing on the alarm clock-3: 25 pm. What. Happened?

I rolled over onto my back, and started to groan. But even groaning was agony. Why did that hurt so much? Oh, I remembered now. OH. I sat upright, and fell off the bed. This was horrifically painful to every part of my body and I curled into a ball, remembering the previous night in flashes.

Moving very cautiously, I took a hot shower and had some bacon in an attempt to be human again before work.

One hour and about five Advil later, I made a mental note to write a will for when I died from liver abuse. Unbelievable. Now I knew why they said a hangover was like death warmed over.

As I made my way across the city, my cell phone rang. The sound was so astoundingly loud it echoed in my head. I narrowed my eyes and stared at it for a second. Nefarious, evil device. Who on earth would have thought this tiny thing could kill a person, a perfectly innocent, hung-over person, where they stood? At the very least, I felt like dropping a bomb on something. Anything.

While I reveled in my violent fantasy, my phone went to voicemail. The relief was so intense that, in a moment of benevolence, I decided to call them back and find out what they wanted. Maybe I could kill them later. Plus, I didn't want my phone to ring again. Ever.

"Hello? You just called, and I've decided not to kill you right away."

"Goodness, what's that all about? You sound a bit... off. Are you hung-over?" I heard Meredith ask, cheerfully. God, I was so glad it was her, but at the same time, the option to torture was not entirely out of the question. No, torture was too involved. Maybe a quick shot to the head.

"Ye-eess. Speak very softly, and I will spare your life. Try to breathe quietly too; the Advil haven't started working yet," I said, rubbing my temples.

She laughed, holding the phone away. Quickly she stifled it.

"Ahem. Well, the bad news is, we need you to come in to the office a little early. Rehka has quit. 'I'm Bored' were her exact words, I believe. We are working a concert tonight, and we are short a girl. You won't be working a regular run like usual. Felix was emphatic we should call you; said you'd never want to miss an opportunity to make a fool out of yourself. Though he said it kind of nasty. I think he's upset with you. Did something happen?"

I filled Meredith in on the second half of the evening, and she was even more amused at the idea that Felix followed me into a bar.

"You've made quite a stir of things, haven't you?"

"I have no idea. I can't even think straight; it hurts too much. I don't suppose Selene would give me the night off, for complications from my lobotomy?" I asked hopefully.

"Well, had you actually scheduled a brain surgery, she might've. But seeing as she's heard every excuse in the book, I'm pretty sure she'll see right through you, and figure out you are just hung-over. That will only make her more determined to get you in here. She might even cuss you out in French. That could be really funny." Meredith was enjoying herself, but I could still blame her. I wanted to stab things.

"Fine, I'll be there. What time?"

"5:45 ought to do it. The trays are built differently and we have to learn new stuff."

"See you soon." I hung up and glanced at the clock. Shit. I barely had enough time to get to the office, and considering how slow moving I was, I was going to need all the help I could get.

¤ ¤ ¤

I made it to the office, and there was a swirl of frenzy going on. Four hot pink outfits were hanging out on a doorframe, and four trays were already set out. They had been stripped of cigarettes, and a pile of candy was sitting next to each one. Selene was seated on a stool, and looking the part of an unforgiving headmistress. I could tell instantly from the moment I stepped in, that 1) Meredith had told everyone I had the rock n roll flu, 2) that this included Selene, who looked pissed off and tight-lipped, and 3) the only person who didn't care about any of this news was Ransom.

I made my way to one of the seats, where Susannah, Lisbet, and Meredith all gave me questioning looks. I shot Meredith a silent finger bang! and she grinned back.

The next hour and a half went a little like usual with a couple of changes. We couldn't carry cigarettes into concert venues, so we doubled the amount of candy and lights in the trays. This changed our tactic for selling, and the profit margin seemed like it would be smaller. Susannah assured me that the profit margin could be much higher; you just had to keep working the room. The trays were also twice as heavy, weighing in at a staggering 35 lbs around each of our necks. For 6 hours. While we did wear a helpful foam roll neck pillow, it tended to get in the way. The lights were more numerous, and there were a few that were quite complicated. Selene began demonstrating the lights' flashing red, blue and green strobe effect for customized messages. I immediately left to get dressed when my hangover that had started to abate came thundering back. When I came back out, Meredith confided that she would teach me about these later.

The other girls were actually being nice. I think it was because they felt sorry for me. I was grateful for it; I couldn't deal with the pressure of getting my look together, as well as being playful in the office. We were dressing all the same, no variation, and our trays also had to be laid out the same way. My tray was so incredibly heavy that I couldn't believe I could carry it around all night in the same venue.

Ransom offered the front seat to Lisbet (figured) and the other three of us piled into the back of his canopied truck, squashed down to lay flat with our trays, trying to get comfortable. Turned out it was impossible. The ride seemed very bouncy back there and I struggled to keep my stomach calm.

We arrived at the Bill Graham Civic Auditorium, where Phil Lesh was playing that night. I had no idea who he was, but Susannah was beside herself. She gushed about him all the way there, so I became curious about him too. Well, soon enough I would either love him or hate him, since I would be in there all night.

Susannah was the micro-manager of our night, and she did an amazing job of giving Meredith and me some last minute tips on how to work a single event with other Tarts all around. In no time at all, we were in a good groove, making good money, circulating multiple floors, and never conflicting in prices or running into each other. The best tip I learned all night was to rest my tray on the garbage cans, since there was nowhere, and I mean NOWHERE to sit down at a concert. The music really was amazing, and the crowd was so friendly and happy to be there. I was feeling recovered from the night before, especially since I almost never had my blinky lights on. Lisbet cornered me at one point, gave me a long stare, and sent me back out with all of them on. Like everyone else, I couldn't say No to her.

We were there for several hours, and shortly after eleven we got the call that Ransom was outside. We were all high from our excellent sales, but happy to set our trays down in the truck. Meredith, Susannah and I all flopped on our backs, tucking our legs in wordlessly as Ransom went to shut the truck canopy door. He looked slightly surprised, but said nothing, as usual.

Back at the office, as we unloaded our stuff, Felix came over to me, and touched me on the shoulder.

"Yeah?" I said, a little stiff.

"Pale, we just got a call. You are going to have to leave," he said, hesitating.

"What? What are you talking about? I did fine tonight," I said, confused.

"It's not that. It's your dad. He's in the hospital," he said quietly. The whole room was subdued, as I stared up into his face.

"My dad?" I whispered. "Is he, wha happen ..." I couldn't get the words out. Tears sprang to my eyes, and I looked away.

"He's fine, but the doctor asked for you to come in first thing tomorrow. He knows it's a bit of a drive, and I told him that you work late hours."

"Fuck that. I'm going now," I said tensely, looking around for my coat and bag. Felix handed me my things, automatically.

"Of course. We'll take care of things here, ok? And Pale ... let me know how it goes, ok? If you want to talk, I'm here." He mumbled this, but gave me a long look, punctuating that he meant it. I melted a little, touched by his caring after last night. Then the crushing worry of my dad washed back over me, and I was stiff as a board again.

Thom patted me awkwardly on the arm as I left, and I gave him a nod of acknowledgement on my way out. I got in my car, and drove straight to Dad's, collapsing and crying myself to sleep in my old room, dawn still many hours away from the horizon.

Chapter 18

I woke, bleary-eyed, and disoriented. The windows told me it was dark outside; the sun hadn't yet risen in the sky. I glanced over at the clock, whose harsh red glow told me it was half past five in the morning. I climbed slowly out of bed, trying to wrap my mind around what Felix told me last night. My dad was in the hospital. My dad, who'd never been sick in his life. He was one of those freaks who never got the sniffles, never had a fever, and never got grumpy. He was just always so...level. So steady. He was not prone to peaks and valleys, physically, emotionally, whatever.

I remembered one time when I was about eight he raised his voice at an incompetent bank teller, and I was so scared and surprised I started crying. He immediately calmed down, and frankly, I couldn't remember another time something like that happened. Then, all of a sudden, he had high blood pressure? It just didn't make sense. Hopefully the doctor would be able to shed some light on all this craziness. Maybe he needed to change his diet? Get some exercise? Wasn't that what they said about getting older? It was important to stay active?

Dismissing the what-ifs, I got dressed quickly in some old work clothes I had at the house, and sped towards the hospital. The sky lightened quickly on my drive; summer had almost arrived in Modesto. It was already bustling in the hospital when I walked in, the day's prep already started for all the accidents, births, fatalities and various managed conditions. Hospitals were hard to be in. They were a place both of power, and of powerlessness. And at the heart of this place, the most inescapable decisions, we either face toward, or turn away from.

I could feel the culmination of heavy decisions and so many human emotions: fragility and strength, anger and loss, celebration and apathy.

I asked for my dad's room at reception, and they directed me to it kindly. They told me the doctor would be in at seven, and would start his rounds. I nodded silently, and headed towards Dad's room.

He was still sleeping, and he looked so much smaller in that bed. His color was terrible, his whitened skin so strange compared to his usual crinkly lined tan. He seemed more tired than the last time I saw him.

I sat with him for a bit, just staring at him, drifting off into nothing-mind.

Eventually he stirred a little, and I sharpened my mind back to the here, as he opened his eyes and saw me. He focused for a moment, and smiled.

"Hello little ghost," he said softly.

He would occasionally say this to me when I looked 'small again', as in, when I got a look on my face that I used to have when I was a kid. Apparently I had a habit of holding so still, I would tell him I was trying to disappear. So he nicknamed me his little ghost. I struggled to choke down my emotion.

"Hi Dad. Felt like staying at this fancy hotel last night?" I smiled back.

"Ja, you got me." He patted my hand, and squeezed me. "I had some weird feelings after dinner last night; you know, my heart started racing, and I got dizzy. I decided to check myself in, and the doctor said my blood pressure was too high, so he kept me here to run some tests. I'm sure I'm fine, just need to change the pills, ok?" he said dismissively.

"Dad, what's going on?"

"It's nothing, honey, I told you before. Let's talk about you. Tell me something cheer-making," he said firmly.

I could tell from the look on his face he was not going to tell me anything else, so I told him about meeting the Mayor of San Francisco, though at this point I couldn't have cared less. His face lit up, and he asked me a bit about the charismatic Flint Lucasey. I told him a few details, but when I caught the doctor passing by out of the corner of my eye, I gave Dad a quick hug, and stepped out quietly to meet him.

I shut the door to the room, and the doctor led me a little way down the corridor, closer to the nurses' station. I had butterflies the size of baseballs in my stomach, and this wasn't making it any better. Shouldn't they take you to a room? With soft music, and a place to lie down and die when they tell you bad news?

"Good morning, my name is Dr. Tuva. Everyone calls me Tuva." He smiled briefly.

"Hi there. I'm Pale, Jeffrie's daughter. I'm a bit tired, I drove here right after work."

"Yes, your dad told me you would likely do that. I'm glad you came so early. We need to discuss a few things. Do you have time now?" Dr. Tuva asked briskly. I nodded my head Yes.

"Well, the bad news is, your dad had a mini-stroke last night. This was caused by his high blood pressure, because it puts added force against the coronary artery walls. Over time, this extra pressure can damage the arteries, which then cannot deliver enough oxygen to other parts of the body. For this reason, high blood pressure can harm the brain and kidneys and, in Jeffrie's case, increase the risk for stroke, which was what happened to him last night."

I was stunned. Dr. Tuva went on in some more technical detail, but I couldn't process what he was saying. I wanted to hear him, but he just started to wah-wah out on me, like white noise. I had no idea it was, or could get, this serious. I broke out of drowning briefly, tasting air.

"Is this something we can fix? Is this related to his diet?"

"This is definitely something we can work on. Since he came in so early, we were able to treat him and run some tests right away. I'm hopeful that if we make some changes to his blood pressure medication, and keep his stress levels down, the outlook is good."

I broke through the waves, able to take a huge gulp of air. There was a good chance.

"When can I take him home?"

Dr. Tuva smiled again. "Later today."

I went in and told Dad the news that we could go home later today, keeping silent about what the doctor told me. We visited briefly, and I told him I would be back this afternoon to pick him up. I headed home to get showered and find some cleaner clothes. I cleaned the house mindlessly, dusting, moving a few things closer together. I considered going in the garage, but decided it was not worth upsetting him. He'd probably booby-trapped it anyway.

Soon enough the day had flown by, and I was back at the hospital picking up Dad, walking him gently to the car, leaving that mortality castle behind us.

Back at home, he was livelier, though easily prone to getting tired. Over dinner I decided to bring up the topic of me moving home, but he wouldn't hear of it.

"Who knows what will happen now that you've met the Mayor! I had no idea this job could be so helpful for your career, little ghost. Try to look up, eh? I want you to do well, that's all." He gave me a hopeful look. I felt the waves lapping at me dangerously again.

"I know, Dad," I said absently, clearing the dishes. I didn't know how to give him what he wanted without making my own life unbearable. But what if my choice to pursue my own dream caused him undue stress? We spent the evening together in companionable silence. I stayed with him for the next week, helping him recover and get his color back. I called Selene, and she understood completely, taking me off the schedule until I returned.

Dad was capable of handling most of the menial things, just a little more easily winded than before. After a few days, he headed out to the garage and dug up an airplane model for us to assemble. I humored him by helping.

Seeing him get his strength back, and that he was able to take care of most of the household chores, gave me hope that perhaps this was an isolated incident. Feeling considerably better, I told him I'd be leaving the next night, and he grunted his acknowledgement.

On my drive back to the city, I decided that it was time to relieve a little pressure and have some fun.

I arrived in the Bay Area close to midnight. I took a deep breath, pulled out my phone and dialed Michael's number.

SUMMER

Chapter 19

The next day showed all the signs of summer in full riot, with flowers blooming, and new green pushing over the top of old green growth on every tree and hedge. I glanced out the window, where I saw that even stubborn shoots coming out of the sidewalk were making excellent climbs towards the sun, and every weed looked like a flower. The sun had risen much earlier than I had expected, though I wasn't surprised; summer could happen suddenly here. I heard music from all sides. The sidewalks were filled with pedestrians in shorter clothes with bright faces, and the polite shuffle of young people moving around the old. Everything appeared in fast motion.

Ruminating happily on the previous night, I remembered Michael calling me, shouting over the phone from the loud club where he had been with the Mayor, both of us straining to hear each other in order to arrange our meet up...

He came over shortly before 5 am? 6 am? Wasted no time in throwing me up against the wall and kissing me passionately. Ah. That explains the upper shoulder pain, my aching head told me.

I hadn't been exactly sure if we were going to chit-chat first, so I had made a quick snack of whatever I could find in the house, which I vaguely remembered included carrots, apples, cheese, peanut butter and cheese poofs, along with a fifth of vodka. That all got thrown aside when he laid me on the coffee table, which I could now see explained the mess of alcohol and sticky peanut butter all over the floor. I winced again. That was going to be a bitch to clean up. Maybe I could cut the carpet out?

I looked around and saw the bedding half on the floor, the other half a small cocoon shape that I had just fallen out of. No sign of Michael, though. I was both relieved and disappointed.

We had definitely had the sexy fun time. The first was a bit rushed, but we also had a nice second round an hour later after a catnap close to dawn. He must've snuck out in the late morning. I wasn't sure if I'd see him again, but it was making my head hurt to think about it, so I shuffled into the shower, before going into work.

By then, Selene had promoted me to four or five nights a week, and I was usually on the North Beach run.

Selene asked after my dad when I got in, and I filled her in on the results with Dr. Tuva, and Dad's strength coming back after the brief time I was there. She was happy he was back to good health, and I thanked her for her concern.

Meredith and I huddled up next to the mirror, gossiping and doing our makeup. It felt wonderful to have someone so immediate to talk to. We were doing things I'd seen other girlfriends doing: fussing with each other's hair, laughing, giving makeup advice--though that was more her terrain. We'd just gotten to the part in my story where Michael wrecked my apartment, as the rest of the office trickled in, getting ready and setting up the merchandise. Felix passed by several times, loading costumes from the back training room to the costume closet.

During my conversation with Meredith, I heard Lisbet talking with Selene and Beth. I overheard snatches of their chatter, and it sounded like they were all going to a concert together.

"What's your next move with Michael?"

I snapped out of eavesdropping, smiling at Meredith.

"Oh, I don't know. I definitely had a fun time. But it was just a fling, you know. Getting my girls some lovin'." I gave Meredith a little sassy shake of my shoulders, making my breasts wiggle in an overdone burlesque gesture. She burst out laughing, which was what I was hoping for.

Felix wandered by, and I decide to play it up even further.

"Of course, if he could get me a job in the Mayor's office, then I'd really be making it, so don't expect to see me around here for much longer!" I dropped my left hand down, snapping my fingers twice for emphasis. Meredith collapsed in giggles on the high stool, curled over the counter in front of the mirror. Felix scowled at us both as he carried more costumes by. Served him right for listening in.

"Pale, Meredith, come over here please. Change of plans," Selene called out, getting our attention. We joined her at the manager's desk, as Lisbet and Beth wandered away.

"Girls, I'm going to change your usual run tonight. There's a private party I need two girls for. The girl we use for almost all of our private events broke her ankle, and can't come in. Lisbet would normally take over, but she wants to work North Beach tonight, and she has seniority." I glanced over at Lisbet, who watched us covertly in the mirror. I looked back to Selene.

"What's the money like? Is it as good as working a run?" I interrupted. I was slightly irritated that I was getting kicked off North Beach. Meredith nodded in agreement.

Selene carried on as if I hadn't broken in. "The client paid a flat amount, and we do the trays by their request. Instead of selling, you will just be providing what they requested. In this case, they have asked for mostly cigarettes, cigars, gum and mints. No candy, no roses, no lights. They also have some special items they want you to carry, lighters I believe. You will dress in the standard uniform for consistency.

"The amount you earn tonight is a flat amount, plus your tips. Parties have several advantages. You make money no matter what, which may not happen on a regular night out, and the people at private parties are always really, really nice. Also, the night is shorter. You will start at 9 pm, and finish by midnight. Ransom will be driving you."

When Selene had mentioned that we might not make money on a regular night out, I had rolled my eyes. I had long since learned that the only kind of girl who comes back after 6 hours with no money in her pocket was lazy, or a drunk.

"You aren't going to say what our take is, are you?" I pressed Selene.

She lifted her eyebrows at me. I knew I was being slightly rude, but I was still not clear on why

Meredith and I were being put out for Lisbet. I knew it was fair, but I didn't have to like it.

"Okay, Ms. Diva, I will tell you. Your flat rate is $85, which is perfectly respectable, along with any tips you make. I will warn you, don't be aggressive about tips. The client has paid for you to be there as part of the theme and decoration. It's not the same hard sales you do in the field." I caught her gentle jibe, and managed to look abashed after she revealed the cut. I glanced over at Meredith, who looked happy with that amount.

Attempting to take it down a notch, I said, "Thank you for this opportunity, Selene."

She rewarded me with my favorite smile of hers, and my heart beat a little faster.

"My pleasure. Have fun tonight."

Meredith and I dressed at a leisurely pace, excited for the new experience ahead. We listened to the office conversation, and were delighted to find out that Ransom and Thom had made our trays for us, since they were adding special product from the client. Now that we had time to kill, we went back to discussing our private lives.

"So, when is your next open-mic? I would love to come and see you, " I prompted, as I was zipping Meredith's top up her tiny spine. Then she faced me, and I turned around obediently.

"Actually, next week I'm singing on Tuesday. Are you working that night?" She zipped me up in return.

I turned back to face her. "Nope! That's perfect. What is today? I lost track of things, being at my dad's."

I was trying to remember what day it was, but it just wouldn't come to me.

Meredith laughed. "It's Wednesday, silly."

"Great, that makes next Tuesday my Sunday night. I'll be there!" I beamed at her.

Ransom came over and glared at us. "Your stuff is ready. Let's go."

Our drive to the party was short and Meredith and I were soon exiting Ransom's inky black sedan. Even though Ransom's presence was often anti-social, bordering on hostile, I couldn't help but enjoy myself; the ride was so smooth and quiet, compared to Thom's sputtering, jerky tobacco-stained rickshaw. Thing looked like a beaten up trash can.

We stepped into a private club off Fillmore and Geary. The building was tall, glass, and modern, set back from the hustle of the Fillmore concert house on the corner. The reception area was silent. I glanced down at the paper in my hands that Ransom had given me which read, "8th floor, Suite 1388."

Meredith and I glided into an elevator, already feeling confident. We arrived at the 8th floor, turning right down a long hallway with beige walls, and dark navy doors to each suite trimmed in white. The carpet was so thick we couldn't hear our footsteps. At the end of the hall, last door on the right, was Suite 1388. Just under the suite number on a gold-plated plaque, was the title, "Recreation Room". Meredith had been leading, and shot me a "look-how-fancy" expression, and we knocked loudly. "Come in!" we heard several people shout through the door.

Meredith opened the door, and we both gasped. The room was easily the size of a small parking lot, with a soaring high ceiling, crystal chandeliers, a black marble bar, and astounding acoustics. The roar of the party was so well shielded from the hall, the sound made me take a step back. Meredith's mouth was still hanging open. A few attendees were smiling broadly at us, but didn't make a move to greet us. As we were getting our bearings, a well-dressed man in a suit strode quickly over to us. He pulled us into a small foyer to our left that I hadn't noticed when we came in, where coats were neatly placed on hangers by an attendant.

"Hi there! So glad you could make it. The party is in full swing. I guess you guys just go to it, eh? Let me know if you need a drink, or anything. Take breaks whenever you want, for however long you like. Feel free to get comfortable," he said breezily. I got the impression he'd been saying this to everyone who walked in the door, since customers didn't often treat us with the same regard as guests.

He looked like one of the patrons I would see on North Beach: tightly curled blond hair almost like dark sand, bright blue eyes, eager for conversation. He had a wiry build, and was constantly in motion, like holding still didn't come naturally.

"Thank you. We'll just circulate and get the crowd loosened up," I offered, stealing a quick glance at Meredith.

She'd managed to close her mouth, but then blurted out, "Is that a pool and Jacuzzi? And a chocolate fountain?"

Mr. Restless laughed at her astonishment. "Yes, it's a pretty amazing space. I would be lying if I said it wasn't a factor when I chose to buy a condo here.

Please, enjoy a drink. And thank you for coming." He wandered off, mingling and toasting his guests.

Meredith and I got over our initial shock and came up with a game plan. Selene didn't say anything about having to work the same space, and I didn't know how big it was, but I assumed it couldn't be very different than working the concert a few weeks ago. Meredith and I decided to do a full lap, crossing over each other as necessary to get the full scope of the size. We headed off in opposite directions.

Having the aspect of hard selling off my shoulders was a relief, and made working the event a real joy. My tray was much lighter, making it easier to navigate tight spots. I could essentially lift it over my head, and even give it a spin for flair. Handing out cigarettes with lighters made much more sense. Unexpectedly, my tip jar did fill, albeit slowly.

The space was ENORMOUS. The front room was already impressive, but what I loved even more were the winding nooks, crannies, small side gardens and fountains, obscuring people and conversations. At first glance, I thought there were about 75 attendees, but after doing a full lap into the labyrinth, I guessed there were closer to 200. There were two smaller bars along my path, compared to the one at the front, and there was no lack of alcohol. Despite this, the party wasn't getting out of hand. There were plenty of things to do beside drink-- all manner of games and equipment: ping pong, darts, pool (water *and* billiards), badminton, shuffleboard, and croquet. I even saw some people roller skate by me on the smooth, concrete path.

I finally caught up with Meredith after 20 minutes. Her tray looked like mine, a respectable dent had been made in her product.

"Whoa," was all she said.

"Tell me about it," I echoed.

"Let's go get a drink in front," I suggested.

"You read my mind." She nodded in agreement, and we took off towards the front. We got stopped a few times, and took our time flirting and providing guests with conversation. Selene was right; all the guests were super nice to us, never pushing boundaries or asking inappropriate questions.

The night flew by. We each had a couple of drinks, and even got talked into roller-skating around the party by the host. We both giggled uncontrollably, trying to hold the tray and keep ourselves upright. This only lasted about 20 minutes before we changed back into our shoes. In no time at all, our trays were nearly empty. We gave the last few lighters back to our host, headed back towards the front to use the restroom, and then went outside to wait for Ransom.

Meredith and I had been waiting outside less than a minute when he pulled up, right on the dot at midnight. The sedan door opened with a whisper, and I sighed blissfully as I settled in. Meredith and I both sat satisfied and quiet on the way back. Ransom finally broke the silence as we pulled up to the office.

"Well? Were they happy? How did it go?" he asked, clearly unused to having to probe for conversation.

"It was amazing. Just amazing. They loved us," Meredith replied, content.

¤ ¤ ¤

The next week passed quickly at work, though Felix was a little distant with me. He avoided talking with me in the van, and we didn't strike up any chitchat in the office. He was all business. I tried asking him once what was wrong, but he just stared at me with a you-know-what's-wrong-don't-give-me-that look. And since I hadn't done anything wrong, I ignored him.

I called my dad to check in and see how he was doing, and apparently the new medication was working out well. He sounded chipper, and told me he'd been able to do more and more each day. I called Dr. Tuva just to make sure, and he confirmed that Dad was out of the woods in terms of a relapse stroke. This was such a relief, I felt even better about going out to see Meredith.

Tuesday night, I was standing in my closet, happily undecided on what to wear, when my phone rang.

"Pale?" a strangely familiar voice inquired.

"Who is this?" I asked.

"It's....Thom. You know, from work?" he said, hesitant.

I was completely floored. Thom. Calling me. What on earth could this be about?

"Hey! What's up?" I asked.

"I have to get away for a night. I can't take it anymore. If I don't get a night off, I'm going to kill someone." He said all this in a tense rush. I could hear the force of his frustration.

"My sister's coming to take care of my mom tonight. I'm calling to ask if...please can I join you in whatever you are doing?" His pleading was so foreign to his gruff nature it sounded strange. I took pity on Thom. It must've taken some serious courage for him to call me.

"Fine. You can join me. But I'll warn you, I'm not up to anything wild and crazy," I cautioned.

"Great. Thanks. Just text me the address and I'll be there." He started to hang up.

"Wait! It's not 'til 8:30 pm!" I called out.

"Okay! See you then!" He sounded jubilant, and then the phone went dead.

Thom was in such a rush to get out, he didn't even care where we were going. Well, I hoped he wasn't looking for a bender, because I wasn't going out to get soused.

I dressed and made a quick dinner at home, climbed into my car and pulled up around the block from Café Boheme in the Mission. The summer sun resisted dropping into the technicolor pink showcase that San Francisco sunsets were famous for, but the moon was winning on its climb higher, and the air was cooling by the minute. I saw the inviting lights of the café on my approach, and its welcome energy and slightly run down feeling looked like a perfect fit for Meredith.

I headed inside, and found her at the counter, ordering a lemon tea, her throat swaddled in a large crochet scarf. I hadn't had time to call her about Thom, and wanted to give her fair warning, in case she had any hesitation about performing in front of him.

"Hi there!" she greeted me cheerfully, hugging me in her bulky scarf.

"Hey. It's sweltering out. What's with the wooly mammoth?" I asked, gesturing to the thick scarf. She laughed merrily at me.

"It's to keep my throat warmed up before the performance. Same with the tea. Believe it or not, the voice is a sensitive instrument. You need to take care of it, as a performer," she said, sipping the tea the barista handed her.

"Wow. I had no idea. Listen, I need to tell you something. Thom called me earlier in a panic. He needs to get away for the night. He's not working, and begged me to let him tag along with me tonight. Do you mind if he joins me? I can always call him and cancel."

"No, it's totally fine. The more the merrier," she said, shrugging.

"Great. He'll be here soon. He doesn't even know where he's going, he hung up in such a rush." I laughed in anticipation at his expression.

"Oh! That's funny," she replied, giving me a sly grin.

We found a table, and the MC soon got up and introduced the open-mic session. People had been signing up over the last half hour, so the list filled quickly. Thom came in during the MC's introduction of the first person and glanced around the room, finally meeting my eyes in confusion. He slunk over and took a seat across from Meredith. She smiled silently at him, then turned back to the stage to give her attention.

Leaning over and whispering, he said, "You didn't tell me Meredith would be here."

"You didn't ask," I whispered back. "And of course she's here. We are here to watch her perform. Now hush," I commanded.

Thom looked slightly miserable, but Meredith shot us a silencing look. For such a tiny woman, she could be surprisingly fierce.

The man who was singing a sweet summer folk song was good, but he was so nervous, huge sweat pockets showed dark stains under his shirt. We clapped loudly when he finished, and Meredith stole off to the bathroom during the pause between performers. Thom yanked on my sleeve.

"What?" I asked, low.

"It's just that Meredith was...she's...I have a hard time..." he sounded strangled, wrestling with telling me something.

"What is the matter with you? Oh. Oh!" I stifled a laugh, shaking my head. I saw Meredith out of the corner of my eye, making her way back across towards our table.

"You like her, don't you? Is that why your panties are all in a twist?" I whispered at Thom. He rolled his eyes at my reference to him having "panties", but the truth in the rest was obvious in his eyes. He pleaded with me silently to help him.

Meredith was nearly back to the table.

"You got yourself into this mess. I won't blow it, but I'm not helping you either," I replied quickly, turning back to the stage, where a middle-aged pair of twins had taken the stage with a tambourine and maracas. It took all kinds, apparently.

Meredith joined us, oblivious to our hushed conversation and her effect on Thom. "These two are great, you are going to love them. So darling," she indicated the twins, as she settled into her seat.

"Oh, this WHOLE night is very entertaining," I said with emphasis. Thom shot me a warning look.

The twins were, as promised, totally adorable. They sang an old Mexican folk song called, "*Besame Mucho*" with real feeling. We all clapped enthusiastically when they sat down. Then the MC called Meredith's name, and she shed her giant fuzzy scarf and made her way to the stage.

She settled and paused briefly, before going into a bluesy rendition of "*Stormy Weather*", which contrasted the warm evening perfectly, raising goose bumps on my arm.

Thom and I were both transfixed.

I managed to look around me and saw that the entire room was frozen in her spell. Her gift really was remarkable, and I soaked up every second of her song. What a blessing!

Meredith concluded on a soft note and thanked us quietly, before we raised the roof, hooting and catcalling. She slid into her seat, quickly surrounded by questions, being pestered by people seated closest to us about a CD. She demurred, to give the same respect to the next singer, and the room struggled to compose itself for the next performance. I felt sorry for whoever was going next.

Surprisingly, the instrumental guitar player pulled me into the rhythm as easily as Meredith had pulled me into the cold and sad fantasy of her song. What a gold mine this open-mic night was!

After 15 minutes there was a small break, and Thom, Meredith and I headed outside for some air with dessert from the coffee bar.

I started in on gushing right away.

"Oh. MY God! That was so incredible. It was amazing! You should be on American Idol! You should win on American Idol! You should sing the National Anthem at the Super Bowl! No, never mind, that's a terrible idea. Too much pressure. STILL! You know what I mean." I finished with the last of my air, taking a gasping breath in. Meredith laughed and shook her head. I was acting like an idiot. I looked at Thom and gave him a nudging look.

"Oh! Hey. That was really. I mean, you did really. Good. Yeah. That was. You know. Good. Good. Great." Thom breathed heavily through his nose, looking awkwardly down at the street. He obviously loved it too, but couldn't seem to get the words out coherently. Meredith just stared at him a moment, giving him an opportunity to continue. Seeing he had no intention of continuing talking, she turned back to me.

"I really appreciate you coming out tonight. Thanks for cheering so hard, and listening to some of the others. I have to get up early, but please stay here and enjoy yourself." She glanced over at Thom's hunched frame. "And Thom?" He looked up at her, resigned. "Thanks for coming out." She gave him an encouraging smile, and went in to get her purse.

I looked over, and he had a hound dog, hopeful look on his face. Sucker. She probably had no idea what she had just done.

"Come on. I need a drink." I said.

¤ ¤ ¤

Lucky for us, it was the Mission. You couldn't throw a hipster cat without hitting a happening bar. We ended up in a booth at Doc's Clock, Thom with three shots of tequila in front of him (two empty, one still full) while I nursed a Last Word on the rocks.

Thom was regaling me with tales of his failure with women. Specifically, he was recounting his stumble with Meredith over. And over. And over again.

"I just can't believe I couldn't even tell her how AMAZING she was, you know? I mean, how hard is it to say, 'Great job'?" He slumped over the bar, grabbed the last tequila shot, and knocked it back, setting the glass down gently on the counter. He signaled to the wait staff to bring him two more.

"Thom, you gotta stop beating yourself up about it. Meredith isn't exactly intuitive about these things. She probably doesn't even know you have feelings for her. She grew up with all those protective brothers; she had to learn to tune it all out. Besides, you can always tell her at work," I said, reassuringly.

"NO I CAN'T!" he said, frustrated. He dropped back two more of the shots as the waitress left them for him. He brought me another Last Word, though it was clear I wasn't getting one in the conversation.

"Work is not the right environment, and I never get time off like this! I blew it, that's all. I blew it, it's over. My chance with her is..." He sighed heavily.

My eyes were trying to focus on Thom, but things were starting to take on that beer goggle haze. I drank deeply from my glass, and decided to put Thom out of his misery.

"Thom? Hey, Thom." I said, since he was distracted watching a large group of women come in.

"Huh? What?" He leaned close to me. His eyes were staring straight into mine, and even in this light, they were very, very sexy.

"Listen. I wasn't going to tell you about this, and you have to keep this under your hat, ok? Don't say an.ee.thING." I punctuated each syllable with a poke on his forehead. He was grinning at me, but nodding yes. He was also staring at my mouth, waiting for what I was going to tell him.

"I'm pretty sure. Don't quote me on this, but I'm pretty sure Meredith. Is a..." I trailed off, lost in gazing at Thom's lips.

"She's a whaaaa?" he prompted slowly.

Whispering, I leaned in, " a virgin." I could almost taste that heavenly bakery smell rolling off of him. God, I could take a bath in that scent. What was happening to me?

"Oh, well. Hmm. I was hoping for something a bit more..imm-ediate-" He broke off, playing with my hair. MY HAIR. Oh my goodness, this was happening. This was happening, right now. I worked with Thom! My brain was screaming at me.

Thom leaned in further, and kissed me gently on the lips. And just like that, a neon Fuck it! went off in my brain, and I kissed him back.

¤ ¤ ¤

Thom and I spent the next 30 minutes having a very interesting conversation. Most of it involved trying to cut off each other's oxygen flow with a passionate mashing of tongues, punctuated by justifications of "It's just tonight" from each of us, a couple of "Don't tell Merediths", and of course, "I just need someone to" which usually got interrupted by whatever that sentence's ending was supposed to be. We threw down some bills and decided to head to my car to continue. On the way to my car, stumbling, he said, "I didn't expect this. Like, at all."

"Yeah, me neither. Like, at all."

We arrived at my car, and I beeped the doors open. Thom climbed in, and we immediately resumed our kissing. But the walk had sobered both of us about the implications, despite our excuses, and we ended up pulling away from each other. Silence fell for a few minutes, and Thom cleared his throat.

"This is a nice car."

"Thanks."

"Listen, I didn't mean for this to happen. I was just upset about Meredith and I—"

"Yeah, Thom, I know. I was there." I sighed, turning to face him. "Listen, I get it. Really. I've been in a space where I need to take my mind off things too. But I think this was a mistake...Do you agree?" I was still a little too tipsy to look at him, and he wasn't looking at me either, but I saw him nod in agreement.

"So, we'll just pretend this didn't happen, and be friends."

"Right. Friends," he mumbled.

We both took a deep breath together, letting it out at the same time. We chuckled about that for a minute, and the tension was broken. Just like that.

"Hey, are you going to be ok to get home?" I asked him. "You've had a lot more than me."

"Naw…I'll take a taxi. Safer," he replied, grabbing his coat from the floor.

"Okay… well. I guess… I'll see you tomorrow." He stole a glance, and gave me a reassuring smile. A real one. For just a moment, I could see him happy, and my heart hurt that he still hadn't found it.

"Goodnight," I said, keeping my thoughts to myself. Too sappy. He wouldn't want to hear that. I started my car, watching him lope up the street.

I figured I'd had enough adventure for one night.

Chapter 20

The next few days were a bit weird. I decided that in the interest of everyone involved, I would only tell Jana about my encounter with Thom. Meredith didn't need to know, and neither did Felix. This kind of office gossip would only hurt everyone. Besides, I didn't want to get chewed out by Selene for "office romance".

Thom had managed to keep up our agreement to act as if nothing had happened. Meredith was still just so pleased we both came, and I was correct in the fact that she still had no idea that Thom had feelings for her. When I got the chance to talk to him in private, I would ask him how he was doing.

Meanwhile, staging that little joke on Felix had given me an idea about trying to get a job in the Mayor's office. The more I thought about it, the more it made sense. Even though my dad's recovery had been going well, he was still not thrilled that I was working as a Tart. I wasn't willing to take some boring job in a cube farm, and I'd been trying to find a compromise that would work. I'd been considering if a job in politics wouldn't be the perfect fit. I tended to get a bit antsy if I couldn't be active at work, and a campaign would definitely keep me on the go. Michael could likely put in a good word for me, and I could intern at the start. Politics seemed a lot like what I was doing now.

I finally heard from Michael the night before my birthday, while in Vesuvio. I had just had a hilarious encounter with a guy who had approached me to ask if I had any bacon, and had continued to go on in ecstatic rapture about the benefits and joys of pork. It turned out he was a comedian, and wanted to try out his bacon topic on me. I told him it was very funny, and wished him good luck, when my phone gave its vibrating buzz. It was a text! Finally! Michael wanted to know if we could meet up later that night. I wrote him back right away, letting him know I was done around 2:45 am, and we agreed to meet at my house again.

His message was especially good timing, as it would be a great birthday present.

Feeling cheerful, I ran into Rehka, who had shaved her head, and was looking amazing from the result. She was with her boyfriend; it looked like things were serious. She seemed happy, and I was glad for her. She sent her regards back to everyone, and while I didn't think we missed her as much as she thought we might (I never heard her mentioned again after she left), I told her I would extend her Hello's all around.

As I approached Fuse bar, the door guy Jim started giving me a neck massage, and I melted under his big, broad hands.

"Girl, you are holding too much tension!" He gave me a piercing look and a little shake.

I had since learned that the door guys and bouncers were a treasure trove of good friendship and loyalty. They appreciated my respect, and in return, were always looking out for me, or going out of their way to make things easier, like this massage. I knew quite a bit about their lives; who was married, who was doing this as side work, who was happy, who wasn't. One of them was going to nursing school, and using his big burly self to pay the whole way through. Sometimes I got little gifts from them, but we were all just platonically friendly. It was a bit like having about 10-15 big brothers. From what I heard, most girls didn't interact with them as much as I did. But I found it too hard to follow the moods of most of the women in the office, and the men made it easy to just shoot the breeze.

My night wrapped up quickly, and I joked with Felix on the way back to the office about what he was going to get me for my birthday, and he sassed me back that he was getting me my own personal chauffeur (my ignoring him hadn't lasted very long). When we got back to the office, there was a sweet little bit of decorating, and they sang me Happy Birthday. Meredith and Selene had presents for me, and we all had some shots together. I was pleasantly distracted and tipsy by the time I got home, and attempted to clean up a little before Michael arrived. I was determined that despite my foggy state, I wanted to pitch my case to him, see what he could do for me.

But when Michael arrived, he was even more urgent than the last time. We had a few more drinks, and the ability to talk fled completely as we started passionately making out. Sometimes the urge to get lost in sex overcomes the need to intelligently and maturely make a life change, I reasoned silently. Plus, he might not go for my plan if I stopped him right now anyway, so I went with it. The animalistic, burning taste of his sweat inflamed me, and I felt like I was folding over and over again, turning away from the past, bolting ahead. He was a dragon, I was a tiger, and I bit him, snarling, while he kissed me tenderly along my hipbones. Despite my slow, clumsy movements, he made me feel like the sexiest creature on earth, his eyes running parched over my whole body, following with his hands, almost in awe.

We were at it for hours, napping softly, reaching through the dreamscape, climbing the dance, playing mirror games, closing and opening the door to mountain peaks of crying-out beauty. He reached inside me and obliterated distraction, reaching further down; we were there, in the tunnel of that great expanse. We drifted away back into sleep, curled under the light of dark shell.

¤ ¤ ¤

When I woke late that Sunday morning, I could feel right away that Michael had gone. I was a bit frustrated with myself for not taking my chance to talk to him when I had it, but at least I wasn't hung-over like before, and I had plenty of good memories from the night before to keep me distracted all day. While I had no plans on my actual birthday, dinner at Dad's was a tradition. Jana was coming down from Chico with her boyfriend, Alex. As I checked my email for birthday messages, and only had a message from a local radio station, and a coupon for a Denny's offer, my phone rang.

"Hello?"

"Happy Birthday, Miss Daisy. Get dressed, I have a surprise for you."

"Felix! What do you mean?" I asked, surprised. Pleasantly, but still.

"Get dressed!" he said, mischievous.

"How do you know I'm not dressed?" I asked, suspiciously.

He laughed a deep belly laugh, saying, "You mean you aren't as lazy as I think you are?"

I was silent as I glanced down at my underwear, tank top, and flip-flops. In the pause, he chuckled again. "Just what I thought! I'll be downstairs in 20." He hung up.

"Wait!" I said, uselessly. He hadn't even said where we were going, or what I was supposed to wear. Sigh. Typical. On second thought, I decided to be happy he went to such trouble. Intrigued and bouncy, I breezed through a quick shower and threw on a summer dress over leggings. Grabbing a cardigan and a coat (this was the Bay area, summer had no meaning to the fog), I headed downstairs 25 minutes later to find Felix tapping his foot at the curb.

"Mi'lady! We will be late for the ball! Did you bring your glass slippers? Into the coach!" He theatrically opened the door, ushering me inside. I burst out giggling, climbing in.

Once we were both in, we turned to each other.

"Where are we going?"

"Are you ready?" he asked.

He grinned. "WE. Are Going. On a. PICNIC!" he announced with a flourish.

I clapped my hands happily. "So, I don't have to make lunch?"

"Nope! It's all taken care of."

We zipped through the streets, chatting about nothing in particular on our way into downtown. When Felix made the turn to head up the hill to Coit tower, I figured out where we were going.

"Oh! I've been meaning to come up here," I said, lost in gazing up at the big tower.

"Best view of the city, you know." He pulled into a spot, and we unloaded the supplies. Felix really packed a great picnic, even bringing napkins and something for us to sit on. We sat on the low, wide concrete wall, the perfect height for gazing out across the bay and around the outlying neighborhoods.

As I was taking in the view, Felix laid out our lunch in short order--lemon chicken sandwiches, pears and cheese, warm, chocolate cookies for dessert, and a spiced wine. Everything looked absolutely amazing and I dug in with delight.

I filled Felix in about Michael, and while he didn't look happy about it, he couldn't say anything, this 'friend' of mine.

I filled him in on Dad's plans for me to work a secure, boring desk job, like he did. I explained how I couldn't imagine that life for me, and how it had been stressing him out, and sending his blood pressure up, which led me to tell Dad about meeting the Mayor, and when he got so excited, that was how I had the idea... "See! It's perfect! If Michael can just get me a foot in the door at the Mayor's office, I'll be golden. My dad will feel like I'm finally working something legitimate, and I will get more excitement than at some corporate soul sucking place. Then he won't be so worried, and his health won't get worse," I finished, laying it all out.

Felix looked dumbfounded for a moment, and I tensed. Waiting for some crack remark about how stupid it was.

"So this Michael guy, you aren't just obsessed with him?" Felix asked.

"Well, don't get me wrong. He's . . .pretty impressive in his own right." Felix wrinkled his nose at me. "But no. He keeps blowing me off. He's a good distraction right now..." I trailed off, uncomfortable.

"I gotta hand it to you, Pale. You sure do surprise me." Felix stood up abruptly and walked a little ways away. I was a bit startled, but stayed seated. I hoped he wasn't going to give me crap about this. We were having such a nice day. I started to put away the supplies, when I heard him turn back and ask, "So, do you even WANT to go into politics? Does it even interest you?"

I shrugged. "I guess. It's all about sex, getting the numbers, and looking the part, right? How is it very different from what I do now? At least I wouldn't have someone tell me they wanted to 'mount me'." I shook my head, disgusted.

Felix roared with laughter, bending over double, holding his stomach. Apparently I had forgotten to tell him about that from a week ago. I thought I was going to punch that drunken guy, but it just wasn't worth it at the time. Of course, it was worth the joy on Felix's face now. Positively priceless.

"I think it's a crazy and stupid idea, and it's bound to hurt you, but I'm done giving you crap, Pale. It's your call. You have more in you than I thought, truly." He shook his head, laughing in disbelief.

"What do you mean? And why do you think it's stupid?" I asked, defensive.

"Now, now, I don't mean it like that. Although I can see why you'd go there, after all the crow I've given you. I didn't say YOU were stupid. I mean I think it's stupid for you to do something without knowing what you are getting into. The politics, I mean. No, I thought you were like one of those girls from Vegas I saw everywhere, working their way to the top, doing anything they could to get attention. And you aren't like that at all. You are willing to drop all the attention, at the drop of a hat, for your Dad. To do something you will probably end up hating. And WHOO Nelly, I bet you will hate it!" He spent a minute laughing again.

"Well, thanks for your support," I said, sarcastically.

"You are very welcome. Because you have it," he said, sincerely.

The drive back to my house was fairly quiet. When we got in the car, I did thank him for the lovely picnic, and he nodded back at me.

When we pulled up to my house, though, Felix put out his hand to stop me before I climbed out.

"Do you want to get a drink sometime? Go out? Just as friends. Thing is, I like talking with you," he said, softly.

I was so floored by this, I just said, "Sure. That would be great."

I headed inside to get ready for my birthday dinner, picking out a dress. My heart had flown up into the corner of my chest, and fluttered there madly. I had to cover my mouth; she was beating so fast.

Happy birthday to me!

¤ ¤ ¤

My birthday dinner was small and understated, but in a really soothing way. Jana and Alex had a good drive down, and it was wonderful to see them together. They seemed to have really found a good rhythm in living together, and were now so integrated, you would never know they had had trouble at the beginning of the move. Some couples were like that; they just fell into an organic pattern that looked easy. I know it wasn't easy, but because it looked that way, it made me wistful for a deeper relationship of my own.

I wondered sometimes how different my life would be if I truly had someone to talk about the future with, to merge our lives together. Two independent forces in Life, navigating family, friends, career, plans for children. Arguing about where to go, but certain that you were doing it together. It had been so many months of chasing Felix, and though I still thought he was a hell of a guy, I was starting to be content to rest in our friendship together, dealing with being a buddy, not a potential sex kitten.

Dad and I made the meal together, since he could be a bit hopeless in the kitchen. He did cook pretty well, but had a tendency to make the food too bland, so he needed a little prodding to add the salt and spices.

They all embarrassed me by singing Happy Birthday at dinner, and we talked easily about life in Chico and Modesto, with only a few bad puns between the men to ruin the food.

Jana and I sat aside for a bit after dinner, and I insisted she fill me in on the changes going on with her. She'd been such a great listener over the last several months; I didn't feel like I'd been giving her much space to vent. We had a happy catch-up session, and she was pleased to hear that Felix wanted to spend time with me, outside of work.

Dad seemed to be doing so much better. There were no further symptoms after his stroke, and the doctor had assured me that the medication was working perfectly.

Back in the city, I tried to reach Michael over the course of the next week, energized by my birthday high, while Felix and I set time on Thursday to go out and grab a beer.

Chapter 21

The late July summer had finally arrived, and though it could still be foggy in the morning, typically the skies were cloudless, and the temperature verged on hot. Everyone was spilling out of houses, cars, and offices, riding mopeds, bicycles, skateboards, and lugging bright baskets filled with lazy indicators: broad hats, low chairs, funny beach toys, simple games, sandals, and of course the universal white-lidded cooler, filled with frosty drinks.

It felt exactly like the right time to get just what you wanted, and I was caught up in the same fever. I dove deep into my closet, pulling out and vigorously shaking dresses, skirts, and all manner of accessories, dust flying everywhere. I was on my way to meet Felix, and even though we were just meeting as "friends", and it wasn't the first time we'd met outside of work, I was a bit nervous about saying the wrong thing. I tried to stop worrying, and enjoy myself. After all, if he was being a jerk, I'd just go home and put his face up on a dartboard.

We decided to meet at a bar that was nowhere near any of the Tarts' stomping grounds, as we wanted the peace and quiet of not being interrupted. He chose Sycamore, and I saw him in the bar through the window as I approached the front door. He was chatting easily with the bartender, who was shaking his hand. They were sharing a joke, and both laughing together. I wondered if Felix saw his effect on people sometimes, he was so good at putting them at ease. He radiated a kind of magnetic confidence; it was one of the first things I had noticed about him. I felt relaxed, yet excited around him. I drew a deep breath, and strode through the door.

"Hey, Pale!" Felix waved me over to his spot at the bar, drawing up a bar stool for me. As I went to take off my light summer jacket, he helped me out of it, hanging it on a hook under the bar. The bartender and I shared a surprised glance, and teasing, he leaned over to Felix and said, "Don't worry. She's impressed." He grinned at Felix knowingly.

"Oh! No, we aren't on a date. Just friends," he said, taking my purse and storing it with the coat.

"Sure, buddy, whatever you say. What'll it be?"

After we consulted for a moment on what we were in the mood for, Felix ordered beers for both of us. I reminded myself silently that he grew up with three sisters, and this sort of behavior came naturally. It didn't mean anything.

We slid easily into conversation, backtracking to my birthday dinner, and knocking back a few more beers as we talked about movies, talk radio, local events, rants about living in the Bay Area, and of course, a little about family. By then, we were both leaning on the bar, and exchanging a few toasts to ridiculous things like spicy mustard and well made leather boots, knowing we weren't as clever as we seemed, but not caring. There was no urgency. There was no agenda. I decided to try a new topic, one that would hopefully shed some light on comments he'd made before, things that didn't make sense.

"So, tell me more about how you ended up in Vegas. I mean, I don't want to press you, but I'm curious," I said casually.

There was a pause, and then giving a sigh, Felix said, "It actually happened by accident."

"I wanted to get away from the 360 degree female influence at home, and decided to man up somewhere I could profit from. I mean, I'm pretty good with math and numbers, but I wanted to try my hand, you know. I sort of got sucked in, and somehow, eight years of my life had passed, and I had a real problem. I couldn't see the forest for the trees, though in my case, the trees were huge debts. Some of those were mine, but not all of them." He scowled for a moment, hesitant.

"What do you mean?" I asked, prompting.

"It's my sister, Audrey. She has a knack for getting into trouble, and I mean real trouble--drugs, jail, fighting, stealing...even, well, other stuff. I love her, but I can't just let her keep tumbling down the hole, without trying to give her a leg up, you know?" He looked at me, questioning.

"Of course, she's your sister," I said, trying to comfort him. He looked so helpless, talking about her. I'd had no idea he was so tied to her difficulties. I wondered what Audrey thought of Felix. I wondered if she loved him for it, or resented him. It wasn't the right time to ask.

"Well, I saw a lot of things while bailing Audrey out. Sam and I took turns trying to help her. Nic-Nic was too broke; she's a kindergarten teacher," he said.

"Nic-Nic?" I asked, confused.

"Oh, yeah, that's Nicole. Sometimes I call her funny names. Nic-Nic, Knick-Knack, Knickerback, Knickerbottom. We don't get a chance to talk much, but she's cool." He grinned at the last one, clearly pleased he'd added a new name to the list.

"That's why I got so upset that day in Tosca. Once you've seen so much of the underground illegal dealings that go on in a big city, you can't really un-see it. And you really didn't have any idea how dangerous it was for you to be there. There was tension going on between two families, and it looked like it was going to get messy. You were in real danger, Pale," he said, softly.

My face burned brightly in the light, as I took in everything Felix was saying. But he continued on, opening up now that he'd already started.

"I had the hardest time admitting I was an addict. I thought I really had a grip on things. It's been difficult to come here. No friends, no family. Trying to get away from the life my sister Audrey seems to crave. I don't want to follow her. I don't want to think of having fun as risking my life all the time. Not just my physical life...my heart...my body...my soul..." Felix trailed off, struggling to keep his conflicted face from breaking down.

"I know that I'm really prickly about the gambling thing. But you have to be, in recovery. For a long while there, I wasn't sure if I could do it. I thought you were just another delusional, ambitious woman, climbing and clawing your way up to the spotlight, for your moment of Fame. That all that mattered to you was finding tools in others you could use. I just wasn't sure about any of you girls. Now I can see it was that I didn't believe anyone COULD be doing it for good reasons, since I'd lost all my good reasons for keeping up the fight.

"You are a good person, and I'm glad we finally came out. Here's to new dreams," Felix raised his glass, and I grabbed my glass hurriedly to toast. I had been so engrossed in his telling me about his past, I had leaned close. I recovered and leaned back, sitting up straight. He shot me another of his sun-bright smiles.

"New Dreams!" we said loudly, clinking and drinking with grins crinkling the sides of our faces.

Felix cheered up considerably after that. He seemed free, as if sharing his story with me had somehow lightened his burden. I thought about all the times I'd been in bars, just like this one, seeing conversations. My mind drifted on how many times young friends had worked out something weighing on them over a beer, spanning the hundreds of years that humans had been on earth. It was sort of staggering to consider that it was trillions of times, over thousands of years, in all of the taverns, pubs, and public houses. Even at the Egyptian Pyramids, slaves must've shared the burden of their masters' wishes over a beer in the hot desert sun.

We played a quick game of pool, backed off of the heavy topics, and went back to our banter. When Felix wasn't making me the target of his teasing, we got along really well. It was a very nice night.

The next few weeks passed very quickly. Work was typical work. I saw my regulars and greeted them all warmly: Coach Bill, Lydia Kim, Ben the Bartender, who loved showing me his abs. They were all part of the big tapestry of my trip around the Land of Oz, where strange wonders awaited. The highlight of my entire year happened at the end of August, when an impeccably dressed, older black man was standing outside the Condor Club, chatting with some smokers. He saw me walking in, gave a very long, very low whistle and said "Mercy, do you work here?" in amazement. It was so kind, and said with such awe, I turned and gave him my best smile.

"No, but thanks for that," I said.

Felix and I continued to hang out about once a week, usually getting a beer and swapping stories. He was genuinely interested in Jana, my Dad, childhood adventures, and especially my adoption. I was a little more reticent to talk about it, but he had a way of worming his way in--damn those charming Texan manners.

It was really nice having a regular person I could call and talk to, but we both kept it cool in the office, just to keep the drama down. Thom was only briefly happy, then back to his Eeyore ways. He hadn't yet said why. Ransom continued to fixate on Selene, and Lisbet continued to pop in every once in a while, and shake things up for everyone. My sales continued to do well, and though I wasn't rolling in a bunch of extra cash, I was doing ok. I kept texting Michael, but he ignored me completely. This was the only blight on my summer.

Things did get pretty intense one night, when Felix got a call at work on his cell. I was busy getting ready for a SoMa run, coupled with the Castro. I glanced in the mirror, and after I saw him bark a few words, he took the call outside, looking thunderous and silent. Uh Oh.

I waited a few minutes and went outside to see what was going on, and he was standing at the curb, hands clenched at his sides. He was turned towards the street, and his shoulders were hunched up, obviously stressed.

"Felix? What is it?"

He looked like someone just shot his dog, twice. "It's Audrey. She's in jail again, and she needs my help. It's bad this time, Daisy. Really bad." He turned towards me, his face tight, eyes bleak and burning. Without thinking, I pulled him into a hug, holding him tight. He stood there shocked, then relaxed slightly, giving me a squeeze, and gently pulling away.

"I have to go. Right now. I have to go to Vegas, and get the ten grand for her bail, or she's in big trouble. I'm going to have to buy into a poker game and win her what she needs."

"What?" I asked, flabbergasted.

"Felix, you can't. You CAN'T do this! It'll ruin all the work you've done. You deserve better than this. Can't Audrey ask your mom, or your other sisters..." even as I trailed off, I could see this was a weak idea. Whatever she'd been mixed up in must have been pretty illegal for her to ask so much of him, especially knowing he'd been dealing with breaking away from gambling.

Felix pried my hand from his arm, which I hadn't noticed was clutching him fiercely.

"I have to. And I have to leave right now. I'll be back, ok? Just, don't say anything to anyone at work." He gave me a quick hug, and looked me in the eye, confirming our agreement. I nodded silently. Felix started towards his van, and I called out to him.

"Hey!"

He looked back, questioning.

"If you need anything, just call, ok?" I knew that it wasn't much, but it was the best I could figure to say at a time like this. He gave me his sunny smile and turned back.

I stood outside a few minutes, thinking up a story for Felix's cover, and headed back inside.

Chapter 22

Everyone bought my story for Felix without comment. It was a sign of how well he was liked that no one questioned that he would drop everything for a 'family emergency.' I knew that the office would run just as well without him, but I felt like the wind just went out of the room, leaving stale air. I tried to rally, and picked out an outfit that was more outrageous than I would usually wear. Susannah gave me a look of approval, and Meredith looked at me like I was an alien. I took that as a good sign, since it was only for one night.

Thom and I headed out with Susannah and Beth, and Thom dropped me off last. I decided to check in and ask him how his time off went. I remembered him saying something a few weeks ago about wanting to get something done.

"Hey, Thom, what ever happened on your time off? When your sister came to help you out?" We were bumping along in his cheap, tinny, frigid car, always such a joy to be seen in. There weren't many things I was proud of in my life, but one of them was not driving a car like this. I shuddered internally.

Thom looked at me blankly for a moment. "Oh, right. Yeah, she came and looked after Mom, and we had a big talk. I sent in some paperwork. For a...school." He looked uncomfortable.

"That's great news! A break, and a change, huh? Have you heard back yet?" I asked.

"No. Still waiting." Thom pulled over in the Castro, and waved me out. Short but sweet. I wanted to ask him more about the school, but he didn't want to talk about it, so that was that. I stepped out, adjusted my tray, and headed off down the street.

Most of the night was without incident, which worked out well, since my mind was on Felix constantly. There was a large demonstration in front of Badlands bar, with protesters, gawkers, signs, megaphone shouting, and crowds spilling into traffic, causing congestion around the neighboring businesses. I stopped one of the sign-carriers, and asked what was going on. He told me they were protesting the bar's blatant racial discrimination. I looked around at the seventy or so people, and shook my head in amazement. Must be a pretty charged up topic, to get this many people out here. I skipped Badlands, and headed into Blush.

I walked up to two gorgeous patrons right as one was saying to the other, "Apparently this Brazilian guy had a cock like this." He held his forearm straight up in the air, fist clenched, while cupping around the bottom of his elbow with the other hand. I had to join this conversation, it was classic Castro.

I laid it on thick all night, swerving and surfing, dipping and flirting, wiggling cash out of reluctant hands, liberating the lonely with a compliment or even a peck on the cheek. I nodded and smiled; I brushed lightly past, and lingered briefly. No one chased me or insulted me. No one threw items. No one grabbed me. No one tried to steal or swindle. It was a remarkable night, in that nothing bad happened. It was the first time ever that things went effortlessly. The evening felt charmed.

I didn't hear from Felix for three days. He called me from the road briefly to let me know it was done, and he was on his way back. I wanted to pepper him with questions, but he sounded beyond exhausted. I went to bed early on my Sunday night, after curling up with one of the Indiana Jones movies, and decided to go visit my dad the next day.

I had talked with him on the phone a few times since my birthday, but that was back in July, and it was now Labor Day weekend. While I was driving to Modesto, my phone rang, and I picked up on the second ring.

"Hey there Daisy chain," a still-tired, but more playful Felix said, and I exhaled loudly.

"Pining away for me, were you?" he joked.

"Hardly. Just worried you had to pay down Audrey's debts by stripping. No one needs that tragedy," I shot back, grinning through the phone.

He chuckled under his breath. "Don't worry," he said, wryly. "It hasn't come to that. Yet."

"Where are you?" he asked.

"On my way to Dad's. Want to see how he's doing," I replied.

Felix reassured me that everything was taken care of, and he was happy to be home. We bantered back and forth, and talked about another picnic and beer date, since the Bay really had its summer right around now, lasting from September to late October, sometimes even into November.

As I got to my Dad's house, and climbed out of the car, Felix was telling me a bit more about the poker game and Audrey, when I noticed the house was eerily quiet. I walked through the kitchen's back door, toward the living room. My dad was lying face down on the floor in front of his easy chair. The TV was muted, and showing some infomercial.

A crack from somewhere below me? Then splitting. A rushing sound roared in my ears, and I could barely hear Felix. He sounded very far away, and I watched as my feet stepped closer to Dad, and I saw my knees fall near his hand. I was drowning in water, icy cold flooding my lungs. I couldn't breathe, I couldn't see. I shook my head, and heard the water icing rapidly over as I reached to check his pulse. Felix was a muffled brush of air. The plates of ice grew thicker, forming layer upon layer, drawing me away from life, drawing me away from pain, from agony. I stopped struggling, lying still next to my Dad's vacant, lifeless gaze.

Chapter 23

It was dark, but I was exposed. Every nerve was cruelly raw to the breeze, which seemed innocently light as a fan whirred by my ears, but was tearing my warm shell off. I was burned? No, frozen. I struggled to find form, to locate my mouth. I had a mouth....yes. It was wasteful and sharp. It was useless. Everything was pointless. I tried for my fingers through the ice, to see if there was a weak crack somewhere. I felt something touching my hand? Then my face.

"mmYouhh arrhhhre layimmmm dwwwn yuuu rmmm. It'sk, uurrhhhh saiiiif. (Focus!) ttt's Feeliks. Can you heaar mee?" All at once, the words broke open like an egg, and I understood.

My treacherous, lying mouth responded, "Yeah." I opened my eyes, and a haze was at the corners, but Felix was clear in my gaze. He was intent on my face, and briefly behind him, I saw a bright blue and purple light, and I felt a distracting wave of strength from it. I was perplexed by this color display... Why didn't he tell me he could do that? Felix was confused, and turned around to see what I was looking at. Seeing nothing, he turned back. The light vanished.

"Pale?" he said softly.

"Sorry. I saw..." trailing off, I turned my head. The icy cold was back, but through the ice, even deep under there, I felt the hot poker of grief. The surreal reason. Tears sprang out, betraying the prison built to protect me. Wracking convulsions took over my whole frame, and curling into the tiniest ball possible, I howled and pounded the bed, over and over. Felix kept a hand on my waist the whole time, sitting silently. Everything was meaningless! White anger took me out of the ice, and I leapt up from bed, my legs wobbly. I grabbed anything I saw, my hands throwing things hard against any surface, the floor, wall, even the ceiling. Felix had moved to the doorframe, and was watching without a word. My shoulders ached from overextension, my legs wouldn't hold me, my anger wouldn't hold me, nothing was here that could hold me together. Several minutes passed? I had no sense of it now. A gasp, a sob, I let go of want, let go of purpose, let go of all the stupidity, and let the love of my father settle over me like a blanket. I was weighted down with the truth of it. He loved me. I loved him. He was gone. My mouth tried to open, tried to use me to free the love, and all that came out was a banshee wail.

¤ ¤ ¤

There were flashes of color in my vision. Red, blue, red, blue. An ambulance. A shiny gold nameplate: "Officer Toestin". An absent thought rose: my dad would've found a pun in that...Made any toast lately? Just that thought took one breath, taken away forever. I didn't breathe every breath; there was a blackness between them. They didn't tell you how hard it was, when your heart had been shattered and spread to the winds. When you wanted to evaporate all the guts and substance that made up You. I guess by the time you are older, you get used to it, but it's actually a tremendous amount of work.

Felix was answering questions, always with his eyes on me. His eyes were a safe harbor, and I went blank there. I didn't try, it just happened.

Felix drove me around and around in circles, never going near the house. I saw fields and houses, gas stations and tire stores. I saw cheap crap being sold everywhere; I saw shit gilded, to make it more attractive to bored motorists passing through. I saw conversations my dad and I had had on certain roads…hearing his laugh, seeing his gentle smile. I saw the sun peak in the sky; I saw its rapid scale down the side of the skyline. Meaningless.

¤ ¤ ¤

Felix decided to drive us back to San Francisco, and he told me many things on the drive. He told me all about Texas, all about his mom. He told me about the color of the sunsets in Vegas, about the ups and downs of his addiction, and breaking free from it. He told me all about his passion for chasing storms. He told me about how much I've been missed at the office. He told me he would help me through this. I only asked one thing.

"How long was I out?"

He didn't answer for a long time, so long I thought he'd decided not to answer.

Finally, he glanced over and said, "You dropped the phone. I called out to you, and you didn't answer. I panicked and drove here, Selene gave me the address.

The door was open, and I found you like that. I would say two hours." He sighed heavily.

We crossed the Bay Bridge, and we took an unfamiliar route. Felix seemed to know where he was going. We pulled up in front of a small duplex, and he ushered me in like a sick person.

It was totally foreign; there was nothing here about my life, and my mouth saved me mercifully from saying something asinine. It was perfect. I laid down, right on the couch, without a word, and fell into a black, comfortless sleep.

¤ ¤ ¤

The next morning, I woke up on the couch and saw Felix crumpled into a chair, snoring. I still felt the ice around me, and the constriction of breathing, but I was starving, and that propelled me into the kitchen. I started to make breakfast from what was around, taking mild interest in how the kitchen was laid out. I brewed coffee, put eggs on toast, fried up some bacon, and by the time I was nearly done, Felix was mostly awake and stretching in the living room. His house was cluttered, but warm. He had great light, hardwood floors, and tall ceilings. There were a variety of storm and cloud posters on the walls, and I glanced up briefly at them, handing the plate of food to him.

"Didn't you make this for you?" he asked. I shook my head No. I had, but the smell of food made me feel sick, so I just slid the toast off his plate and nibbled at it, testing the taste. It tasted terrible, but I had to be strong today. Stronger.

Felix told me about his fascination with storms and clouds, how you don't know where they will go and what they will do, sort of like a poker game, and I zoned out on his voice briefly. I saw a familiar bag, and opened it. It was a duffel from my apartment, filled with my clothes. I thought a former me would be upset he went through my purse, got my keys, went to my house, and packed me a bag, all while I was asleep. But at that moment I just didn't care. I dug through the bag for a change of clothes, and looked up at him. I nodded my thanks, and he nodded back, still tucked into his breakfast. He was watching me, though.

"I have to go back today," I said, wincing. The words sounded raspy, my voice still vulnerable from the...from yesterday. With great effort, I willed myself to breathe and concentrate on the moment.

"I will call the office and let them know you will be out for a few days. Does that sound ok?" he asked, standing up and taking his dishes to the kitchen. I nodded as he glanced at me.

"Can I come with you today? Would that be ok?" he asked quietly. I nodded again, relieved.

In short order, we both changed clothes and were headed back out the door. Felix made some calls on the way, finding out the funeral home, calling us both out of the office, even searching through my phone to call Jana. I was numb, and though I was aware of what needed to be done, I was gripped by terror at what was coming next. I could hear Selene's frantic questions when he called to say we would both be out a few days, but I couldn't talk to her. Felix was firm that I was in no position to come to the phone. I felt like he kept reading my mind, and I was grateful.

We reached Modesto, and went straight to the funeral home. I drifted through the conversation, handing my credit card to the director like a drone, feeling Felix's strong body holding me upright. I felt like water trying to escape through a leak in a balloon. I slowly drained away, acutely aware that somewhere in that building my dad lay cold and lifeless. I arranged for a cremation, and left as soon as possible.

Felix drove us without a word to my dad's house, and sat in the kitchen as I walked slowly and wordlessly from room to room, drinking in memory after memory. Despite the fact that Dad was always a quiet man, the energy of the house was never this quiet, and I felt compelled to turn some music on. Felix put on a CD, and it lulled the roar of grief that bit at my heart. Hours passed that way, broken only by Felix making lunch and attempting to get me to eat. His phone rang regularly, but he steadfastly ignored it.

In the early evening, I went out to the garage and stood in front of the door, willing myself to enter Dad's truly happy place, his cave. To enter without his permission, to casually invade his space and make it abruptly my own. My feet on his floor, my hands on his light switch. No fanfare, no celebration. Just a violent transfer of ownership, mechanical as a coin drop. I couldn't bring myself to go in.

Back in the house, I told Felix I didn't want to stay here, so he took us to a hotel, and we slept in separate beds. He went to the drug store, and bought me some over-the-counter sleep aids, and I took them without question. I ate some applesauce that tasted like ash, and went to sleep to the sound of the weather channel.

The next few days passed in a haze. Felix asked the occasional question so we could put something in the newspaper, and a small memorial was held at the funeral home. My dad only had a few friends, so it was a brief affair. I had no plans to scatter his ashes yet, though it had occurred to me that I should go up in a plane to do it. I didn't speak at the memorial, but received flowers and the kind words his friends had for him. Jana also came for the memorial, and was wonderful in her non-demanding nature, never intruding on my thoughts.

Felix and I spent the rest of our time either at the house, or driving around. The bright sun was so rude, glaring at every thought, blanching every privacy. At night, and only after I was truly exhausted, we would go back to the hotel. He often babbled on our drives, telling me all manner of random things about the sky and clouds, likening them to life, to people, to animals. He made up haiku poems, and mumbled them to himself. I concentrated on breathing in and out, knowing the ice would have me for a while. I tried to keep it from covering my mouth and ears completely. Every day I woke up and thought how meaningless my life was. How stupid my plan was. I couldn't care less about Michael and politics now.

I kept trying to go into the garage, but just couldn't face the wall of grief that came to me when I would open the door and see so much of Dad. I would quickly shut the door, and go back in the house. Felix's sad eyes followed the ritual.

On the morning of the fifth day, I told Felix I wanted to go home, and I meant my own house. I wanted to distract myself with work, and to see my own room. He drove us back, and went straight to my house.

As I climbed the steps and opened my door, I felt a constriction on my heart, and had to grab the doorframe to keep myself upright. There were strong memories here, more than I'd realized. Photos, clothes, memorabilia.

Felix was just behind me, and quickly looped my arm over his shoulder and brought me to the bed. His face was so close to mine, for a moment we shared a thread of desire, and he stayed there, close to my face, drinking it in. He touched my face with his hand gently, and let out a breath. I could feel something stirring deep inside my heart, past the blackness, past the meaninglessness. It was faint, but fluttering. Felix pulled me close in a hug, and I closed my eyes, letting his heat try to melt the ice around me. He pulled away and climbed over the top of me, curling into the big spoon position, wrapping his arm over my waist. Surprised, I lay still.

We lay like that for a long time, until our breathing fell into the hypnotic, heavy rhythm of sleep.

FALL

Chapter 24

I threw myself into work that fall. The days swept into weeks, and the cold and fog mercifully arrived in late October, obscuring me from the sun's mockery. A perfect wall of sadness still clenched my heart. I felt the cold inside, radiating outward. Strangers asked if I needed a coat and I replied with a blank look. Why did they ask me that? They repeated themselves, as if I was uncomfortable from the outside. I didn't have the heart to tell them that there's no reason for it.

"I'm not solid; I'm hollow," I said sometimes, and got peculiar looks. I said this one day to an old man on the pier. He nodded his understanding; and he took my hand and held it gently, stroking the skin, as if coaxing a fire. For a moment, the ice around my heart thinned, and I could see through the prisms to that old man's face. I could feel an urgent push from inside, and tears sprang to my eyes, spilling silently down my face. The old man saw my tears, brushed them away with the back of my hand, still held in his, and kissed it. He gave my hand a squeeze, and walked away.

As I approached the office one day, I paused to step back and look up at the building that I had entered for the first time so long ago, almost a year now. I remembered that thrilling day, so full of rich opportunity and rebellion. It still looked completely boring, but I knew it to be my reluctant home. It was home for my real self, a safe distance from the persona I'd developed while out with the public.

I was both surprised and dismayed by the reactions around my dad's death. It seemed to have brought out the best or worst in both friends and strangers. Thom and Selene had been surprisingly gentle, but Meredith had been avoiding me and gave me awkward smiles when I saw her. Susannah also kept her distance and acted as if I had some contagion. Ransom was irritated.

Felix was...well, he was the male equivalent of honey and superglue. I saw him every day or he called when he couldn't come by. Even when I didn't see or talk to him, he'd leave me some gift on my door or in my car. Once, after I had driven to Modesto alone, and was trying to get the courage to go in the garage, I found a note tacked to the door, with the words, "Hi Daisy." I couldn't have survived any of this without him. His sister (he told me while babbling one night) made it out when he posted her bail but had since landed herself into further trouble. He and Sam had a discussion and decided to stop bailing her out, since it was costing their family more than financial trouble.

Their mother and the other sister Nicole weighed in with their thoughts, and they had an intervention for Audrey. From what I heard, she yelled and stormed out, but at least she knew that her family cared, which was more than some could say.

One night I was scheduled to head out with Thom, and was a bit relieved that he didn't scrutinize my every move like Felix did. I appreciated Felix's friendship and presence, but I needed a small breather.

Thom and Meredith got in the car quickly and tried to stay warm in the autumn chill. It didn't bother me, so I climbed in the back, breathing in the comfort of bakery smells, a respite from my thoughts. Meredith chatted easily with Thom about surface matters, and when she probed deeper about his personal life, he answered her reluctantly. He seemed startled by her direct questions.

I mourned Meredith's easy chats with me, but she didn't seem to know what to say, and I didn't have the energy to reach out to her. It was hard enough to find the energy to work at all. Once we dropped her off, Thom motioned me forward, which was a surprise. Usually he had us stay in our seats, 'no point in moving around'.

I climbed in the front seat and closed the door. Thom just sat there, absent-mindedly tearing his steering wheel cover. Since we weren't moving, I waited for him to say something. I assumed he was figuring out how to convey his condolences, but he surprised me.

"Pale. I want you to be the first to know something."

"Ok, sure. Tell me whatever you'd like."

"Do you remember a few weeks ago, God, maybe it was longer, a month or two, when my sister came to take care of my mom for a weekend?" I wasn't sure where this was headed, but I nodded in agreement.

"Well, I applied to a culinary school in Paris that weekend. Specifically, a pastry school. I've been wanting to go for a long time but didn't have the money. And what with Mom..." he trailed off. I nodded again, a stab of pain against my chest. I ignored it, as he continued in a rush.

"Well, I sent in all the paperwork that weekend, and was waiting to hear back on whether I got accepted or not. It's a very prestigious school. I wouldn't ever have to take driving jobs like this; I could do what I want, cooking and baking. I would have more time to visit with Mom, and my sister could stop badgering me about getting a real job. I might even have time to ... meet someone. Date," he paused, looking astounded at the very idea.

"Well, I got accepted. They want me to start right after the New Year. My sister and I have to put Mom into assisted care living, anyway. I'm too exhausted and not able to take care of her as well as I once did, as much as she needs. I've been doing this for two years now; I'm so exhausted and burned out. I hate my job driving. I hate the bakery I work for. I hate this car, I hate that I hate so many things. I need a change, you know? I need to do something that matters. Everything can't be this fruitless!"

Thom's words shot through me and shattered the last thin sheet of ice around my heart. He had the look of a man who has truly seen an oasis in the desert, not just the illusion of one on the horizon. He was unconcerned about us being late, if he'd been good enough, or loyal enough. He had tasted freedom and wanted to chase it. He was warming my whole body from the inside. I could see his self-respect, in the way he stood up to his sister about his mother. I could see him discarding the work he didn't enjoy to pursue his passion. I felt naked in my grief next to his purpose and started to cry at the sheer waste of my time and energy.

Thom broke out of his reverie and patted me awkwardly on the shoulder. But he was beaming, and his smile was very beautiful.

"You've been one of the better parts of this job, Pale. I know I don't really make friends, but I appreciate you not taking it personally, and your professionalism. I know things are horrible and shitty for you, and there's nothing I can say to change that. But it will turn around, I promise. And Felix certainly isn't going anywhere. That has to be a comfort." He smiled encouragingly, and I laughed weakly.

I moved his repetitively patting hand and said, "Thanks for letting me know. I truly hope everything works out for you, Thom. I will miss you. No, scratch that, not really." He gave me a playful punch in the arm and turned back to concentrate on joining traffic.

I decided not to mention the breakthrough to Thom. He had enough on his plate and so much to do, moving and going to school in a foreign country, leaving his Mom and sister. But later that night after work I told Felix about it.

"I think I'm ready to try and tackle the garage," I told him over a cup of warm tea at my house. This was our new thing, instead of going out for a beer we would stay in and have herbal tea. Felix was determined to help me sleep at night, and he knew that other than at work, I'd had a hard time being around a lot of people.

We were curled up on my couch; a dim light from the kitchen cast a gentle, cozy aura around the apartment. Felix had put up some corny decorations for Halloween as well as an autumn leaf garland over my front door. His attempts at decorating were pretty pitiful, but it was a sign that he'd been here often.

"Do you want me to go with you?" he asked softly, his hand holding mine. I stared at our hands entwined. When did that start happening? His hands felt wonderful ... to be touching like this was suddenly intimate to me, though I was sure it had happened before. I couldn't believe I had let it slide past, but I was suddenly aware of it. Something about Thom's decision and life change gave me courage.

I looked up at Felix, not answering, just taking in his face. He saw me searching his face, and his gaze intensified. We leaned in to each other, magnet-drawn, and he released my hand to touch my face. His hand gently tipped my chin, and we brushed lips, breathing in and out, the spark of the other. Our lips hovered there, and then suddenly we were wrapped around each other, pouring and tumbling all the energy and longing of months of being apart. He made his way across my face to my ear, down my neck, then buried his face and murmured something I couldn't hear into my hair. I held him tightly, afraid to feel anything, least of all this dangerous Hope. But I'd wanted Felix for so long, I wasn't strong enough to think wisely in that moment. He rose to a standing position, and tugged on my hand. I stood up with him, never leaving his eyes. He gestured to the bed, and I nodded slowly.

We walked over, never letting go of each other's hand, and lay down together.

Chapter 25

The drive to Modesto went by quickly, and I concentrated on the road during the drive. The music was loud, and Felix and I held hands. Occasionally I glanced down at the seemingly innocent touch and marveled at how lucky I was to have finally broken through the barriers that had kept us at arm's length. Remembering last night, I started to grin slightly and felt a small slap on my hand. I looked over at Felix, and he grinned back, also remembering.

"Why did you slap me?" I asked.

"Concentrate on the drive," he said, wryly.

There was a pit in my stomach as we approached Dad's street, but I also felt a determination to try and plow through the barrier I'd been up against. I was still a long way from normal, but at least I wasn't having suicidal thoughts. At least, not that much. My birth mother passed through my thoughts a few times, as well as some strangely intense anger at my adoptive mother for having left us. I felt really alone, most days. Felix certainly helped to battle that, but he didn't have any more answers than I did. Which is why it was time to go through the garage and find out as much as we could.

We pulled up in the driveway, and instead of automatically going into the house, I turned off the engine and sat in the car, staring straight ahead.

"You want me to wait here?" he asked.

"No, I want you to come in, but give me a minute, ok?" I said.

"Of course."

I stepped out of the car and hesitated outside the battered wooden sliding door. I thought of how much my Dad had loved it in here, how it contained the essence of his passion and comfort. How much of the little kid in him was in here still. And it pained me that he wouldn't be in here again, tinkering away. How we wouldn't watch *Star Wars* together again. How he would never again pilot a plane or make those terrible puns he loved so much. Tears welled in my eyes. But I wanted to drink in these parts of him, to swim through the pain and feel him around me again. I took a deep breath, gripped the handle hard, and yanked the door.

I fumbled for a moment in the dark and found the switch for the overhead lights. The room was immediately bathed in a warm glow from above. I activated the smaller, sharper halogen lights over the workbench where Dad assembled his model airplanes. The desk was both wide and long, a converted workbench moved to the middle and facing the door. The top of the workbench held a scattered variety of tools as well as outdated bills and a few plane sketches. His computer was also there, the tower and his filing cabinet tucked underneath. The shelves on the side of the garage were packed with boxes of all sizes, marked "Christmas Decorations", "Model Parts", "Doorknobs", and "Knick-Knacks". Dad had never let me into those boxes, saying they were not for children.

There were a few chairs, a liquor cabinet, a fridge with brick-hard sandwiches, and a few blankets.

I was overwhelmed by the gentle masculinity in here; I felt as though I was seeing this room for the first time.

Felix was a few moments behind me, and was standing near the door, taking it all in.

"Are you ok?" he asked.

"Yeah. Whatever that means," I replied, shaking my head.

He nodded silently, and headed over to one of the boxes on the shelves marked "Model Parts", as I leaned down to the filing cabinet and opened it up. I pulled out a variety of marked files, and stacked them on the desk. I figured I might as well check and see what he kept around, see if there was anything in there I needed to worry about.

A few minutes later, both Felix and I said simultaneously,

"You need to see this."

I grabbed the files and came over to the box he was peering into. Instead of model airplane parts, there was a huge pile of newspaper clippings, all apparently following some traveling circus show. In the files I found and passed to Felix, there were a variety of letters between the adoption agency and Mom and Dad, as well as baby pictures of me, report cards, essays, and other projects.

"Pale, did you see these?" Felix asked, astonished.

"Yes. It looks like Dad was actually in correspondence with...my birth mother all these years. I'm not sure what this means; I thought the adoption was closed."

"Did you two ever talk about your adoption? Didn't you search for your birth mother?"

"Dad explained it to me when I was very little, and though I brought it up a few times, it was clear he didn't want to talk about it. I didn't want him to feel betrayed any further. I mean, after Mom left ... " I staggered slightly and felt light headed. Felix grabbed my arm to keep me from falling backwards.

"Ok, maybe this is enough for one day," he said firmly.

"No! I can handle this. I want to know everything. He lied to me. He lied!" I could hear that I was shouting, but I didn't care. Felix gave me a long appraising look and sat down a little ways from me.

The next few hours were both painful and illuminating. As Felix and I pored over letters and newspaper articles, reports, court papers, and other legal documents, I found an entirely different man than the one who raised me.

The adoption was actually semi-closed, where the birth parent still had contact with the adoptive parents, though it was kept fairly limited. Dad made duplicates of everything I did and sent along relevant stages of my childhood to my birth mother. There were letters back and forth between them, where my birth mother asked a few times if she could see me, but my Dad always told her "No." After my adoptive mom left, I think he felt that he couldn't handle the risk that my birth mother would've posed, inserting another mother figure into my life. Plus, I bet he felt threatened that she might petition the courts to reverse the adoption. Such things can be done in California. Dad had a whole FAQ on adoption in California in one of those files. There were several newspaper articles that tracked where the traveling circus went, and all of her correspondence was from different towns, coinciding with the newspaper chronicling he had done.

Reliving my childhood, seeing the secret relationship between them, finding out my mother was in the circus, was staggering. I kept shaking my head and rubbing my temples. Felix gently pulled me away after six hours, and we went down the street to my favorite Mexican restaurant to process and eat something.

"I can hardly believe it. My birth mother is a carnie. My Dad had a secret relationship with her all these years. No wonder he wanted me to get a regular job and settle down--he was worried I would end up wild like her! And why did she give me up? Does she know who my father was? Why did she stop asking to see me so long ago? Why didn't he let me meet her? My whole life, I could've had a mother? Is this why my adoptive mother left?"

I slumped over the table, exhausted by the sheer intensity of how many questions remained unanswered. Piercing through the haze of hurt and disbelief was the grief again, that I couldn't confront him. That he wasn't here to answer these questions, explain his thinking. I felt so totally alone all over again, I couldn't bear it.

Felix sat through my rant in silence, only reaching out to hold my hand. I reluctantly gave it to him. It was hard to feel trust just then, and I didn't know what was real anymore.

"Listen. Your Dad loved you very much. It sounds like he kept in touch with her because he thought you might want to look for her one day, and since she's so hard to track down, he just kept tabs, for when you did ask. We know that she wanted to see you, but we don't know more than that. We need to look over the rest of the letters. And we certainly don't have to do that today, or even here. Why don't we pack up the lot of it and bring it back to San Francisco. That way you can look it over without dealing with...you know, Modesto." He waved in a general manner around us.

I looked at him bleakly. Our food arrived, and I picked at an enchilada while he wolfed down a burrito. "I can't believe he didn't talk to me about it. I mean, he knew he was getting worse and didn't tell me that either. I thought he trusted me-" I broke off as sobs caught in my throat. I covered my face and pushed away from the table, bolting outside. I sat on the curb in the shade and buried my face in my knees.

Felix came out a moment after me, and sat down next to me, not touching. He said quietly, "He was just protecting you, that's all. That's what this whole thing was about, Daisy. It wasn't that he didn't trust you. It sounds like he pretty much ONLY trusted you. He was your father. He wanted to protect you for as long as possible, until you were ready. And it's unfair, and it sucks, but Life doesn't wait 'til you are ready. Which is what makes acts like this, on his part, all the more precious. I never had a dad, so I don't even know what that feels like. But I recognize it, because my Mom was that fierce, especially since I'm the baby in the family." He flashed a grin.

"I'm so sorry all this is happening at once. I think this crappy town brings you down. I think this crappy Mexican food isn't working its magic. And I think we should get out of here, play music really loud, and get drunk." He nudged my legs, and I put out a hand, to keep from falling over.

"Felix?" I said, lifting my head.

"Yeah?" he asked, looking off into traffic.

"I don't know who I am, or where I come from. Everything I knew is a lie. Everything that mattered to me, is crumbling. If you are just here to swoop in because you see some wounded bird, then just don't. I don't want this thing with you, to just be happening because of all this shit going on. I want a real thing with you. I don't think I'm up for giving much, but..." Felix leaned in to me, and gave me his shotgun look. The one that shows me he's got me in his sights, and there's nowhere for me to go.

"You really are a bit of an idiot sometimes, Daisy. It's not like that at all. I trust you; I've told you things I haven't shared with anyone. You let me be there for you, even though you have other friends who can help. You have a good heart, you are damned sexy, and you keep surprising me. I want the real thing, too. Let's just get you through this, ok? Then we'll talk again."

I'd been holding my breath and didn't know it. It was bad enough that my whole family and past were coming apart. I couldn't have handled it if Felix wasn't genuine. I had to make sure. I spent a few minutes getting my breathing under control, and Felix held me in a tight hug. It seemed ridiculous, that in a cheap Mexican food parking lot we cinched our bond together, but I had needed something to anchor me, and so I was glad regardless of the where.

We drove back to the house and put everything back in boxes and loaded his van. I called Jana on my cell and filled her in on the garage findings. She was speechless when she heard about the letters and cautiously asked if I was ok. I told her the plan to take everything back to SF, and she was relieved that I would have time to go through everything on my own. She offered to come down in a day or two, and I accepted. I had a few days off coming up and planned to dive in at that time.

We managed to get nearly everything packed up and left all the real model airplane parts behind.

Once we were back in San Francisco, we went straight to a pub and spent the next few hours forgetting my burdens. Felix and I played a few games of pinball, then tripped down the sidewalk to my place, clumsily made out and crashed. Our night before was so tender and beautiful, we had spent it leisurely exploring each other's bodies, making out and going to 'second base'. We had decided breathlessly we weren't going to fully seal the deal yet. This time, I wasn't sure if we were paying attention to such rules. But by the time we were mostly undressed and fumbling around, the sexual oomph had gone out of both of us. We were almost comically knocked over the head by the Sandman and collapsed in an ungraceful heap on top of the covers.

In the late morning, we both woke up like sleeping cats, stretching and yawning on top of each other. Without a word, we both rubbed sleep from our eyes, groped for the aspirin and headed in to brush our teeth. I finished and walked back into the main room to pick out some work clothes to get dusty in.

Felix aimed into the kitchen, poured two bowls of cereal, and sliced a banana into them. He handed me a bowl and said, "You know, I'm glad we didn't, last night."

"Me too. Not yet."

We grinned sheepishly at each other, and ate our breakfast in the gloomy November light.

Chapter 26

Felix got dressed and started bringing boxes up to my apartment. My fragile good mood vanished, and I felt fear, anger, and curiosity, all battling in my heart at the sight of them.

I started pacing and fussing, and pushed items back against the wall to make room.

As he brought the last box in, I made a decision.

"Thanks," I said as he dropped the box on the floor, giving it a shove with his toe.

"Listen. I'd like to go through these on my own. I just think I'm going to want to fully digest things, take notes, you know. It's going to take a long time, and I want it to be private." I watched his reaction carefully.

"Oh, duh! That makes total sense. But if you want to take a break, or need to talk, it's no trouble, just call," he said, giving my arm a squeeze. I leaned in for a kiss, and we lingered there, sharing a moment of connection. He grabbed his bag, and headed out the door.

I spent the rest of the day going through the boxes as methodically as possible. I separated out items from my own childhood, and concentrated on creating piles for the legal adoption papers, the correspondence, and the newspaper clippings in order, by date. I learned that my birth mother went by the name Shake, though I didn't know if that was her real name. According to a few enthusiastic reporters, she was named that for her signature trembling during the knife-throwing act. Apparently she and her knife-throwing partner had been in a long-term relationship. I studied his picture carefully for signs that he was my birth father. There was no mention of him, dating back to about two years ago, and I wondered what happened as she was billed with a new partner in the act after that.

I saw glimmers of myself in her face, though the pictures weren't very good, being both faded and newspaper print. I got lost wondering what she was like, if she knew about my Dad's death. Although, of course no one would think to tell her. I felt a pang of fear at the idea of reaching out to her.

I could also see from the letters that, while my Dad was forthcoming and even shared information freely about me while I was growing up, he never discussed what happened with his wife, nor any of his personal feelings with Shake. She would occasionally inquire after him, and he always said he was fine and well. It was just so typical of him to not allow people to worry, and seeing his handwriting brought tears and grief to the surface. Despite how unremarkable my dad was, he was totally remarkable to me in that he was kind, fatherly, and so totally pedestrian about it. He had strived for normality, and I'd always thought of normal as boring. I could see now that he had been gifting me with a sense of honor and family. A sense of belonging to someone.

My anger at him began to fade, as I saw him secretly scheming to get as much information for me as possible. I was angry that I didn't have him to share it with, but I wasn't angry with him directly, not anymore.

By the end of the day, I felt wrung out, especially after my long night with Felix. I gave him a quick call to let him know I was ok, and I gave Jana a call to make sure she was still coming. She confirmed she'd be there early in the morning. I was grateful, and fell into bed early after a light dinner.

In the morning, Jana rang the bell and came quickly into my studio. In a heartbeat, she took in my face, the apartment, the boxes everywhere, and my mental state. I couldn't hide anything from Jana; it was a gift of hers. She pulled me tightly into her arms, and we sat down on my bed, just hugging for a few minutes. Finally, she said, "I'm not sure what to say, but I'm sorry this is all happening at once. When it rains, it pours, huh?" She shook her head.

"I'm just glad you are here. Thanks for coming. You know I love hanging with Felix, but he's...new. And intense. I don't know who or what I can trust, and you are one of the things that doesn't shake me." I started laughing bitterly, realizing the pun on my mother's name. Jana looked alarmed. I composed myself, and filled her in on the details of yesterday. Jana had to close her mouth a few times.

"I can't believe he never told you, or left you a note, or anything. Honey, I'm so sorry," she repeated, looking around at the boxes.

I explained my system to her, and we picked up where I had left off yesterday. We sat in easy silence, occasionally rustling papers, or smiling at each other in comfort. Just having another woman with me helped my sadness. Without asking, Jana went into the kitchen after a few hours to throw together some lunch. She came back with a few slices of cold pizza and some lemonade. We ate companionably and discussed our findings. It was more of the same with a few extra details. We found out that in the last few letters to Dad, all dated within the last year, Shake had referred to a brief brush with cancer and renewed her request to see me. Dad's letters back to her admitted that I was of age to be contacted, but indicated that the stipulation of the adoption contract showed that I had to initiate contact in order for her to see me. His letters were dated less than six months ago.

"Oh God," I whispered, the pizza slice forgotten in my hand.

"What is it?" Jana asked, concerned.

"It's just ... I thought that his health problems were coming from him stressing out about my career, and not pursuing a more normal job. I kept thinking it was my fault that he had that stroke. I already know you are going to tell me I'm being ridiculous. But it looks like he was worried about Shake reaching out to us, getting more demanding about meeting me! It's just so stupid he didn't talk to me!"

Frustrated, I got up and walked over to the window, yanked open the latch and slid the window back, cold air rushing in. It braced me and kept me from breaking down again. I heard Jana's voice behind me.

"That's a lousy thing to do. He lied and coddled you. As if you couldn't handle it," she said calmly. I turned around, stunned.

"That's exactly right. I don't want to be mad at him. I'm trying to understand why he so obviously didn't trust me to handle this like an adult. It's not as if I haven't had my own doubts, wondering, making up stories and daydreams my whole life. I get that he was disappointed in the direction he saw me going, but it's my life, and I have to make my own mistakes and choices. Holding this relationship hostage, arranging for a semi-open adoption, then not letting me even know about her, it was too much. It IS too much."

I made a decision right then. Turning my back to the window, I announced, "Jana. I want to meet her."

"Just like that?"

"No, not quite yet. I need to get through all this information, make sure there aren't any other surprises. But soon."

"Wow. Talk about surprises."

"Do you think it's a good idea?"

"I do, honey. I support you no matter what. But it really is totally your decision. You can't undo anything you hear or experience, so make sure you want to do this."

"I hear you. And thank you. But I think it's time. Worrying about this obviously contributed to bringing him some pain, maybe contributed to his death. I don't want the unknown to hold me back like it did him." Jana came over to me, and hugged me tightly. I hugged her back, and we both took a deep breath.

"Let's finish our pizza, ok? I love that pesto chicken," she said, poking me in the arm.

"Yeah, I know. That's why I buy it. Love you," I said, softly.

"Love you too jelly bean," she said, toasting me with her lemonade.

Chapter 27

Sometime in the late afternoon, the sun dipped down on the horizon and bathed my apartment in the last bit of weak light. We had spent several hours working our way through the last boxes, and I was taking a break while Jana went through the final file box. My phone rang at the same time that Jana said, "Pale. You need to see this."

I gestured with my hand that I'd be one minute, and flipped open the phone.

"Hello?"

"Is this Pale Baumann?" a strange voice inquired.

"Yes. Who is this?" I asked, guarded.

Jana frantically waved some papers at me then walked over and thrust them under my nose.

"This is David Cliffstone. I'm calling from the Northern Californian Life Insurance Company. I want to express my condolences and make an appointment with you to discuss your father's estate."

I stared numbly at the papers in my hand. I felt slightly light-headed as I tried to read them. "What?" I said into the phone.

"This is in regard to your father's estate and will," David said patiently.

"My father doesn't have an estate. He has a house in Modesto that hasn't seen good taste since 1976. I'm not aware of a will," I said faintly.

Jana shook her head vigorously and pointed at the papers in my hand. I focused away from David's legal talk, and saw the words "Last Will and Testament" across the top of a copy. I dropped the papers and the phone and sank down to the floor. Jana crossed the room quickly and scooped up the phone.

"I'm sorry; Pale's not prepared to talk right now. We are still recovering from the last few weeks. I'm her best friend Jana, can I help you?" Jana scribbled a few notes hastily on the pizza box nearby while she watched me anxiously.

"Great. She'll be there. And thank you." She hung up and leaned down.

"Are you all right?"

"I don't think I am. I can't take any more of this, Jana. What's next? Are you going to tell me I'm really a black kid from Detroit, or that Darth Vader was my father?"

I buried my head in her arms and cried out my loneliness, frustration, grief and shock all at the same time. I felt the waves trying to pull me under, and I wanted so much to believe my life would go back to normal one day. All my earlier bravado had faded. I just wanted to crawl under a rock and die.

Jana helped me up, and got me into bed. She went into the bathroom and found some over-the-counter sleeping pills. Jana gave me two to knock me out. She sat with me, cuddling, murmuring kind words and reassurances until my head felt drowsy and heavy. I sensed her leave the bed and turn on the TV. She curled into the chair and watched me out of the corner of her eye. I drifted off dreamlessly.

Chapter 28

In the morning when I woke up, all the boxes were gone. I found Jana in the kitchen, working with some pancake mix I didn't know I had.

"Good morning. I made breakfast."

"Thanks. Sorry about last night. Got overloaded and emotionally vomited," I mumbled.

"There's no need to apologize. But, I do have to get back to school. Honey, I made an appointment for you to meet with that insurance company guy later this week. But I also want to give you some advice."

"Ok, shoot," I said slowly.

"Just try and get back to normal. Go to work, make some money. Spend time with that sweet man of yours. Don't make any hasty decisions. Just let the feelings about your birth mother rise up and drift away. Then, later this week, go to that appointment, and find out what Jeffrie had planned for you."

"Okay. That actually sounds pretty good. I think I can do that." I even meant it.

"Good," she said firmly.

"And the boxes?" I asked.

"I had Felix swear on pain of death he wouldn't poke around, but he does have them. I think they would be painful for you to have here, and there's no need to make a special trip home."

I released a breath I didn't know I was holding.

"Jana, thank you. Really. You thought of everything."

"Oh, you would've thought of it eventually. But you have plenty going on."

She gave me a long hug, grabbed her overnight bag, and headed out with a wave.

I forgot how wonderful it was having her around. I had to get used to sharing her with Alex.

As soon as she left, only emptiness remained. I decided to take her advice and throw myself back into work.

As I stepped into the office, Thom waved me over to the training room. I followed him wordlessly and was surprised when he shut the door firmly.

"Pale. Hey. I, uh, I have something for you. But you can't tell anyone."

Thom seemed both nervous and sad. I gave him a puzzled look, and his usual irritation came back for a moment.

"Oh, don't look at me like that. I won't keep you here long. I just...felt bad for you. About...your dad. I wanted to give you something to take your mind off things."

He abruptly reached into his jacket pocket and pulled out a small box. I saw a white rectangle made of a thick cardboard. The top flaps were locked into each other, and as I tugged them open, a heavenly smell, so faint, drifted up from the tiny wax paper. I couldn't believe Thom was finally sharing a baked treat with me, especially one that smelled as amazing as this. It was a Madeleine in a perfect golden color. It was a little bigger than the ones you buy in packages. I glanced up at Thom, and his face had that sad look again, but he nodded at me encouragingly.

"The ones I make are filled with a sweet date paste. There's a secret ingredient, too. I hope you like it. It's one of my signature pieces," he said, shyly.

It smelled so good, at first I didn't want to bite into it. And then, just as abruptly, I reached down and impulsively lifted it to my mouth, sinking into a bite. The complexity of flavor flooded me, and warmth spread through me like magic. I was transported straight out of my troubles, straight out of winter, and drifted along the simple cakey fluffiness, buoyed by sweet dates, and a sharp smoke of . . . what was it? Clove? Ginger? I had no idea. I didn't remember eating the next two bites, because I was awash in the waves, a sense around the edge of memories, of childhood summer afternoons with imaginary friends, of being loved, and of a simplicity to the world.

I opened my eyes and saw Thom looking anxiously at me. I threw my arms around him, surprising us both.

"Thom, that was so wonderful. Thank you so much," I mumbled into his shoulder.

He pulled away after patting me awkwardly on the arm, and said, "Just don't tell anyone."

I grinned at him, and he went out the door. I sighed, and walked out behind him.

I saw Felix, and walked over to give his hand a quick squeeze. We weren't working together that night, and I saw from the board I would be on a run with Lisbet.

A few of the girls were giving me looks about being in the back with Thom, AND coming out to hold hands with Felix, but I couldn't have cared less about those things now.

Lisbet hadn't said a word to me about my dad, but that was fine by me. First, I didn't know if anyone had even told her. Second, I was tired of people working out their own issues about death through the critical one happening in my life. It was exhausting. I preferred to keep it to myself and work it out with the friends I knew I had. I had quite a bit to distract me as it was.

In no time at all, we'd gotten dressed and were fanning out to different parts of the city. Thom's car had finally kicked the bucket about a week ago (seemed to me it was perfect timing for that thing to crawl away and die, right as he was about to go live abroad), and he was driving his Mom's vintage 1966 Lincoln Continental convertible - an absolute joy to ride in.

Lisbet took the first run of North Beach, while I took Grant and Green Extended. I think I'd gotten this run out of pity, but I didn't care. I decided to play the game of Faces, which was something Dad and I used to do together. It helped me to be around big crowds of people when I got anxious, and recently I'd been getting anxious a lot more often.

In the game of Faces, instead of getting caught up in what people are saying, you slide your focus to some part of their face, like their nose, or the chin, or their ears. Eyebrows work too, and foreheads.

You still respond in a vague way to conversation, but really, you are keeping track of who has the most interesting nose, or the smallest chin. Who has attached earlobes, wrinkly foreheads or dimples. It's a great way to detach, to check out of being witty or particularly interesting.

I'd learned by now that the job didn't always require the persona I'd built. There were plenty of places and people who didn't need me to talk at all. I'd been doing this more and more at work, as my interest flagged.

I played the game of Faces for quite a while, until Lisbet and I switched, and I was on the North Beach run. The people were tiring, always looking, tugging, toying with me. I felt like a pinball pushed around, and what little energy I had began to dwindle quickly. The bouncers all helped keep me afloat, but they must have sensed some of the new chaos in my personal life, because while they still gave me a squeeze and a comforting arm to help me in and out, no one said anything.

I ended up at Crow Bar just before last call, feeling dazed, and at a table of belligerent older punk rockers. They were vicious in their teasing, but I was too far behind in sales tonight to not try to score a last $20. The bartender started screaming Last Call! and throwing bottles into the trash. Through the din of the bar's loud music and shouting, strangely I heard the glass shatter into a thousand tiny pieces against the metal. I saw a flash of hot pink out of the corner of my eye, and I recognized Lisbet, without her tray. Shit. I must be late to meet Thom. I wiped some sweat from my head, and turned back to the table of Neanderthals. Lisbet crossed over to me quickly. Muttering, she said, "What's going on? You ready?"

"I could use this last sale, but these guys are being hard on me. I'll just try one last time."

As I turned back to the table, the skinniest guy in the middle looked up under the harsh light hanging low over their drinks.

"Say, who's your friend? We might be interested in two or three items, if ah, she's included." He chuckled meanly, and his friends joined in. I knew I should leave, but I couldn't. I couldn't seem to move my legs. I glanced over at Lisbet, whose eyes flashed anger, but she said nothing. "So, what's your problem anyway, Creepy? Who let the air out of your balloons?" He laughed uproariously, slapping the table. I realized a little too late that he was talking to me.

There was a lull in the cacophony of the room. A cold anger rose up in me and without pausing, I leaned down, reached out and pinched his Adam's apple with my free hand and said, "My fucking Dad just died. What's your excuse, you sad little piece of shit?"

I had never spoken to any customer like that, but I was beyond exhausted and my feet were burning, I hated this place, and it was exactly the time of night to pick a fight.

He jumped to his feet and pushed toward me. Without changing position, Lisbet hauled back her right arm and popped him in the nose, right when he was getting out of the booth. He crumpled to the ground, and we heard a roar go up in the bar. The bartender and bouncer rushed over and shoved the rest of his friends outside. Lisbet and I stared at each other.

"Thom just told me in the car. I'm sorry. I didn't want you to be alone in here. I could see on your face that you weren't going to get that sale."

She looked at me deadpan, and we both laughed loudly, then hysterically. I was laughing at the fury and chaos. I was laughing because it felt like I hadn't done it in a long time, and here, in a dark punk rock bar where I used to be so scared, I had just insulted a customer, and was nearly clocked in the face.

I laughed because I was so over this whole experience. Lisbet threw her arm around my shoulder. We walked out together and climbed into Thom's car, accompanied by the red and blue lights that always seemed to flash in North Beach.

WINTER

Chapter 29

The rest of the week passed in a similar fashion, only without the fighting. Lisbet did get into a bit of trouble after what happened in Crow Bar. But there were so many witnesses to the escalation and, just because she was Lisbet, she ended up with a warning. She shrugged it off.

I still couldn't shake my dissatisfaction with the job, and it showed in my sales. I did poorly all week, no matter what my efforts were to hide my true face. I felt lost as new girls came and went, looking to me for advice and enthusiasm. I could sense my time there was drawing to a close, but had no idea what to do next. I limped through my week, and felt wrung out by the time my appointment with the life insurance company loomed near.

I had filled Felix in on what Jana had found and the phone call, and he asked if he could accompany me.

We headed back to Modesto and easily found the company's office off the interstate. Felix and I had passed the office a few times on our drives around town; I felt that I knew Modesto so well I could give guided tours. Of course, that was assuming anyone would come here on purpose.

I'd dressed simply for the meeting but was wound up like a top. I was so tense about whatever was going to jump out next that even Felix didn't tease me in the car ride over.

When we stepped in through the door, he rubbed my back reassuringly, and I relaxed slightly into his touch. I glanced at him, and he gave me a warm smile, reminding me that we were in this together.

The office had a small reception area that was deserted. No one greeted us when we arrived, but the soothing sounds of a cleverly hidden fountain did the work of helping me feel comfortable. Large, leafy indoor plants stretched toward a skylight and were shiny from loving care. There was a good collection of art on the walls, and I was surprised to find it had a more modern feel than the rest of Modesto.

I couldn't picture Dad ever coming in here, but a tall man in his late 40's came striding out of an office, holding out his hand like we were old friends.

"I have a bell that tells me you came in, and my receptionist took the day off to accompany her son on a school trip. You must be Pale?" he said in a friendly manner, giving my hand a vigorous shake, catching me off guard. Felix bumped me, and I looked back to see he was holding me up slightly, and laughing at me behind his eyes.

"Easy there, Daisy," he murmured.

Turning back to David, I said nervously "Yes. Hello. You must be Mr. Cliffstone? Can you tell me what this is all about? Why am I here? Oh, and this is Felix."

"Please, call me David. Where are my manners? My apologies, a client on the phone distracted me earlier. We have much to discuss. Please come into my office and we will cover everything. I've prepared all the paperwork. Can I get you anything to drink? Water? Coffee?" he prompted, gesturing to a beverage station I hadn't noticed. Felix helped himself to coffee, and poured me water without asking. He knew me well.

We walked into David's office, which was a more intimate version of the front area, only with even more plants and some lovely furniture. Despite the large room, David's desk only occupied one corner closest to the window. We took seats opposite him in comfortable chairs. I wasn't sure what to expect or what sort of conversation was coming. Did my dad have unknown debts? Did he have a secret collection of gold bricks? Did he lie about anything else? I took a few deep breaths, which David noticed quickly.

"Please, be easy. This sort of conversation often starts off with so many unknown factors, but also just as often ends happily, if not bewilderingly. I am thorough and totally confidential. You can say anything, express anything. My job is to make sure you understand what's happening, can figure out what to do next, and in general, support you through this unbelievably tough time." His eyes were bright green, and he looked at me with compassion and intelligence. He had an air of confidence and decisiveness.

He had captured my thoughts exactly, so I only nodded in encouragement.

"First of all, I knew your father, Pale, and his sudden loss was a tragedy and a shock. I don't know that I will ever achieve his masterful level of puns. They were so terrible." He smiled gently, remembering. I felt a wave of sadness and understanding.

"Your father came in to see me shortly after I had just opened my practice here, 20 years ago. He was one of my first clients. It was after your mother had...left, and he was concerned that being the sole provider for you would be too fragile of a life together. He wanted to explore his options. I advised him to write a will, and to invest in a stock portfolio. He had a shrewd mind, and I am pleased to say he did both of these things. He came back in over the years, making adjustments to the will in relation to his earnings, and always keeping his expenses in check, despite his passion for one day flying his own plane. An expensive hobby, I might add."

"I'm summarizing here, obviously, because it was evident to me on the phone the other day that you had no idea that he had set aside anything other than the house. I am not sure if you have gone through his papers, since I know he kept meticulous notes, but if I recall, everything related to the stock portfolio was being held in a safety deposit box at the bank. They are not authorized to give you the key; that's my job."

David reached into his desk drawer and handed me a key with a square silver head. A number was stamped on the top. I took it wordlessly. He paused, letting this sink in.

"Does this also have anything to do with the relationship Dad had to my birth mother?" I asked, confused.

David's face showed surprise, as he answered, "What? No. He's left no instructions or provisions for her, only you. I see that you've had your plate full." David looked at me thoughtfully.

"No, I am here to make sure that you understand the details of your inheritance, as well as make myself available, should you wish to continue some of the investments he has in place. Naturally, I don't handle that personally, but I'm in touch with his investment broker, and she's anxious to meet with you." David paused.

"Pale, your Dad carefully nurtured the small amount of money he started with over many years, so he could share with you the fruits of that growth, to help you while you are on your own. He started with only $500, and it's bloomed quite substantially since then. First, and only if you are ready, I'm going to read you the will, and second, we will discuss the details of the provisional statement he left. Lastly, I am to give you the letter he left for you."

Startled, I said, "Letter? He left me a letter?"

"Yes. But he asked that you receive it after you have heard the entirety of the will," David said. I nodded my assent.

David then proceeded to read the Last Will and Testament of Jeffrie Hugo Baumann, my father. I would be lying if I said it didn't bring all of my grief up to the surface. Felix held my hand the entire time, when I wasn't blowing my nose repeatedly.

It detailed that his property and earnings were all left to me, 100%, and he requested I give 5% away as charity, preferably to a flight school. He also requested that his ashes be scattered in the air, which I had already been thinking about arranging in the spring. He left only one request about his financial portfolio, which was that his investment broker continue to make the primary decisions until I'd had six months from the time of the reading of the will to become familiar with his strategies, and that I take over making primary decisions at that time. Dad was adamant that the investments continue, and I had no disagreement about that.

The end of the reading strangely relaxed me. I guess I had feared there would be some deep dark secret, lurking in another part of my Dad's life that I was clueless about. This didn't seem so much blind protection, as smart planning and careful study. Sure, I was sad that once again he didn't feel like he could talk to me, but I could see that he felt I needed a bit more time to be open to such things.

And if I really thought about it, it was not as if I'd been the most mature about my decisions. Becoming an adult is not always something we choose in Life; often the timing of it is chosen for us, and not usually when it suits our plans.

I'd been selfish and careless, and while I didn't regret my past choices, it was time to be more mindful of my choices. We never know how much time we have left with the ones we love the most.

Breaking out of my reverie, I saw that David and Felix were both watching me patiently. I leaned forward and took a long drink of water.

"I apologize. I was lost in my thoughts," I said, my voice stronger than when I first arrived.

"As I said, Pale, I'm here to help you understand. I can see by your face, though, you understand your father very well. You both make the same face when you concentrate." He smiled broadly, and I smiled back in gratitude.

"So, now that we've talked about the provision of keeping the investment portfolio running, was there anything else?" I asked hesitantly.

"Well, yes. There are your earnings. A certain amount of the earnings were set aside when Jeffrie...passed on, as an inheritance. I assure you, the investment portfolio is still healthy, and can manage as you go through your educational process," David said, rustling through the file on his desk.

"Ah, here are the numbers. The total amount available is approximately $50,000," he said, looking down.

I stared blankly at David, and looked over to Felix. Felix looked at me questioningly.

"That can't be right," I said faintly.

"Oh, well, that's give or take a few thousand. The exact total is $54,377.20. If you want to look at the last report-," David broke off when he saw my face. I stood up, my jaw hanging, and held on to the chair for support. Felix jumped up in alarm, and held my arm, and rubbed my back. I shook and held my hand over my mouth. David came out from behind his desk, and held out the glass of water to me. I took a few cool gulps, gasping on the last one as it went down the wrong pipe. David encouraged me to take a few calming breaths.

I felt like one of those women from the 18th century, always fainting at the sight of a mouse or a man without a proper hat. It was ridiculous that I kept having such jumpy reactions. Embarrassed, I sat back and tried to gain my composure.

David and Felix returned to their chairs and were looking away to give me a moment. I was grateful to both of them, and cleared my throat obviously so we could continue.

David began, "I've seen grief reveal itself in the strangest of ways, Pale. Don't be embarrassed by it. You've been dealing with more than most, completely on your own, with no other family to help share the burden. I suspect you've even been handling the last few weeks better than you think, as your friend here will likely attest." David glanced at Felix, who nodded firmly in agreement.

"Again, I'm sorry for adding to your plate. But your dad was quite clear that he wanted you to feel that you have the freedom to start over and do what you want. Is the amount not to your satisfaction?" he asked.

"No, David. Quite the opposite. It's more, much more than I thought would come out of your mouth. In my wildest dreams, I never had any idea he was up to this. It's so much to take in, to accept. If you don't mind, I'd like to stay overnight in Modesto, and get back to you tomorrow. Can we talk again? Do you need me to make an appointment?" I asked, dazed.

David laughed slightly, clearly happier that the news was received well, and said, "No, you can just come in anytime. I'm here from eight in the morning until about three in the afternoon. The bell for the front door rang, and he jumped up. "Excuse me, I am expecting a delivery that will need to be signed for."

When Felix and I were alone, we turned to each other in total disbelief.

"Are you ok?" he asked.

"Believe it or not, I think I am going to be ok. I feel strange. Surreal, but lifted up. I feel above the pain. David has been really helpful," I added.

"Yeah, he seems to really care about his work, and about your case in particular. Do you have more questions right now?" he asked.

"No, I want to get out of here soon, maybe get some dinner. Can we stay at a hotel tonight? I don't want to be at Dad's," I said, distracted. I could hear David coming back in.

"Sure thing," Felix replied. David entered and closed the door. He sat down quickly at his desk. He focused his green eyes on me.

"How are you feeling? Do you have any questions?"

"You said there was a letter for me?" I asked, reminding him.

"Oh! Yes, of course. He filled this out after his first stroke. He said you would want to read this in private." He handed me an envelope I recognized from my dad's desk. It had his scrawled handwriting on it, with my name across the front. I stood up, and Felix stood up as well.

"David, it's been a pleasure to meet you. Thank you for being so friendly and professional. You've been very easy to talk to. I'll be in touch tomorrow." I shook his hand, and he gave me the same vigorous shake as before. Felix and I headed out the door and into the parking lot. I stood next to the car just holding my Dad's letter. Felix wordlessly opened my door and walked around to get in the driver's seat.

I got in, deep in thought.

"Can you drive us to the house? I want to open this there," I said. He nodded, and turned down the interstate.

As soon as we arrived, Felix turned off the car and gave me a stop-and-pay-attention look.

"Pale. I want to tell you something." He leaned in close to me, hypnotizing me with his eyes. I was pulled into his yearning and momentarily forgot about the events of the day.

"Yes?" I said, breathless.

"It's just...I've always wanted..." he started, breaking off as he nuzzled my neck.

"Oh?" I said very faintly, not really paying close attention as his breath passed up to my ear.

"I've always wanted a sugar mama. Will you take care of me now?" His tone was joking, and he nipped me playfully on the ear. I blew out an exasperated breath and gave him a shove. He cackled, and his joy made me smile despite myself. He scooped up my hand, giving it a gallant kiss.

"Don't worry, Daisy. I'm not that kind of Texan." He gave me a tender kiss on the cheek. "I'll be in the house, just holler when you're ready to go get some dinner."

As I watched him walk in the house, I was amazed at the transformation between us. A few months ago, we were barely managing civil conversation. So many changes, so fast. What did I do with all this new information?

I looked down at the letter in my lap again. So many of the answers might be in here. Or none of them. I wasn't sure if I wanted to read my dad's last words. I didn't have to open this now. But part of me knew that I would, which is why I had directed Felix here.

I opened the sliding door and walked into the garage, switching on the lights and shutting the door behind me.

I went to the workbench and sat down. I thought about him for a few minutes, still deliberating. Then, before I could stop myself again, I tore open the top of the envelope and pulled out one page.

My beautiful daughter,

There are many things I could say about my life. It's so hard to face the cruel white paper before the enormosityness of my feelings for you, and for this life we have together. Nothing is as important to me as your happiness. From the moment I saw you, and your eyes that looked through me, I knew you were family. It was hard to know, as a father, what was best. I think sometimes I bully you like Han Solo does to Chewy, but it is because I want so much for you.

The only thing I can try and help you understand are my letters with Shake. Your birth mother was a part of your life that you can never replace. No matter how you came to me, no matter how close we are, you two deserve to know each other. I waited until I thought you would be ready, and not restless, to meet her and not lash out. You have some of my German steady-mindedness, yes? But you also have impulsiveness. I love that in you. I love it so much, even though it drives a father crazy. You drive me to the store; you drive me crazy, ha!

Please know that all I want to say was like Obi-Kenobi, I will see you again. I love you, my daughter, my love,

Dad

I folded up the letter and collapsed onto the table, laughing, crying, and shaking with emotion. The sun streamed in the window and hit the bench, illuminating his little kingdom, the place he plotted and schemed his whole life just to better mine.

The letter was so inimitably him; I felt a hundred facets at once, my love and exasperation, his planning and his wisdom, his grace and teaching. I saw myself in him so much. No one ever knew me like he did. I felt all of this and a sweet sense of symmetry in the universe, a place of knowing more about who I am and where I come from than I ever had. He clearly wanted me to know Shake, so I would honor his wish.

I pulled myself up from the bench and touched the letter to my heart.

"I love you too, Obi-Wan," I whispered.

Chapter 30

Felix and I headed to dinner after that, and had an easy conversation about trivial subjects. A tension had eased, and I found a way to laugh at some of his jokes. His eyes were relieved, but he didn't mention the meeting, or the inheritance. Back at the hotel, as we were getting ready for bed, I decided to bring it up.

"I'm thinking about taking some time off," I said when I finished spitting my toothpaste in the sink. I rinsed out my mouth, replaced the water cup, and crawled under the covers. Felix was catching up on the score of some football game on TV, but switched it off, as well as the light on his side. We had curled up close to each other, and his hand was enveloped around mine. We looked like cuddly arm wrestlers.

"What do you want to do?" he asked softly.

"I don't want to do the Tart thing anymore. And now, I don't have to. I want to take a road trip to meet Shake. Find where the circus is staying, go and see her, face to face. After that, I don't know. Maybe do something with the house, take those education classes to get caught up to speed on the investments." I laughed softly. "I don't know the FIRST thing about investing."

"Neither did your Dad. But he managed. And you are just as smart as him." Felix pulled a few loose hairs from my face, leaned in, and kissed me tenderly. I kissed him back, savoring the moment of quiet and intimacy.

"I'm going to miss you," he said finally.

"I'm going to miss you too. But, I need to do this. I won't be gone long," I whispered reassuringly.

"It's not the time, it's the depth of what you are doing. I trust you, but a lot can happen on the road. What if you meet some drugstore cowboy who sweeps you off your feet? I hear Texans can be very charming," he teased me, melodramatically waving a hanky in his own face. I pinched his arm.

"Ow!"

"Serves you right. You know that's not going to happen. One Texan is handful enough." I sighed and put the back of my hand to my forehead. He pinched me back gently.

"Ow!" I declared, faking.

"Serves you right."

As we settled deeper into the covers, I began musing about what my birth mother would be like, what sort of traits we shared, and where the circus must be right now. But soon enough, Felix and I were distracted with each other, and slipped into a slow dance of warm hands and quickening breaths. We wordlessly agreed to put off knocking boots a bit longer, but we explored tickle spots, surprising erogenous zones, and massaged each other's belly, legs, feet, and back.

Time slowed, as we loved each other in the dark, meeting gaze for gaze, fingertip to fingertip. I felt an unspeakable impatience I had no desire to satisfy. I wanted to know him, over and over. I touched his lips with my nose, lifting my face to his. He whispered my name, and gripped me suddenly, his desire strong. The urgent wave crested, and both our hands were between the other's thighs, guiding each other to climax. It was over in seconds, our buildup from weeks, culminating in an agony of sweetness. We calmed our breath together, steadily coming from off the peak. We drifted happily into sleep, sheets tangled, a steady heartbeat in each of us.

¤ ¤ ¤

In the early morning, we were clumsy with happiness, bumping into each other, grinning like idiots, taking three times as long as normal, fumbling trying to get the other dressed. Giggling stupidly, we climbed into the van and drove back to David's office.

Once again, we were only in the lobby a few minutes before David came in, pumping my hand again. I was not as composed as yesterday, and let out a giggle as David yanked my hand up and down. He startled and pulled his hand away, looking closely at us both. Then smiling broadly, he gestured to his office, and we took our seats again.

I filled David in on my decision to see Shake and the details of the letters I had found. He responded as supportively as I thought he would, I just hadn't been sure yesterday if I could trust him. He complimented my perseverance and decision, and we discussed options on whether or not to keep the house. He also gave me the contact information for the investment broker, as well as several other web classes to begin my education on financial investing.

Felix and I headed back to San Francisco close to noon, and stopped at his house to move the boxes back to my house. We took a break for lunch, discussing the details of the road trip, and he had several great tips for me, having traveled a bit more than I had. I had never taken a road trip, and despite my nervousness at the goal, I was elated to be doing this on my own.

I spent the afternoon going back through the boxes, making sure everything was organized and in order. I stacked the boxes neatly near the door, ready to go back to the house in Modesto.

I contacted Jana and filled her in on my meeting with David. She was naturally shocked, and we discussed my decisions in detail. She was very happy that I was going to meet Shake, and requested I stay in touch with her whenever possible from the road. I laughingly reminded her that email should be easy enough to do, but she insisted I call her. This was what I loved about Jana; she bullied me about the things that were important. I told her I loved her, and moved on to my next call, to Selene.

I said Hello when she answered, and she replied, "*Bonjour*! Will we be seeing you tonight, are you working?" I heard her pause as she checked the board.

I filled her in on the details of my adoption, the meeting with David, and my budding road trip. I told her that I was giving my two weeks notice, and she protested.

"But *ma biche*, why not just reduce the days you work? I'm sure you just need some more alone time ...

how about only one or two days a week instead of 4 or 5?" she haggled with me.

Shaking my head, I said, "I suspect this won't work long term, but I will try it your way. Either way, I will definitely be gone for about eight days as I track down Shake."

Selene loved that my mother was in the circus. "Tsk, of course. But we will be here when you get back. Plus, Thom is leaving us too, it's tragic! He's going to Paris, I can't believe it!" She babbled faintly to someone in the background.

I wrapped up with Selene, and sat back in my chair. I felt strangely free, knowing I had some financial and professional buffer to allow myself to take this trip. I turned on my computer, and spent a few hours tracking down the circus, who posted their schedule on the web, as well as contacting the management to ask about visiting the employees. They assured me that as long as a staff member was expecting me, they could let me behind their security measures.

I agonized over what to write in the letter; apparently many of the circus staff didn't care for email. I guess it's part of the carnie life, so I typed out a simple Word document mentioning briefly that my dad had passed away, and I wanted to meet as soon as possible. I offered a few show dates I could attend, and printed it out, signing carefully. I posted it in the mail, and decided to take a walk.

The grey of the last week's late January sun had given way to a warm snap in early February, and my sunset walk was well rewarded with warmth, and a beautifully shocking pink and orange light as the sun dipped down once again. I looked out over the city, and its sluggish nightwalkers, coming out of the woodwork for the hustle of the game, the dodge in the dance. I knew so much more than I ever had before. About people. About myself. I didn't have the same naiveté as I'd had before, and I was glad for it. I was a little harder, but it seemed like a good time to cut loose of the things that might make me harder still. I was happy with my decision, and a little surprised by that fact.

I spent the next few days restlessly prowling around the city as I waited for a response in the mail. Fortunately, there's plenty for someone to do and see in San Francisco. I passed the time enjoying the strangely warm weather in Golden Gate Park's Japanese Tea Garden, walking along the Embarcadero, even tourist watching in Union Square. I even headed up to Coit Tower, remembering the birthday picnic, this time going to the top of the tower in the quaint old elevator with the attendant. The view was breathtaking.

I got home that evening and saw the awaited letter in my mailbox. I hurried upstairs and ripped it open. It was short, but good news. She expressed her condolences, and a great desire to see me. She thanked for me letting her know, and listed the next five cities she would be in, and recommended visiting her in Albuquerque, Phoenix, or Las Vegas. She signed it "Fondly, Shake."

I sat with her letter, reading her handwriting over and over again. Looking at the shaky loops on the q's and g's, and the bold scrawling of her S. I set the letter aside, and typed a quick response, and printed it out. I dropped it in the mail, and called Felix to fill him in. We both agreed that Phoenix would be a great city to visit at this time of year, as Albuquerque might still be cold, and Vegas would be highly distracting.

The next few days were all preparation for the trip: washing clothes, buying a cooler, packing it with snack food and drinks, and even getting a proper haircut. I made a trip to Modesto to collect a few photos, just in case. I dropped off the boxes there, and spent a long time in the house by myself. It was the first time I'd been there on my own since Dad passed, and while my grief was no less difficult, it was now supported by the love and care he put into preparing for my future. I strove now to measure up to what he had wanted for me, the woman he had hoped for.

The night before I left, Felix came over and we made a pleasant dinner. We discussed the details of my planned route, and conversation eventually swung back to family. I realized I never had the chance to ask him about his trip to Vegas, and the bailout of his sister, and brought up the topic cautiously. Felix smiled at my reluctance, and filled me in on what had happened during the three days he was away. He told me about the poker game, some of the techniques he had used, and the discussion he'd had with Audrey, once the two of them were out of the police station and on their way back to her house.

There were still so many things about him I didn't know; and yet he'd shown me his true nature over and over again. His devotion and kindness. His passion and humor. I listened closely as he blended his news of his sisters and Mom from then into now. It really drove the point home for me how intense the last four months had been, and how fast they had gone.

I asked Felix about what it was like to have to deal with his addiction once he had come back from Vegas, but he just shook his head.

"I'm not going to lie, it was a bit of a struggle. I thought it might be, but what happened to you on the phone that day ... it just went clean out of my head as I came after you. I wish I could've talked with you about it more, but you weren't in a space for it. I'm a work in progress," he said, smiling sadly at the memory. I felt a sense of disappointment in myself, and even though I wasn't sure I could have been more supportive at the time, I still felt bad about it now. I reached for his hand silently.

The next morning, in the faint light of sunrise, I packed the trunk while Felix stood sleepy-eyed in my driveway.

He was holding an iPod, and handed it to me, saying, "These are some great road trip play lists I put together for you. They will help during the boring stretches. Just you wait until you hit the cattle ranches along I-5." He grinned at me; breaking into a huge yawn, stretching his arms above him like a cat. He looked unbelievably sexy like that, guard down, in only his pajama bottoms.

Composing myself, I said, "Thanks. I will be back soon enough. I will call you from wherever I decide to stop tonight." I bounced on my heels, anxious to be on the road.

"All righty Miss Daisy! Think you can drive yourself this time?"

"Definitely. But thank you Hoke." I was pleased to see his shocked face as he recognized that I'd finally seen the movie, which I had watched a few nights ago on the sly.

I jumped in the car, revved the engine, and rolling down the window, gave an exuberant wave as I left the city by the Bay.

Chapter 31

Most of the first hour of the drive was the same as the route I took to Modesto, but then I had to turn onto 580S to get to I-5, the main thoroughfare that runs up and down the entire west coast. In short order, the lovely and familiar landscape of the Bay Area had dropped away, and flat irrigated fields lined both sides of the freeway, with no picturesque landmarks to distract me. I pulled out the iPod, and plugged it in. The first few songs set a great mood for the first leg of the drive, and soon I was singing along and pounding away my anxiety by drumming my hands on the wheel.

The day slipped away, and the repetitive miles continued to zip past my window, until I saw a dismaying sight. Cows, thousands of them, were lined by the freeway, mingling around each other, miserably snuffling along the ground, looking for the tiniest blade of grass. The smell was God-awful and permeated everywhere, despite fiddling with the air controls. Without meaning to, I started crying. I decided to just keep driving, and focus on the music. Felix had tried to add some up-beat songs for this leg of the drive, but nothing could take away the despair all around me.

I finally pulled away from the ten or fifteen miles of cattle ranch, and slumped back in my seat in guilty relief. I spent the next several minutes wondering if I could give up meat, just to stop participating in such blatant disregard for life. I decided to stop for a rest break to get some air, and I pulled over a few miles outside of Bakersfield at a gas station.

I checked the maps of where I was going, and saw I was about an hour and a half outside of Los Angeles, where I would turn off of I-5 to Highway 10, on my way to Phoenix. I felt the thrill of the unknown, and decided to try and push further before stopping for the night. I could try and drive all the way to Phoenix, but there was really no rush. I wanted to enjoy the drive.

I hit some traffic in Los Angeles, and was held up an extra hour or so. I played the game of Faces in the car, watching the Southern California drivers and remembering all the crazy stories I'd heard of road rage down there. Slowly and steadily, I made my way to my split off to Hwy 10, and traffic picked up. I decided to stop in Palm Springs for the night.

I called Felix from my hotel room, and he teased me about the cattle ranches, and my weepy reaction. I could hear he was at work, rustling inventory, and the background laughing of a few unfamiliar voices. I felt a stab of anxiety for my solitude, and perversely, wanted to turn around and go home. I told Felix I would swim in the pool and think of him, and he cleared this throat in pain. Smiling through the phone, I told him to sleep well.

I headed into town to find some dinner, but changed my mind at the idea of sitting down in a restaurant by myself. I changed my order to be taken to go, and took it back to my hotel room. I sat on the bed, eating a deliciously large green salad with almonds, beets and lemon vinaigrette. I felt better about those poor cows, and curled up in front of a movie. I was too full of food and too comfortable to go to the pool, but Felix didn't need to know that. Grinning wickedly, I fell asleep to the flickering story.

¤ ¤ ¤

I hit the road again in the late morning, after having a mediocre breakfast. I drove through more flatlands, passed by the Joshua Tree National Park, the desert many shades of brown, with rising green hills around Blythe. Soon enough, the Arizona border loomed in sight. I felt a personal triumph that I was leaving my home state for the first time ever, and doing it all on my own. I made a mental note of the terrain, and felt a stab of sadness that Dad wasn't there to witness my adventure. I thought of him more and more, now that I could trust myself to do so. A month ago, thinking of him would've threatened me with near-catatonia. I wished he were with me.

Arizona was not what I thought it would be. It was more rugged and textured than I'd imagined. I had assumed it was a scorching blond sandy floor, with no hills or vegetation. But there was depth to the colors around me, and plenty of vegetation, even if the blooms were dormant at the moment. I sped straight through to Phoenix, aiming to arrive in the mid-afternoon. I wasn't sure what to say when I met Shake, and my thoughts turned from the outer terrain to my inner landscape. I checked the map a few times, and headed for the visitor information center in the downtown area.

A very nice older lady gave me the information on where the circus was located, and how to get there. I thanked her, and drove across town to the convention center. As I made my way through the labyrinth of the parking lot, there were trucks being unloaded by teams of people, all working like a well-oiled machine. Men and women bustled back and forth, ignoring me completely. My nerves were already at a fever pitch and I was too intimidated to ask them about Shake directly. I felt light-headed, foolish for driving all this way, and especially for facing her so soon after Dad. I kept pushing my way through the layers of movement, and found a semi-official looking RV with OFFICE written on the side.

I stood in front of the door, suddenly feeling very alone and terrified. A few minutes passed, and a gigantically muscular man pushed past me, glaring, and knocked on the door. The door opened quickly.

"Yes?" said a tall man with sharp eyes. He had the look of a chameleon, and I could see he would change his demeanor in a second depending on his mood.

"I need the key to the pass through for the tiger, to get him set up for the show."

"Fine, wait here." The tall man shut the door, and the muscle man looked at me suspiciously, without a single word. A few seconds later, the tall man came back, saying, "Return this to me in 15 minutes. Who is this woman?"

"No idea, sir."

They both evaluated me, looking me up and down. Realizing how ridiculous it was that I'd allowed the conversation to go on as if I wasn't there, I cleared my throat, and stood a little taller.

"I'm looking for Shake. She knows I'm coming, and told me to check with you."

The tall man's eyes sharpened, and he stepped out of his trailer. He shut the door firmly, waving off the muscle man with a nod. He took my arm and started leading me deeper into the maze. I considered yanking away from him, but didn't want to be rude. He was clearly taking me directly to her. I tried to calm my breathing, reminding myself this was my idea.

We arrived in front of a small RV, and he knocked impatiently at the door.

I heard rustling inside through the same open window from which a golden light spilled. "Just a second!" I heard a woman's voice call. My mother's voice. My. Mother.

He had released my arm, and I felt unsteady on my feet.

I held my breath.

The door opened.

Chapter 32

Standing a few feet above me was my older sister. No, I shook my head slightly, trying to clear a strange sound from my ears. An audible click had fallen into place. I felt a sense of alignment, an ease deep in my bones. The man was gone, the RV was gone, the light, hell, even Arizona was gone. In front of me, looking through grey eyes, through grey eyes! was my mother. The woman who gave birth to me. Her mouth was making the same O of astonishment; her eyebrows mimicked mine as they shot up in surprise.

And in that same instant, everything around us came rushing back, the man, the afternoon heat, and the sounds of a working crew assembling the night's entertainment.

The man said something, and I could only pick out the end of his sentence, " ... sure to be done within the hour, ok? We have a lot of work to do." She nodded in agreement. He walked away, disinterested.

She stepped down the stairs, and reached to take my hand. Startled, I looked down at our hands. We shared the same, short, slender fingers, with the same shaped fingernails. I was marveling, and felt like I was in shock. Or in molasses. One minute, everything went so fast, and the next, everything slowed.

"I'm so sorry about Jeffrie, Pale. Please know that I understand your grief," she said gently. I took my hand away hastily, discomfited by the concern. I cleared my throat.

"Thank you. I appreciate that."

"Would you like to come in? We can talk for a little while."

"Yes, that makes sense. I drove here from Palm Springs," I said stupidly.

"Oh? Is that where you live now? I thought you were in San Francisco."

"No. I mean, Yes. I don't know why I said that. I meant that I stopped at a hotel last night on my drive, and stayed in Palm Springs. It's not important." Embarrassed, I sat down at the small nook table as soon as I stepped inside. Shake bustled around the small kitchen, pouring juice into glasses, and set one down in front of me. We both sat in silence for a few moments.

Finally, I said, "So, you are in the knife throwing act?"

"Yes, it's a good spot for me. I've always loved the immediacy of the danger, and the trust you have to have in your partner. It demands total intimacy. My new partner and I are still learning each other. It's a slow process." She smiled sadly.

"New partner?" I asked.

"Yes, I was with a man, romantically, for many years, and he was also the other half of the act. But, he passed away two years ago. My new partner and I aren't together, you know, and it makes the act, less, diverse. We can't do as many dares, we are still learning each other's moods and throws."

I wasn't sure what to say. "I'm sorry."

"Thank you. That's very kind. But enough about that." She paused, searching for the right words. "Will you tell me about you, a little? I know I haven't earned the right, Jeffrie was always careful about that. I tried to reassure him I wouldn't interfere..."

"Yes, I know." I said abruptly. "I read your letters."

She looked surprised momentarily, then understanding dawned. "Yes, of course, you probably found our correspondence."

"Can you tell me ... " I started. I wasn't sure how to phrase my next question.

"Anything you'd like. To the best of my ability." She encouraged, gently. Her eyes were downcast, and I could tell she was expecting the next question.

"Who was my father? My biological father?"

Shake drummed her fingers on the table softly, so softly that I could see her hand was actually shaking. I had thought it was just a name, but apparently it's also part of how she responds.

She saw me watching her hand, and put her hands in her lap.

"Yes, that's why I took the name. I actually do start shaking when I get nervous, or scared. In this case, I just hope for your understanding. I guess a part of me didn't believe you would actually come today."

She leaned back, and settled in. She gave me a long stare, and then began trying to answer my question.

"I was with that ... partner for a long time, but we had hit a bad patch when I was much younger. I ended up sleeping with another man during that time, who was only with the circus for a short while. When I got pregnant, I told my partner, and we mended things between us. We both weren't sure if the baby, you, were his, or this other man's. He desperately wanted me to keep you, but I felt so guilty. I just wasn't sure if I wanted this life for you, or if I could face a paternity test. What if I never found your father? What if you hated me, or hated this life? I had already seen so many people try it, and hate it. Or worse, have accidents, sometimes ending up with life-long injuries. There aren't many children raised this way, at least not while we are on the road. Many of the kids are raised by grandparents who've retired, so they can have some semblance of a normal life. Yes, many of them come back into it, but that's when they are older, and can make the decision for themselves."

She continued. "My partner respected that I wanted something better for you, less risky. It was the hardest thing I've ever done. I have never stopped thinking about you." She broke off, choking up. I felt a wave of compassion for her, but didn't reach out.

After a few minutes, Shake was able to speak again.

"I am sorry for all the pain you've gone through. Losing Jeffrie, finding out about me this way. I did my best at the time, and have had to live with the decision every day. When I had my own scare with cancer, and lost my partner, I guess I just wanted to see you, see how you turned out. Jeffrie was sympathetic, but still thought it wasn't the right time. Despite the circumstances, I'm glad you wrote to me." She gave me a smile, meeting my gaze.

I was so overcome with complex feelings; I wasn't sure what to say. I wanted to be angry, but looking into her eyes, I saw her plea for acceptance. Those eyes that were just like mine. And she had been my age, blundering around just like I've been, trying to figure out her place in the world. She had been confused, scared, and there were too many volatile factors to raising a child that were in the way.

Finally, one emotion surfaced above the others, barely dominant, but definitely the emotion I could grip to, and speak from. Closure.

"I understand. At least, I'm trying to. I am really confused right now, but, mostly, I'm glad to hear what happened. It really helps me to feel ... closure about something I've longed to know. I think I got used to not ever knowing, but it's never stopped ... twisting in my heart, even if the twist was slow." She nodded in agreement.

We talked for the rest of the hour, gaining slightly more comfort. We talked about her partner, and why she liked being in the circus. She asked about my job, and I told her a story or two. She drank in the information. She asked if there was a man in my life, and I just told her he was from Texas with three sisters, and his name was Felix.

"Oh, that's Italian for lucky, you know."

Smiling, I said, "Yes, I know. He's been pretty lucky for me."

"Hey, would you mind staying for the show tonight? I can get you a comp ticket. I would like you to see what I do. That is, if you are interested."

I agreed to come back, and we stood up. I reached out to shake her hand, and she shook mine back with a feather light touch. A faint tremble remained. She looked at me, and we moved in for an awkward hug. Feeling better, I left and headed back to the car.

As I made my way back through the maze to where I was parked, my head was in a daze of information. I'd never felt as light as I did now. I felt like dandelion fuzz, lifted above all the events around my birth, around my adoption, around my adoptive mother's abandonment of me and Dad, and the awkward stumbling of my youth. I saw my restlessness and sense of adventure, and how my whole life led up to that moment of moving to San Francisco, and how much I'd learned. I drove around in a fog, looking for a hotel near the convention center. In no time at all, I was secured in an innocuous room, and laid down on the bed, drinking in my meeting with Shake.

After an hour or so, I decided to call Jana and Felix and give them a general overview of the meeting. Both of them listened attentively, and were supportive and relieved to hear it went well. They both peppered me with questions, but I told them I was reeling too hard from it all to go into details. I promised to call once I was back on the road. They both accepted this, and wished me well.

I spent the next few hours killing some time by having dinner in downtown Phoenix. My thoughts returned again and again to my dad. I so badly wished I could talk to him about today. About how much I loved him. About what a great dad he was. I missed him so much; it was an ache that would never go away. But coupled with the pain of the things I never got to say, was the promise of the things I could still say to my birth mother. The relationship we could have, which was foreign to me. I hadn't grown up around other women-- no sisters, aunts, or grandmothers. I'd tried to understand the unspoken rules and minefields that come with other women, but more often than not, I just didn't get it.

I wasn't certain that I would ever get it; but having a place to start with Shake just made it seem possible. Jana was one of the few women who had always understood that about me, and didn't try and make me interpret invisible signals. That was another reason why I loved her.

My thoughts were all a jumble, and I had picked at a plate of sub-standard sushi without enthusiasm. I had gotten so used to eating well in the Bay Area, it hadn't occurred to me that the fish here wouldn't be as fresh. I paid the cashier, and walked back to the hotel to get dressed for the evening's performance. I wondered what kind of preparation Shake had to do to get ready for having knives thrown at her, and whether or not she was nervous that I would be there.

I made my way back to the convention center, where the chaotic jumble of trucks and equipment had miraculously vanished, leaving a clear and well-defined path to the entrance. I asked one of the staff where I could pick up a ticket, and I was directed to a smaller booth with an old-fashioned sign above it, the hand-painted job reading 'Will Call'.

I was handed a ticket by a sweet old man, who gave me a wink and gestured through a heavy piece of the canvas wall. Seeing my hesitant look, he motioned again. I pushed through the wall, and it opened up to a designated walking path, separate from the main crowd, leading to a small seating area in the very front, where approximately twenty seats were roped off with a thick red cord.

People looked down at me curiously, and I avoided their gaze. I was the only one in this sitting area, and I took a spot in the middle toward the back row. A few minutes later, the canvas wall flipped open again, and some important looking business people stepped through it, and strode purposefully to the same sitting area.

I was relieved to not be the only one, and they ignored me completely, chatting amongst themselves in a foreign language. It sounded like German, and I quietly tried to pick out words my Dad might have taught me when I was little.

The lights went down, and the show started. There were animal acts, acrobatics, fire breathers, and clowns. I wasn't sure when Shake was going on, and about an hour into the show, they finally wheeled out the wall she would stand at, and the knife throwing man walked out to applause, holding his knives high in the air. Shake walked out behind him in a sparkly outfit, waving and smiling warmly. I could see a slight tremble as she looked for me, but when she caught my eye, she waved excitedly directly to me. I gave her a shy smile, and waved back, a strange happiness coming over me.

The act was a good one, but I could see what Shake meant about getting used to her partner. He popped balloons around her while she trembled against a brightly painted female outline, pinned playing cards, and even split flower stems, but I heard a few voices call out, 'Wheel of Death!', which the man ignored. Overall, the show was a good one, and I stayed until the end, caught up in the performances. I dropped by the Will Call booth, and found the old man was still sitting there, smiling at me.

"Could you give Shake a message for me?" I asked him.

"Of course, little lady. What's the message?" he asked genially.

I wrote down the name and number of my hotel, along with my room number. I folded it in half and handed it to him.

"This is where I'm staying. If you could have her give me a call, that would be great."

"Absolutely," he nodded, like he does this all the time. For all I know, he does.

I walked back to my hotel, my thoughts swirling around. I reveled in the solitude of being on the road by myself, but I also missed Felix terribly. I decided to leave it up to Shake, which was why I left her my number. I headed to bed without a message from her, dreaming of exotic animals, journeys, forked roads, and of course, Dad.

Chapter 33

In the morning, I got a call as I was getting dressed.

"Pale?" Shake said, uncertain.

"Yep, it's me," I replied.

"You aren't leaving today, are you? I wanted to talk with you more, and I have most of the morning and afternoon free. Maybe we can go somewhere? Take a walk?" She sounded eager to see me again, and I smiled in return.

"That sounds great. I wasn't sure if you wanted some time to think things over," I said.

"No, I've had plenty of time to think things over. I want to spend as much time with you as I can, until you are sick of me!" She laughed merrily. It was a good sound, very lyrical.

"Well, I do have to get back to San Francisco soon, but I can spare a day. I would love the time to talk, too," I reassured her.

We arranged to meet in a park near both of us within an hour, and I notified the hotel that I would be staying another night. It was still a shock, walking up to someone who looked so much like myself. We fell more easily into conversation, starting with last night's performance. I complimented her on her dramatic moves and good nature with the crowd. She accepted my compliments gracefully, and described some of the background and history of knife throwing acts, as well as what originally drew her to it in the first place.

We talked easily about culture and illusion, our mutual restlessness, our ease with men over women, and a myriad of other things we discovered in common. The hours flew by, and soon we were laughing more naturally. My heart soared, adrift on a playful wave of Fate, high above my previous worries. We decided to get some lunch together, and the more serious topics looped back around. My playful wave came down a bit as we discussed Jeffrie's sudden death, and I opened up about Felix and his steady presence in my life.

It was during the gossip about Felix that my cell phone chimed urgently. I paused and she nodded, encouraging me to answer, so I picked up on the last ring.

"Hello?"

"Daisy, have you run away and joined the circus, or did you forget the gas pedal is on the right?" Felix teased me.

"Oh! I'm sorry. I meant to call you this morning." I gestured to Shake that it's Felix, and she gave me a wink and gestured that she's going to the bathroom. I nodded to her, telling him, "I got caught up today talking with Shake. We've had a great day together." I couldn't keep the beaming out of my voice, and he heard my happy tone.

"Well, I'm delighted to hear it. But tomorrow is Valentine's Day, and unless you get in that car and haul ass right now, you are going to miss what I have planned for us."

"Oh NO! I'm so sorry! I had no idea you were doing anything..." I started to stammer.

Felix interrupted me mid-sentence, "-which is WHY I took the precaution of including a secret present in your glove box, in case such an eventuality were to take place." He was grinning through the phone, the smug bastard. Always thinking of everything. Still, a present!

"What kind of present?" I asked, fake suspicious. "Is it a box of exploding glitter?"

"Tsk, tsk, I can't tell you that. But I will tell you that you will want to open it alone."

I gave him an abbreviated version of the day's events, and promised to call from the road.

Shake made her way back to the table, and I told her about Felix's call. She smiled warmly.

"I'm so happy you have someone in your life who seems to truly care about you. I want you to know that you are not alone. I'm interested in being in your life as much as I can be, considering my gypsy lifestyle. I'm never going to be a mother in the traditional sense, but I would like to be your friend."

I took her trembling hand.

"That sounds like a start."

¤ ¤ ¤

I headed back to the hotel, the list of the circus's planned route in my hand. Shake had promised to write me at every other city, so we could get a semi-familiar writing relationship going. It was bizarre to me that she handled correspondence this way, but when I suggested email, she just shook her head No.

I got to the car to check for Felix's present, and as expected, there was a brightly wrapped box, sitting on top of the registration and user guide.

I sat in the passenger seat, running my hands over the paper. I smiled to myself that he had gone to the trouble to do this. I hadn't even noticed what day it was, truthfully.

I tore the paper off the box, and flipped open the lid gingerly. There was a bracelet inside, made from opals and bluish pearls, set in a beautiful silver chain. I gasped involuntarily, holding it up to the late afternoon light. From inside the lid of the box, a note fell onto my lap, and I glanced down and opened it tentatively.

'To the lovely Pale,

I'm not a man of many flowery sentiments. I get things wrong, I am impulsive. But when it matters, I can be very direct. So let me be direct now. You are the kind of woman that hides her strength to her advantage, uses grace in front of buffoons, and spends her love wisely. I tried to fight it, but am helplessly in love with you. This token is a small gesture, meant to say, I want to dance with the one I came with. Will you dance with me?

Hurry home,

Felix'

A rush of desire and love overcame me as I held the note, shaking in my hand. I dropped the bracelet and box in the car, and ran to the hotel lobby. At the desk, I asked the clerk if they have my credit card on file, and he responded yes, bewildered. Running out the door, I shouted, "Put it on my card, I have to go!"

I sprinted back to the car, climbed in, and snapped open my phone as I roared out of the parking lot, racing to the freeway.

I dialed Felix's number, hitting 75 mph.

"Yes?" he answered in a drawl.

"I got your note. Put out the lanterns, I'm coming home." I said, in a voice choked with desire.

For once, Felix was not joking. "I love you, Daisy. Hurry back."

I nodded in agreement, then started laughing, remembering he couldn't see me. "I...I love you, too. See you soon."

Chapter 34

I raced to Highway 10, the miles stripping away, pumped onward by the second half of the iPod play list Felix had given me. It was about 3 p.m., and by my estimate, I could make the drive if I went all night. I'd arrive around one in the morning.

I arrived in the Los Angeles grid traffic just after dinnertime, and while it was congested, it was only a Wednesday night, so it wasn't too bad. I stopped and grabbed some fast food and caffeine in Bakersfield, then hopped immediately back in the car. I thought only of Felix, and what I wanted to do to him when I saw him. I prayed I would be able to keep this burning animal desire for him in check; otherwise, he would not expect the pouncing I had in mind. I grinned at the thought of tackling him by surprise, and the white stripes fell under my headlights like a timer ticking down.

It seemed only a blink of an eye, when I saw the familiar turnoffs to the Bay Area, and opened the driver's door window to let in the cooling air to keep me awake. I'd been off the Tawny Tart work schedule, so my body had reverted to a natural rhythm of making me sleepy around midnight. I turned on to the East Bay/San Francisco Bay Bridge with relief, and a third wind coursed through me as I neared Felix's house.

I saw a light go on in his house as I put the car in park, yanked the emergency brake, and barely had the door shut when he opened his front door, and was coming toward me, the same urgency echoed in his eyes. I ran to him and he picked me up. Without saying a word, we went into the house, bumping into doors and walls, and as he kicked the door shut, I beeped the button to lock the car over my shoulder.

As I nuzzled into his neck, biting on his ear, I heard a rustling sound that told me he'd shed his robe, despite holding my legs around his waist. He pushed me against the wall. Some part of my mind marveled that he was wearing only his pajama bottoms as I ran my hands down his chest and back up and around each side of his face, cupping his neck. The heat intensified, and I could tell that we were done with waiting. We were done with exploring. We had moved to the final leg of the hunt, to the prize.

Felix growled under his breath with impatience, and wrenched us off the wall, whipped around and collapsed with me onto the couch. I looked into his eyes, and saw raw, animal lust. His love was there, but it was buried beneath. I reflected the same sentiment, encouraging him by flinging my clothes off as fast as possible. He had grown still, watching me ready myself. I leaned back, and he dropped his clothes with finality. He crouched over me, all of his glorious nakedness, pausing briefly to allow me one last hesitation. I responded by pulling him into me, and we both gasped with surprise and ecstasy. We moved in a synchronistic wave, a rejoicing and an unspeakable togetherness, at last joined, the final step taken.

We continued together, riding our bodies' demand, not stopping for poetic license. My vision exploded into stars as I climaxed around him, his expression fierce and tender at the same time. He was a moment behind me, letting out a groan as he spasmed against me, his back arching toward me. Felix crumpled in a heap, both of us out of breath and sweating hard.

After a long while, he leaned over and kissed me tenderly on the neck.

"So. How was the drive?" he asked in a normal voice.

I cracked up laughing, and once started, couldn't seem to stop giggling. I was so happy; I didn't think I'd ever been so happy. In a moment, I regained my composure.

"Oh, nothing special."

"Mmhmm, mmhm. And, did you want to tell me something?" he prompted.

"I think I just did." I grinned at the implication.

"So, you mean to tell me, you didn't get me any jewelry for Valentine's Day?" he asked, indignant, rolling off of me and crossing his arms across his chest. It was hard to focus on the top half of his frame--his lower half, even post-coital, was magnificent.

"Hell-o! My eyes are up HERE." He gestured to his face with two fingers.

"Mmhmm. I know that," I said absently, my gaze remaining fixed on his groin.

"Pale!"

"I guess there is something of importance I should tell you. You know, in person." I said seductively, sidling closer to him. His posture relaxed, and he automatically lifted his arm to curl around me as I snuggled closer to his chest, drawing circles with my hand.

"You. Really Have. The Most ... " I breathed low, caressing his nipple.

"Yes?" he said, slightly undone.

"The Most Beautiful. Chorizo. I've ever. Seen." I finished, tweaking his earlobe.

"My what?" he asked, affronted.

"Chorizo. Spanish for sausage. You know, your-"

"Yes, thank you," he snapped, pulling away, looking for his robe in the hall.

I stood and joined him there.

"Felix," I said softly. He glanced up at me.

"I've never been in love before. I think that's what I'm feeling, but everything has been so crazy lately. You've been amazing to me. Amazing. More than amazing, actually. You've become my best friend, and I missed you terribly when I was away. I never, never could've done any of this without you. When I saw that note, I drove all night. I keep thinking this has to be a dream, that it couldn't possibly get any better, and then you grabbed me, and we ... " I broke off, because Felix had come closer to me, and was staring down at me intently.

"I love you." I managed to get the words out, but he'd picked me up again, this time gently, and we were headed to his bedroom, where he set me down, so softly. We scuttled under the covers, and lay there for a long time, touching, arousing, making love for hours. We drifted off to sleep, curled around each other, and I slept deeply for the first time in many, many months.

Chapter 35

In the late morning, we stayed in bed, while Felix occasionally hopped up for a few breakfast snacks of pop-tarts, bananas, coffee, and yogurt. We talked at length about my trip, about the future, and about what we wanted for ourselves. We agreed to respect and listen to each other, to stay present and keep it surprising, and most of all, stay devoted and keep communicating. We shook on it, and just like that, I had a boyfriend. We also did more than shake on it, seeing as how we opened the door last night to all the delights we could experience in each other. The day passed quickly, and I was so blissed out, I could hardly get up in the late afternoon to hop in the shower.

My last night of being a Tart was tomorrow, and Selene called me to sorrowfully ask if I could come in tonight as a last favor. I told her my legs weren't working today, I was having some problems with my knees being all watery, giggling silently to myself and Felix. She said she understood and would see me tomorrow night.

I drove home and did some basic clean up. I managed to leave Phoenix with only my purse, so my overnight bag was left at the hotel. I called them, and they assured me they found it, and asked if I wanted it shipped to my home address. I told them not to bother, and went out to buy new toiletries. Rushing home to Felix was the better decision, by far.

Felix was also not working tonight, so we went out on a "date" together, hamming up the Valentine's Day celebration a day late, by wearing red, and going out for a touristy date on the wharf. We had an extravagant dinner of fresh fish, good wine, and a lovely chocolate mousse for dessert. Around dessert, he got that gleam in his eyes again, and we got it packed to go, leaving with less leisure than when we arrived.

Back at his house, we had another night of tortured slow caressing, but this time it was joined by the orchestra of our intercourse, ending after multiple, varied orgasms. We added to the complexity of what we had done before, and seasoned it with new sensations.

"I didn't know you could do that with chocolate mousse," I said at one point, as he licked it in slow, terrible circles around my breasts.

He chuckled evilly under his breath, reaching up to run his finger tantalizingly near my mouth. I sucked the excess chocolate off his finger, and he groaned in agony when I showed him what else I could do, if he would just cooperate.

Much of the night passed in similar fashion.

Another morning dawned, and I was a bit grateful for somewhere to go. I had begun to worry that Felix's house was a bit of a vortex, sucking me in and keeping me there.

Briskly, I hopped out of bed, and he groaned in protest.

"No, no sir!" I swatted his grabbing arms away, dancing out of range.

"There's no rush! It's your last night!" he complained.

From a safe distance, I started locating my flung clothes. "Yes, but I want to leave plenty of time to look my most amazing, and to say goodbye to everyone properly. I have a SPECIAL dress in mind." I smiled at him wickedly. He groaned again, swiping at me as I passed close by, leaning down for my pants. I glided away from his attempt.

I headed home, and went through my closet, looking for the dress I had in mind. It was a very expensive dress, one that Dad bought for me a few years back for my birthday. I also pulled out the beautiful bracelet Felix gave me, and managed to find some complimentary earrings. I threw it all in a bag, and stopped by a costume shop to buy a few peacock feathers for my hair. They were cheap enough, and would really top off my look. I smiled in anticipation.

As I pulled up outside the office, I sat back and stared at the buildings I'd grown so accustomed to. I thought about the people I'd met, the confidences we'd shared. I thought about those who'd stayed closed to me, and I wondered for the umpteenth time what Dad would say if he could see me here. I drank it in, and silently said my goodbye before stepping in the door.

Chapter 36

Selene was sitting behind the desk, rustling a bottle of chilled champagne in a bucket.

"*Ma biche!*" she exclaimed, coming out from behind the desk, holding my face with her icy fingers, and kissing me passionately on each cheek.

"What does that mean anyway?" I asked.

"My dear! That's how I got my little crush on you when you first arrived, your big eyes, so wide with excitement." She pinched me in the arm, and pulled me closer.

"Did you bring something special to wear?" She smiled at me knowingly, taking in my garment bag.

"Yes. Of course!" I replied, smiling at Felix and Ransom, who were both in the office early to go over the inventory room. Selene popped open the champagne as the women filtered in quickly. There was a buzz as she filled plastic glasses, and the ladies who'd been working with me a long time, participated in the toast, while the newer girls who'd just started grabbed their glasses and went to hover at the mirror, giggling to their reflections. Just as well. They would learn soon enough.

We downed our drinks, and got to work. I did my makeup, hair, and even tray first, leaving the unveiling of the dress for last. I went into the back room after a little while, taking the garment bag with me. I opened it with a sigh, and straightened a few wrinkles.

The dress was deceptively simple; it was short and slinky, with a touch of ruching along the arms and along the legs; the gathers pulled up the material suggestively. It was the material itself that was the masterpiece--a medium blue, with traces of different greens, and even some pink highlights. It matched the peacock feathers and my bracelet perfectly. I looked much fancier than I ever had while working this job. I realized I forgot to check the board for where I was working tonight, in my haste to get ready.

I stepped out of the back, and the entire room fell to a hush. Even Ransom let out a long, slow whistle, which I appreciated.

"Where am I working tonight, Selene?" I asked her.

"Oh, of course you are working North Beach. Especially looking like that."

She admired me appreciatively, and I could see that I'd made the deal with Felix too soon. Tragic! It just figured she wanted me now. Grinning, I turned toward the mirror, and was astounded at the change over my features. I looked like a woman, a mature, confident, self-assured woman. I adjusted my hairpieces a bit, and saw Meredith come up behind me hesitantly. I made eye contact, and turned to her.

"Hi there," I said, surprised.

"I know I've been an ass, Pale. I'm really sorry about, you know, your dad. I just don't handle that sort of thing well." She reached for my hand, and I took hers.

"It's ok. I understand," I said quietly.

"I'd like to stay in touch, if that's all right with you?" She looked at me while asking the question.

"Sure, I'd like that too." I smiled at her, and we embraced, all traces of our previous tension gone. I felt much better, knowing we were leaving each other on a good note. I wasn't sure if we'd stay in touch, but at least we'd agreed to try.

Felix came out of the back inventory room, where he had missed my grand entrance. We locked eyes, and the love that surged between us blocked out everyone else. He glanced down, saw the bracelet on my wrist, and broke into the heart-breaking grin I knew so well.

"They don't stand a chance," he proclaimed loudly. The room laughed with him.

Ransom was my driver that night, and I'm not sure what it was, but I seamlessly moved from bar to bar in a protective bubble, away from bullshit, mean drunks, and creepy situations. Not everyone bought from me, but my dress, coupled with my demeanor, made me a bit magical. People asked me what the special occasion was for, and I mastered a Mona Lisa smile, only saying, "Must be the love in the air."

Even the most die-hard cynics didn't have the heart to rain on my parade.

I glided through my route, dipping and swaying, winking and nudging. I rode the surf of the evening, and conquered it. Never had I felt so confident, so purposeful, as I did in those last moments. The call of humanity, the push to know one another. It fascinated and repulsed me. It had given me despair; yet it had also given me a safety net.

And as I walked into Tosca, I saw the close of an unfinished loop. This was one of those moments when I knew there was a great force at work in the Universe, as I spied Michael standing sentinel over the Mayor. I walked past everyone else in the bar, giving a quick wave to Ben, whose jaw had dropped, and walked straight up to their table. Michael didn't have any time to react, he was so stunned. I leaned over, and said, "Flint daa-hling. It's been such a long time," in a voice that left no question.

Mr. Mayor looked me up and down appreciatively and reached out automatically for my hand. I gave it to him, and he kissed it, tenderly.

"I remember you. You were that little trembling flower I met, what was it, six months ago?" he pondered.

I smiled at the trembling flower part; how true it was. "And I remember you. You were kind enough to help me out. I wanted to thank you, and let you know it's my last night. I'm sure you'll find other ... entertainment in the future." I said, raising my eyebrows. He chuckled knowingly, tapping his finger to his nose.

"Yes, indeed. Well, I for one am devastated I won't be seeing you again. Good luck with all your endeavors, Ms...?" he asked.

"Pale."

He grinned again. "Pale. Of course."

Michael had recovered his composure, and was reaching for my hand. I took a small step back, and he flinched.

"Thanks for everything, Michael," I said softly.

He nodded mutely, turning away with a thoughtful expression.

I headed back to the bar, and ordered a shot from Ben. He happily obliged me, and while we were catching up, Michael approached me again.

"Boss wanted you to have this. Said good luck." Michael thrust five, one hundred dollar bills on top of my cigarettes, and I raised my head to him. He and I nodded to each other, and he walked back to the booth.

Ben gave me a huge grin, and I plucked one of the bills off my tray. "Here," I said, shoving it at him.

"What for?" he asked.

"For showing me that lovely belly." We both started laughing, and he leaned over, hugging me goodbye.

I strode out the door, back into the river of the night, giving away each of those hundred dollar bills to my favorite actors of this stage.

SPRING

Epilogue

The rest of February tripped into March, cherry blossom trees exploding in bloom with the warm snap. Felix's birthday was coming up, and he decided he wanted an old-fashioned, outdoor BBQ to celebrate with a small group of friends and family.

Thom had left Tawny's on February 1st, but was still wrapping up moving his mom to the assisted living home, and was headed to Paris at the end of March. Meredith had called to say she was getting a second singing gig, at a quality jazz bar, and I congratulated her. Singing in a college coffee shop was never going to be tough on her, and if she really wanted to make that her career, she needed to be seen by people who cared about talent.

Since I'd stopped working, it took me a while to get used to having my time for myself. I spent more time in Modesto, packing up boxes and figuring out what to keep and what to throw out. Felix and I had plans in April to go up over the Bay and scatter Dad's ashes, but there was no rush. I wanted the weather to be clear, for Dad's sake.

Felix and I were spending most of our time together, and despite the crazy sex fest that seemed to be ongoing, we were falling into an easy routine. We'd spend two or three days together, then spend two or three days apart. We each spent one day exclusively on ourselves, no phone calls or communication with the other. I spent many of those days at Coit Tower, mostly because of the view. For some reason, I felt like Dad would've loved the city from up here. It's not the highest point of the city, but it's the prettiest, and it almost seemed like you were flying.

We had been talking more about next steps, and I felt that addressing my restlessness was going to be a part of it. I had gotten a real taste for travel from my brief road trip, so I was considering something that would involve that. I had decided I wanted to go back to school, but where was a question. Fortunately, on that point too, there was no rush. Felix was ready to leave Tawny's, and broke the news to Selene. She wasn't surprised to lose him right after me, but she certainly did her best to convince him otherwise.

Felix wanted to pursue his love of all things storm and cloud-related. He said it helped satisfy the adrenaline rush that gambling gave him. He was researching jobs or internships closer to the weather and research stations peppered around the country.

As March came and went, the weather dawned beautifully for the day of the BBQ. Felix and I had hunted down the finest of Niman Ranch burger meat, along with veggie patties, cheesy puffs, local beers, and some veggie munchables. He had asked his landlords if we could borrow their back patio and grill, and they were happy to accommodate, since they were spending spring break with their kids in Hawaii.

Felix was wearing a ridiculously high chef hat, and I was overjoyed that Samantha and Nicole, two of his sisters, had decided to come out and celebrate. Both of them had greeted me warmly, and assured me that they had heard the highest of praise from Felix about me. I asked after Audrey, and Samantha ('call me Sammy') answered me with a shake of the head. I took that to mean it was a work in progress.

At one point while Felix was distracted, I stole Nicole back into the house to show her the gift I'd gotten Felix, and to see if she thought it was something he would like. I had splurged after talking with David Cliffstone, and had bought both of us tickets to Boulder, CO, to visit the Center for Severe Weather Research. I thought this might help our decision on where to go, and give us a chance to check out Colorado. Nicole's eyes lit up, and she nodded emphatically and just said, "Cool!" when I showed her the card, the note, and the tickets. Felix was right; Nicole really didn't talk much.

We re-joined the party, and I slipped my card on the present table. Felix had been opening them slowly while the party went on, clustering near the gift giver, so he could talk to them personally right after he saw what their gift was. Despite his audacious manner, he didn't like being the center of the room, chef hat to the contrary.

I glanced around the backyard, and saw smiling faces among our friends. Felix and his sisters were all obviously cut from the same cloth, laughing together easily with their same chin, hair, noses, and smiles. I wished my dad were here, and even briefly felt a pang for Shake. I had gotten a few letters from her, and while my letters were shorter, they were getting longer, as we learned more about each other.

Felix scrambled back over to the grill, and announced it was time to eat. We all made our way to the buffet station, and heaped plates high with good, simple food. Thom had brought some of his heavenly madeleines for dessert, and I was guarding them for the end of the meal. I had already had to slap Felix's hand away from the box a few times, as he kept leaning down and smelling the intoxicating vanilla inside.

As we all settled into our seats, Felix held up my card like he would a wine glass, and the table quieted down.

"This is from my lovely Miss Daisy, which I started calling her when I started driving her around town. Thank you." He nodded his head toward me, in all seriousness, and I got choked up suddenly. I nodded back to him, smiling.

He opened the card, read the note I'd written to him, and smiled privately at the dare I'd flung at him for our sexy fun time. He raised his head and nodded at me to let me know the game was on, and the rest of the table caught the raised eyebrow, and howled as I blushed and looked down.

But as he opened the plane tickets, and saw the invitation to Boulder, he jumped up, and started shouting with happiness. I was so overcome, everyone was clamoring around us, "What was it? What did you get him?" I just couldn't stop staring and laughing with him. I'd never seen him so spontaneously joyful. It was an amazing sight.

He finally calmed down, raised his beer, and gestured for quiet. Despite not liking the spotlight, he certainly has a flair for the dramatic. It was one of the many things I loved about him.

"My darling, my Pale, will you chase this storm with me?" he asked softly, his words carrying weight across the distance.

In those words I felt the caress, the hope. The devotion and the love. The adventure.

"Only if we do it dancing," I replied.

The End

Made in the USA
San Bernardino, CA
14 June 2013